THE
WOODS
OF
HITCHCOCK

To Elizabeth ~

I hope you enjoy
my latest! Miss you!
Best,
Ann

Praise for *The Woods of Hitchcock* and Ann W. Jarvie

"5 out of 5 stars! – Ann W. Jarvie has written a complex and intriguing novel in *The Woods of Hitchcock*...fascinating metaphysical information...an engaging read from the first page to the last!" —*Readers' Favorite*

"A compassionate and intriguingly constructed novel of transcendental awakening." —*Kirkus Reviews*

"It's unusual to find a thriller that weaves paranormal and psychological tension into its murder mystery, but Ann W. Jarvie achieves this with detail and depth...a thoroughly engrossing story that's hard to put down." —*Midwest Book Review*

"*The Woods of Hitchcock* is a wild ride and fun read from beginning to end!" —Lesley Ward, former Editor-in-Chief, *Horse Illustrated* and *Young Rider Magazine*

The Soul Retrieval: A Novel by Ann W. Jarvie

"Riveting!" —*Pacific Book Review*

"A masterpiece...I look forward to much more from Ann W. Jarvie." —*Paranormal Romance & Authors That Rock*

"Enticingly written...portrays the boldness within to seek inspiration and truth." —*Readers' Favorite*

"The author has a gift for crafting striking images...consistently evocative...sharp characterization, and haunting, gorgeous imagery." —*Kirkus Reviews*

"An amazing book...you will find yourself searching within yourself as well..." —*Undercover Book Reviews*

"The writing is top notch with some charm thrown in." —*Lilac Reviews*

THE
WOODS
OF
HITCHCOCK

A Thriller
By
Ann W. Jarvie

![Jazz]

JazzComm Publishing

Cover design by Girard-Creative.

ISBN-13: 978-0-578-94981-9 (hardcover)
ISBN-13: 978-0-578-93200-2 (paperback)
ISBN-13: 978-0-578-93201-9 (ebook)

For Paul, Dane and Luke

Chapter 1

Suzanne Clayborn woke up in darkness, mouth taped shut.

Jerking only made the ties around her wrists and ankles tighter, but it wasn't just the bindings holding her down. Her muscles weren't working right, like her whole body had fallen asleep. All she could do was lie there on a floor, heart pounding in terror, listening to the eerie bangs of pipes hidden somewhere behind the shadowed walls.

Her body trembled, despite an overwhelming heat, heavy and putrid, falling on her face and neck like the terrible breath of a monster. She had no memory of what had happened to her or where she was now. She only knew she was immobilized, maybe paralyzed, and every inch of her head ached. She might've welcomed another blackout, but the fumes were acting like smelling salts, forcing her to remain awake.

Yet she preferred consciousness—she didn't want to die. It wasn't that she feared the afterlife. That was actually the only good thing about the tragic accident years ago, when she was thirteen, when she'd felt her soul float away in bliss. It was the coming back that was the scary part. What she'd seen and felt when she'd woken up, and almost every day since then, could not be unseen or unfelt. It was a secret horror, her life irreversibly altered with strange, new abilities she didn't need or want. Still, she didn't want to die—not now, not like this— because she was struck in this dark moment with an awful knowing, a bothersome niggling in the deepest part of her soul about something important she had to finish in this life. It remained unclear, buried in sub-consciousness, waiting for some future self-discovery, but she understood she'd been running away from it, wasting precious time on ambitions that didn't really matter. And given the things she'd seen and felt, she would not, could not risk dying only to become one of the miserable ghosts she saw, lingering in earth-bound limbo, troubling the living with the stuff of nightmares all because of their unfinished business.

With excruciating effort, she craned her neck to peer at her surroundings, helped only by a small ochre-colored light at the very end of the space. It looked like she was lying in a short hallway. It led to a square room about twelve-by-twelve feet—the size of a horse stall, and she recognized the smells of dirt and fertilizer. Was she in a barn? Some kind of underground bunker? As she strained to keep her head lifted to look around, she decided it was something different. Shelves held spray cleaners and the kind of bathroom supplies found in office buildings. This discovery gave her unexpected relief, but only for a second.

In the middle of the square room were two tarp-covered mounds. The bigger one was the height and width of a large desk; the other, low on the ground, looked like a body bag at a crime scene. Her heart nearly stopped at the sight, and she felt the tears rising, but she willed them to stay put. It was hard enough to breathe already.

Her arms and legs started to tingle. And she could now move them ever so slightly. Shaking her head, she blinked, feeling her right shoulder throbbing. The pain was from an old wound, but having the sensation as well as some mobility in her neck were encouraging signs, that the numbness in her muscles was fading. Sluggishly, she started to remember… her office, a big client presentation, but her thoughts took a turn and she remembered the dirty barn smells, yellow rubber gloves, whispers…crying…then blackness. She shook her head again. These things didn't go together. They didn't make sense.

She rolled her head around in every direction, searching for movement, and some reason to hope. A closed door was behind her, and a video camera on a tripod sat to her right. Both were out of reach. A light the size of a fly glowed bloodred on the camera's top. She could sense someone watching, no two people, no it was three, and their combined energy was more than creepy. The awareness rushed into her body without warning, like a midnight draft blowing in through cracks in her soul, biting and pinching as it traveled.

Most people didn't understand how she felt the emotions of others or how they affected her physically, even hurt and make her sick. Hell, she didn't understand it. Psychics had told her she was a strong empath, like her grandmother. Yet she wasn't able to perceive or understand the emotional energy of others one hundred percent of the time, nor was she always able to pick up on everything someone else was feeling. At other times, she couldn't turn off the thoughts of others, often in crowds, where her senses could be easily overwhelmed. Most times, she didn't know how to interpret or control her empathic ability, but she'd often wondered if it was possible to learn. In this moment, however, she knew she was picking up on the fears and confusion of the watchers—and it only added to her own.

Let it go, Suze. Use it to get out. Focus. You must get out!

Taking a moment to analyze her situation, she now realized there was a pillow under her head and that she was lying on a mat, which was incongruent and possibly alarming, until she intuited one of the watchers felt sorry for her and what they were doing to her. Maybe they didn't mean to kill her, just scare her. *But why?* She couldn't fathom any possible answer. Guessing was useless anyway. She'd know when she'd know—truth was something she felt in her heart.

The smothering blackness was as hot and humid as a sauna. Her silk blouse and jacket were soaked through. At least the moisture was starting to loosen the tape on her mouth. Struggling with her good shoulder, she managed to curl the tape halfway off her lips. She took in a deep breath, finally, but just as quickly coughed from the fumes scorching her throat. Tears resurfaced, and this time, she didn't stop them.

She could wiggle her fingers now, so she balled her fists and pointed her toes, breathing in the room's dark heat slowly, cautiously. Tugging again on the bindings, she heard three rings, like those from a cell phone, coming from the direction of the tarp mounds, in the middle of the adjacent room. There was a click, and she flinched, her eyes bulging. The digital numbers of a LED clock burned fiery orange.

30:00

In a blink, the numbers started to change—a count down. She gasped. The dirty barn smells. The fumes. A mix of fertilizer and gasoline.

Oh my God!

She kicked and screamed.

Chapter 2

Just when she thought she'd be blown to bits, Suzanne felt a snap. Then another. With adrenaline shooting through her body, she sat up—the ties on her wrists and ankles were made of mere masking tape. Had she not been in such a terrible predicament, she might've laughed, but she couldn't waste time thinking about how stupid the watchers might be. She freed herself, as every impulse to escape exploded within her, and she jumped up to the door.

But once there, her fingers twitched as she reached out to grab the doorknob, feeling the hope was almost better than the knowing—because she already knew the door would be locked and no one was on the other side. Turning the knob would just confirm that she was trapped in this smothering blackness with a ticking bomb.

With no alternative, she did it anyway. The slow twist, then frantic rattling, as tears poured, mixing with the sweat on her cheeks. She pounded the door. She was so sure she was in an office building. Why wasn't anyone on the other side of the door? Wait, what was that? A moan. She stood motionless, staring at the unmoving doorknob, on high alert, holding her breath. The moan came again—behind her. She whipped around. The smaller tarp was moving, like someone coming back to life in a body bag. The groans turned into muted coughs and cries. *Someone else is in here with me!*

Her eyes snapped to the LED. *27:10.* She ran, jerked the smaller tarp off its contents, and gasped. "Jill!"

Jillian O'Neill, the administrative assistant for their advertising agency's creative team, had not come to work on the morning Suzanne last remembered, nor had Jill called in to explain her absence. The entire team had been angry about Jill's uncharacteristic behavior because it was the day before their big presentation to their key client, Americos Oil. It was plainly obvious what had happened now, but there was no time to feel bad about it. "Oh, Jill. Get up! We've got to get out of here," she cried hoarsely, ripping the tape off Jill's mouth and pulling her up to a sitting position.

But her coworker was in much worse shape than Suzanne had been, with a gash under her left eye and large bump on her forehead. Dried blood covered most of her blouse. Jill was semiconscious and unable to move on her own.

"Hold on, Jill! I've got to get the door open first." Suzanne cradled her clumsily back to the floor. Frantically, she searched the room for something, anything, to smash the doorknob. *Nothing!*

As she stood panting and trying to think about what else she might try, she felt a cell phone in her pocket vibrate. Fearing another explosive device, she pulled it out tentatively. Her initials were on the case.

Even with the clock ticking away, Suzanne remembered leaving her phone on her office desk before going down the hall to the bathroom. It had been about ten o'clock at night by the time she'd completed her team's ad campaign presentation to be given the following day. As she left the bathroom, she'd been grabbed from behind by someone with yellow rubber gloves, and something awful had been put over her mouth and nose before she'd blacked out.

Why would I have my cell on me now? Maybe the watchers are just playing with me, and it's rigged to explode. All of these thoughts flashed through her mind in a second. Her phone screen said it was Dan Brunoski calling and it was five a.m. It was the first time Suzanne was truly thankful that her boyfriend, a Chicago commodities broker, started work so early in the morning. She answered it.

"Where the hell have you been all night?" he shouted before she could say anything.

"Just stop and listen, Dan!" But as she was trying to quickly explain the situation, her cell phone died.

Chapter 3

A chill ran down her spine, despite the gripping heat. She whipped back to the LED. *13:15*. She prayed Dan would call for 911 and that she'd guessed correctly—they were maybe in the Americos Building in Chicago, locked in the storage closet on the fifty-second floor. But she wasn't sure she'd gotten all of that out, that she was even right or that Dan would understand. She was trying to hold onto hope. But she and Jill would die in this locked room unless he did and help arrived in time. And there was so very little of it left.

Dear God, please let us get out of here. And please let me get back to Hitchcock Woods...just one more time.

Within seconds, fire alarms went off with piercing shrieks. She almost couldn't believe it, but someone was rattling the doorknob from the other side. Suzanne stared wide-eyed at it, her heart leaping as she heard the faint clatter of keys. The LED showed 10:07 as the door flew open.

"Jill, it's open!" she yelled, backtracking to get her. Even though Jill was petite, and Suzanne was strong and tall at five-foot-nine, she was still in a weak state, and it was impossible to heave up Jill's dead weight. Hastily, she grabbed Jill beneath her armpits and dragged her through the open door. "Thank you!" she shouted. But she didn't see anyone on the other side; the floor was deserted. It didn't matter—they were out.

Pulling Jill's body to the elevators, she slapped at the down button, just as she remembered elevators might be shut down during emergencies. *Crap! Everything's frozen!* "The stairs!" she shouted to no one. Fresher air and blood surging to her recovering muscles, Suzanne found she was finally able to lift Jill. She started toward the stairs, opening the door to the stairwell just as two men rushing down offered to help.

In a blur, the four of them mashed in with others coming in at every landing. By floor twenty, despite going down and being in what she perceived to be good cardio shape, Suzanne's entire body was racked with side-stitch pain and raw-throated hard breaths, her head still aching from shock or some inhaled drug or chemical. Ignoring it all, she continued on, others thundering behind her and a clock ticking down somewhere above.

Chapter 4

Blasting out of the stairway and into the gigantic marbled lobby, Suzanne and hundreds of others ran past the front desks and out toward the covered plaza on Wacker Drive. Alarms continued their soul-chilling screams. Frantic voices braying into cell phones mixed with incoming sirens.

It was still dark outside, but Suzanne was too overwhelmed to shiver in the cold rain or wonder why so many people were in the building at five in the morning. The men placed Jill on her feet, and although wobbly, she'd regained enough consciousness to stand. Suzanne wrapped her arms around Jill, and together, they just stood there, adrift in a sea of people, until Suzanne guided them to a concrete bench.

Fire trucks, ambulances, and police cars with lights blazing lined the sidewalks. Chicago Fire

Department cruisers disgorged a variety of uniformed first responders, including men and women wearing bomb squad tactical body armor. They rushed past Suzanne and Jill, not yet realizing the role the two women had played in the terrifying events.

With Jill sitting up on her own, Suzanne reached out to one of the armored men and shouted over the pandemonium, "Hey, stop! I've got to tell you... There's a fertilizer...um...I mean a bomb on the fifty-second floor! In the cleaning supply closet. Set to go off any second." She looked down at her watch. "Wait," she said, quieter now. "It should've gone off by now."

A deafening explosion sent a fusillade of debris crashing onto the plaza's gazebo, which thankfully seemed to stop it, as the uniformed man shielded them with his body. Seconds later, he called some city policemen over.

"She has information; they're both involved. Medics needed," he said to the police officers encircling her and Jill.

"Are you aware of any other bombs in the building?"

She shook her head, and he instructed them to go with the officers before repeating what Suzanne had said into a walkie-talkie attached to his vest and dashing off.

The police officers marshaled them through the crowd to an area being taped off for emergency triage.

Suzanne tried to answer their questions as Jill was assessed, loaded into an ambulance and whisked off.

"We, uh, were taped up in a dark room…uh, I mean a cleaning supply closet. And Jill … was under some kind of tarp. I could smell fertilizer and gasoline. The fumes were awful. And there was a countdown, on a clock, a digital clock, but we somehow got out…"

The questions kept coming, but Suzanne, in shock, her wet clothes icing over, swayed, too cold and stunned to continue. A paramedic caught her and eased her onto a gurney. She trembled as he covered her with an emergency blanket.

"What day is it?" she asked.

"Friday, March 19," replied one of the paramedics.

Her team's client presentation was supposed to be today, meaning she'd been locked in the closet, unconscious, for about seven hours.

Shane Morgan, the other writer on her creative team, who was arriving earlier than usual because of the day's presentation, raced up to Suzanne. His face was beet red and shiny, as if he'd run the entire five blocks up from his L stop on Lake Street. He was wearing his customary black and gold Missouri Tigers knit hat and a dark blue flannel business coat.

"What happened, Suze? Are you okay?" Shane shouted, bending down next to her, but his voice was like a soft echo.

"We were kidnapped, Shane. Jill and I were locked in a cleaning closet…on our floor…with a ticking bomb." She couldn't tell if she was yelling or whispering. "They've already taken Jill to the hospital. She was hurt…bad."

"We're asking the questions now," an officer said, interrupting Shane. "You'll have to move behind the caution tape." He forced Shane back.

As another wave of exhaustion hit her, Suzanne turned her head away from Shane, only to see Dan jumping out of a cab and running toward them. The police stopped him, like the rest of the onlookers and pushed him into another taped-off area. She turned back to Shane, who was now, incredibly, answering the incessant questions of news reporters.

"Yes, the blond woman there and another colleague, Jillian O'Neill, who was apparently already taken to the hospital. That's Suzanne Clayborn. No, not married. She's a copywriter and associate creative director for us, for Darby, Banter & Brenton Advertising. You probably already know that we're Americos Oil's agency of record. Background? Originally from the South. But she went to Northwestern's journalism school…summa cum laude… Hey, we work together. I should know, right? What? Oh, she's originally from South Carolina. A place called Hitchcock Woods, well, actually, the town is Aiken. Have you ever heard of it?…Her full name? Suzanne…um, her middle name starts with a Q…"

Why do they have to be so damn nosy? She figured Shane was trying to be helpful, but why did he have to be so cooperative?

Within seconds, the reporters left Shane and moved toward her. They leaned over the yellow police tape, stretching it.

"Ms. Clayborn, we're told that you were locked in a supply closet with a bomb on the fifty-second floor of the Americos Building. Is that true? Do you know who did it? How did you get out? Ms. O'Neill was critically hurt and could barely walk. Did you save her life?"

"No—I mean, no comment," Suzanne mumbled, feeling too exposed to the myriad of probing eyes, and not just those of the unyielding reporters. She was relieved when several city policemen separated them from her with another yellow caution tape.

"But we have questions, and she's obviously involved," said a perky, bronze-headed woman from one of Chicago's local TV news stations. Behind her stood others with microphones bearing logos from a variety of networks.

"You'll have to wait for da press announcement," said another policeman in the clipped, thick accent of Chicago's South Side.

"Oh, dear God," Suzanne said as the paramedics took her vitals right out in front of the media and everyone holding a cell phone camera. She didn't want this to be broadcast on the six o'clock news, and the thought of her haunted face being posted on social media made her want to throw up. She draped her arm over her eyes to block it all out, feeling hopelessly drained and disappointed, knowing there'd be no more beautiful and hard-won anonymity for Suzanne Quinby Clayborn in Chicago.

Why's this happening to me?

She answered her own question with the words of her sage-like grandmother, Henrietta: *You haven't been minding your thoughts and emotions, Suzanne. You know they draw your experiences.*

Suzanne continued to deliberate on Gran's words during the ride to the hospital. *What've I been focusing on, other than work? Or, what have I not been focusing on?*

Suzanne cursed under her breath, admitting that she'd never really faced and reconciled the past. After graduating from Northwestern and starting her career in Chicago, instead of returning home to South Carolina, her grandmother had warned: "You can't run away from who you are." She'd looked deep into Suzanne's eyes before adding, "Or your ghosts."

Suzanne had sighed heavily. "I know, Gran. I just need a break from it all, at least for a while. I want to be normal. I want to be serious about my career and to be taken seriously. I want to focus on my work and put together a first-class creative portfolio in Chicago, so I can work anywhere in the world."

"There may be a day of reckoning, but we'll hope for the best," Gran had said ominously.

No one in Chicago knew Suzanne's terrible secret: that she could sometimes see, hear and feel the emotions of ghosts. Living in Chicago had helped to keep them at bay—or at least far enough away from her for comfort— and mostly in the peripheries of light. It seemed the energy, vitality and anonymity available in the big city did indeed help her to forget about them and focus on her career. But now, she knew the perfect and safe world she'd created in Chicago had probably been ruined, just as her life in South Carolina had been derailed when she was thirteen—in a tragic blink of an eye.

Chapter 5

At the hospital, two police officers recorded Suzanne's and Jill's recollections of the janitor and main bombing suspect, who was the only one both women had seen. Detectives came the next morning, for further questioning, and offered updates on the case.

Unlike Jill, who had a concussion, required stitches on her forehead, and suffered from severe dehydration, Suzanne wasn't physically hurt apart from also being dehydrated. She would probably be released after her lab work was completed, assuming all was well with it. Jill would have to remain another night or two, but Suzanne was relieved to learn that Jill was expected to recover completely. Meanwhile, Suzanne had made sure Jill's parents were contacted, and was relieved to see them when they arrived. She'd been unable to reach her own.

Her right shoulder was throbbing again, which could mean ghost trouble. But it also happened when she was simply picking up on the sad emotions of another person. The last time she remembered her shoulder pulsating like this was when she was bound and lying on the floor in the dark room. At the time, she hadn't known Jill was in there. But something in her had. She smiled at herself and thought: *Should pay better attention to it.* Looking up, she saw a dozen orbs floating into her room. *Ghosts this time*, she thought, rubbing her shoulder. A shadow passed and lingered near where Dan was sitting. She sensed feminine energy, a worried young mother, as a form began to fill into one of the orbs, and the ghost's electric-sparked eyes fixated on her. There was another shadow, pointing and nudging at the ghost to get closer to Suzanne, but the ghost batted it away. Suzanne took in a deep breath, choosing to ignore the drama no one else could see and focus on the two detectives. She pushed the bed's control button to raise her head. One of them informed her that she and Jill should expect a visit from other investigators already on the case, as well as the Chicago Field Division of the Bureau of Alcohol, Tobacco, Firearms and Explosives. As they left, her freshly charged cell phone, thanks to a nurse who had an extra cord, pinged next to her hand.

"That was Clyde," she said to Dan after concluding the call with her boss. "He's concerned about

Jill and me. Thankfully, to his knowledge, it was a relatively small explosion as these things go." She took a sip of water. "No one else was hurt in the blast, but the office is pretty messed up from the sprinkler system. Some windows were blown out." She motioned with her hands. "The hall had some damage, nothing too serious. The agency is closed until it's officially confirmed there are no more bombs in the building and a suitable temporary office space is arranged. Our files will be retrieved from the server and presentation materials will be recreated. But he said that I should take off as much time as I need to recover."

"I think you should hire an attorney," Dan said. "And sue the hell out of the agency and Americos." He removed his coat and rolled up the sleeves of his white shirt.

"Dan, I can't think about that right now." Absently, she picked up her cell phone to check it for messages, hoping to see a return call from her parents. But she saw only numbers she didn't recognize. *Reporters*, she thought, grimacing.

"What do you mean? You were nearly killed because of them." He waved his arms and paced.

"I guess so," she said, sighing. "But despite all this, I think I'd like to keep my job after I've recuperated. And suing my employer and its most important client aren't exactly good career moves." She felt a sudden stomach cramp, but was uncertain about how to interpret it.

"No one would blame you," he said. "We could probably get millions."

"We?"

"I meant you. But we're a team, right?"

"Clyde will make this right. He'll make sure I'm taken care of." Her stomach tightened in pain again.

"No, he won't." To Suzanne, Dan's tone seemed to signal the start of an argument, which he regularly liked to start and win. "Unless we push it."

She felt the churn and fire of Dan's agitation and his ego-driven need to be right. She put her hands over her stomach, to stem the tide of a rising nausea. "Can we please just talk about this later? I'm exhausted and I don't feel good."

He crossed his arms in a huff.

A doctor entered, and Suzanne breathed a sigh of relief.

"Hello, I'm Dr. Nesbitt. I have your lab results." His delivery was deadpan as he proceeded to tell Suzanne that her urine contained zolpidem metabolites, and her blood revealed elevated liver enzymes. That meant she'd most likely been drugged with an inhalant such as chloroform or some other form of anesthetic, and that she might possibly have some mild side effects of drowsiness for another day or two. Overall, though, she was in excellent health. Concluding, the doctor added, "A discharge nurse will be in momentarily to prepare you for immediate release."

Dan drove her home to her condominium on Armitage Avenue in the DePaul area of Lincoln Park. At the building's street entrance, two special agents from the Chicago Field Division of the Bureau of Alcohol, Tobacco, Firearms and Explosives were waiting as promised, flashing badges and credentials as she and Dan approached. Reporters also were waiting, and had parked illegally along Armitage.

Although unfamiliar with the protocols required of such official visits, Suzanne led the way, navigating the cheerless agents through the exterior glass door and a narrow vestibule lined with mailboxes, before guiding them up a short flight of stairs.

Dan used his key to unlock her door, since her key was in her purse, and was presumably still in her damaged office. As they entered her condo, the agents' eyes darted around the space as Suzanne invited them to sit in her small, but tidy, living room. The feeling she was getting from them was a disturbing mix of concern and suspicion. Dan brought in glasses of water, and they sipped in silence for a few seconds. Like most visitors, the two agents found it challenging to locate a place to set the water glasses down, as almost every available surface in Suzanne's home held some sort of plant. Perhaps she'd overdone the greenery a bit, but against the backdrop of snow often seen on the other side of the windows, the foliage was medicine for her soul and, surprisingly, was an effective antidote to ghostly haunts.

Special Agent Boyd Griffin, an unsmiling middle-aged balding man, asked her a series of standard questions: name, date and place of birth, how long she had lived at this residence and so on.

"I'll be recording your account on this tablet," said Carl McMann, the other agent.

"We've got a team of investigators on this case. But right now, the reason we're here is we'd like you to give us your full account of what happened in the Americos Building, Ms. Clayborn," Agent Griffin said. "Let's start with the day before the explosion. We want to hear everything you can remember."

Chapter 6

Three days ago, she explained to the detectives, her entire focus was on the advertising campaign to be presented the next morning. At first, Suzanne had paid no attention to the putrescent odors when she stepped off the elevator and onto the fifty-second floor. The smells were faint, and her mind had been on the work ahead. She continued her recollections.

That morning, she arrived at work, pushing through the glass entry door, holding a cup of coffee she'd bought in the concourse. She headed toward her office, as others dashed around her. Like most ad agencies, Darby, Banter & Brenton's internal rhythms and rituals were not ones that stood on delay. Its inhabitants were restless and never satisfied nor still, throwing themselves into creative frenzies with a twitchy, almost panicked energy, like trapped birds in a cold, dark attic. At times, Suzanne relished and thrived on that rush, although in this moment, she wanted to remain calm and poised—like a swan.

Even before her childhood accident, Suzanne could easily conjure vivid images and stories in her mind's eye. It was her true superpower, and she chose to build on the swan image gliding in her imagination now, noting it as an elegant metaphor for her day. The swan's strong, web-footed kick was below the surface, like her invisible mental work, as she continued to busily compile her last-minute to-do list. She smiled. The efficiency of her creativity made her heart happy.

Unlike most ad agencies, this one was located in a building named for its most important client—Americos Oil, the building's owner and largest tenant. It pleased Suzanne that she was somewhat unique among the tall building's denizens; at twenty-six, she'd become the youngest copywriter/associate creative director and the only southerner that she knew who worked in the world-class ad agency's Chicago office. As such, she co-managed a highly talented creative team consisting of one other copywriter and three art directors. There were dozens of creative teams within this large agency, but hers was the only one that had been the focus-group winner for Americos Oil's midgrade gasoline. Tomorrow's presentation of her team's ad campaign would be the most important meeting of her professional life—and she could hardly contain her excitement.

Suzanne loved the life she'd created in Chicago. The guy she was dating, Dan, was a successful commodities broker, who knew how to make her feel special and charmed. His eyes were as green and alluring as a cat's. She was attracted to him, and not just because he had a body to die for, muscular and hard in all the right places. He loved showing her off at Broadway in Chicago performances as much as at his beloved Bears' football games. He was fun and adventurous.

Her boss on the Americos Oil account, Clyde Darby, was also the agency's president of client services. He had fast-tracked her promotion and given her plenty of leeway after her first big win with one of Americos Oil's engine lubricants; her copy and concepts had played a strategic role in catapulting the brand into the number-one slot in market share. Looking back on her initial career success, Suzanne felt the vainglory of being recognized for her creative abilities—gifts that had absolutely nothing to do with ghost stories or having come from a peculiar southern family—and it felt simply stupendous.

As a reward for their work, last fall, she'd gotten approval to fly her four-member team—Shane,

Kate, Jim, and Ira—to South Carolina for a weekend of horseback riding in Hitchcock Woods, an equestrian forest preserve. In addition, they enjoyed yummy southern foods and the high-octane energy of a Friday night high school football game, southern style. *It had also worked to make them into an even better team*, she thought. Their latest work was a testament to it.

But recently, something did feel quite right, which may be why her once-thick mane of blond hair had started to thin, and her hands were chapped and peeling, the latter a blush-inducing embarrassment when shaking hands. She attributed her skin and hair issues to stress; she'd had flare-ups on her hands before. They usually coincided with a big move or career event. But, she thought with a twinge in her gut, it could also signal the approach of a significant and unseen entity that was about to materialize. *Please, no.* She shook her head, choosing to ignore these annoying distractions until after tomorrow's presentation.

She hung up her red spring coat and purse-like briefcase and kicked off the sneakers she wore to and from the L, Chicago's elevated rapid transit train, and slipped on a pair of black dress pumps from the small collection of designer shoes she kept underneath her desk. Taking a sip of coffee, she wrote down and reviewed the mental to-do list she'd made on the way in.

The first order of business was to gather her team for a final assessment of the campaign's digital layouts before printing and collating them for client handouts. She opened her computer and pulled up the overview, reviewing the creative concepts and plans for digital, print, TV and social media.

Yeah, I still love it. Our campaign's still singing to me.

She reached over to the desk phone and buzzed her assistant, Jillian O'Neill. "Jill, could you get everyone in conference room A for me?"

No answer.

"Hey, Jill? Are you there?" *How odd*, Suzanne thought, trying another number.

"Where's Jill?" she asked Shane Morgan through the speakerphone. Shane was the other copywriter on her team.

"Isn't it obvious?" he answered, standing behind her. She jumped before swiveling her chair around to face the doorway. Though he'd wear a business suit for the presentation, today, as most days, Shane stretched the meaning of business casual, wearing a black T-shirt with a punk band logo, faded jeans and a wool-lined leather bomber jacket he'd yet to shed.

"Not at all," Suzanne said, looking up. At six-foot-two, Shane had an athletic build, like her father. But instead of playing polo as her father had, Shane was a journalism student who played football at the University of Missouri until a knee injury permanently rerouted his future and focused his career on deadlines rather than the line of scrimmage. He had a keen intellect, an admirable way with words, a wry sense of humor and a handful of creative awards, earning him the distinction of being the cutest, most quick-witted smartass in the agency—Suzanne had liked him immediately. Their relationship was strictly business, but Shane often felt more like a brother to Suzanne, and they regularly engaged in politically incorrect mocking. When he added a good idea to a brainstorm, she would say, "You're pretty smart for a football player." And he'd return with a wisecrack about her being surprisingly clever for a southern blonde.

"I don't understand how you fail to see the obvious," Shane continued, frowning. "Hashtag Saint Paddy? No? How about hashtag Chicago River is garish green?"

"What are you talking about?" She really wasn't in the mood for one of Shane's comedy routines. They had way too much to do this morning.

"Oh, come on. It's the day after St. Patrick's Day. Jill's a redhead from the South Side. Hello?"

Shane tapped his foot and waved his large fingers spastically in a respectable imitation of the late great Robin Williams.

"Don't be silly. And you know how I hate stereotypes." Suzanne crossed her arms.

"A southerner who hates stereotypes. Yeah, okay, we'll just leave that one right here." He pointed to the floor.

Suzanne waved her hands dismissively. "Stop it, Shane. Our Jill would never be late for work, not for all the green beer in Chicago. And especially not today."

In fact, the petite twenty-two-year-old administrative assistant was always the first to arrive at the office and usually the last to leave at night, a regular eager beaver. She had never even missed one day of work.

Suzanne buzzed the front desk. "Bev, has Jill called in sick by chance?"

"No, dear, I haven't heard from her," came the friendly reply.

"Would you mind trying to contact her and letting me know what you find out?"

"On it," Bev said, clicking off before Suzanne could thank her. She looked back up at Shane. "While she's doing that, would you please ask everyone else to be in conference room A in five minutes?" Her tone was polite, but assertive.

"Yes, ma'am," Shane said prissily, mimicking her southern accent. Because he'd played football for Mizzou, of the Southeastern Conference, he'd been exposed to many southern campuses and their accented colloquialisms. But Shane was originally from Barrington, a Chicago suburb known for its excellent horse properties, including the one his family owned. Suzanne had been both shocked and pleased to discover this big man was a good rider during their team reward weekend in South Carolina.

She pursed her lips. "Come on, Shane."

"Hey, y'all. I might be rude or ticked off," he said, continuing with the annoying mocking, "but you'll never know it. 'Cause I'm from the South, so I always aim to please. Bless your heart." He flipped imaginary long hair from his face and exited swishing his hips, a surprisingly graceful move for a man of his bulk.

Suzanne laughed as she got up. She walked to the window and stared out at the breathtaking Chicago skyline. As she turned back to her desk, her eyes paused on the framed quote she'd hung above her desk: "A picture is worth a thousand words." It'd been written not by Confucius like everyone just assumed, but by an ingenious advertising copywriter named

Fred Barnard in 1921. He'd written a line with profound clarity and brilliantly labeled it as a "Chinese proverb" to give his ad for bread more credibility. Suzanne couldn't have been more impressed and inspired by his oft-quoted copy.

A buzz snapped her back to the present.

"Suzanne, I'm sorry, but I've been unable to get in touch with Jill," Bev said. "She isn't answering her phone."

"Oh no. This, we don't need today," Suzanne said, exhaling heavily. "Will you please let me know the second she calls or comes in?"

"You bet."

"Thanks, Bev," Suzanne said, hanging up. *Maybe Jill did get drunk last night.* But as she gathered up her presentation tablet and notes, Suzanne's hands burned and she felt a rising nausea. She looked around and breathed out. *At least there are no ghosts*, she thought, putting her things down for a moment to apply hand lotion. But something definitely felt off about Jill.

On the way to the conference room, she noticed Shane still in his office. "Aren't you coming?" she said, popping her head in.

He was finally hanging up his jacket on a coat rack that also held a couple of business suits still in a dry cleaner bag. Next to it was a large backpack.

"What's the extra set of clothes for? Afraid you'll spill your coffee during the presentation tomorrow?" She smirked at him.

"Um," he started. "No."

She then remembered Shane wasn't a particularly good public speaker, despite his office theatrics. "Hey, I was just kidding," she said. "Your part in the presentation will be stellar. Come on, football boy!"

"Yes, ma'am," he said with a southern accent, returning to his previous jauntiness.

After reviewing all the work with her team, rehearsing their respective roles and making a list of minor changes for the PowerPoint presentation, it was almost noon. They usually ordered in lunch on the hurried and entrenched days before a formal presentation, but because they had everything in such good shape, she was able to say at last: "Okay, I think we all deserve to take a breather. Go out; get some fresh air and something to eat. We'll reconvene afterward for a final rehearsal, but I think the home stretch is looking really good. Thanks, guys. Great job!"

The team headed for the door, while Suzanne sat back down.

"Aren't you coming with us?" Shane asked, turning back.

"Nah. I want to go over everything one more time. And hopefully, I'll be able to round up another admin person to make the presentation booklets. Y'all go ahead." She smiled widely. In truth, she wanted them to leave without her so she could have some quiet time to herself.

The door opened and Clyde, her boss, popped his head in. He was fiftysomething with the clean good looks of a TV news anchorman. He had a full head of salt-and-pepper hair, an amiable smile, and an avuncular Midwestern way about him that had made Suzanne feel comfortable from the start. "Slaying the dragons alone, Suzanne?"

"Not quite, although Jill's out today, so there's more admin than I anticipated. But there's nothing to worry about. We're ready." She paused. "Actually, I'm feeling pretty confident about it, so I encouraged the team to go out for lunch and a break."

"Based on what I saw earlier, I'd say good choice. I've already signed off on it."

"Yes, thanks, Clyde," she said, feeling his trust. "We won't let you down."

After he left, she went back to her office to change into her sneakers and grab her coat, purse, and cell. Once outside, she headed down Wacker Drive toward Michigan Avenue, thinking about having a Brie

sandwich, which she'd found helped to settle her
nervous stomach.

As Suzanne traveled the cold sidewalks, always
the observer, she took in the splendid grid and
geometry of the Wrigley Building, the carved neo-
Gothic gray beauty of the Tribune Tower, the
exquisite blue-glass contrast of the Trump Hotel and
the surreal sight of the Chicago River temporarily dyed
a shocking shade of green for yesterday's St. Patrick's
Day festivities.

Despite the severe chill in the March breeze
and the ever-present potential of violence in some
Chicago neighborhoods, spring break tourists
abounded in these relatively safe and vibrant Loop and
downtown areas. They looked down at the flowing
emerald and up at the iconic architecture, pointing and
posing for their pictures. Armies of men wearing wool
business suits and trench coats trooped hurriedly
toward their meetings while giving rapt attention to
their cell phones. Women wrapped in scarves, also on
phones, wore dress coats, both fashionable and not so
much, although like Suzanne, most of them were in
some sort of comfortable tennis shoe or boot. They
moved briskly through the frosty air with shoulder-
strapped purses or briefcases draped diagonally across
their chests. Deliverymen zipped by on ten-speeds.
The usual homeless people, each wearing about five

layers of clothing, were out and about doing their requisite panhandling.

Her coworkers had told her to never give them money, but Suzanne couldn't help it. She found it nearly impossible, painful even, to walk by when someone was lying pitifully on the sidewalk, perhaps ill or wounded and definitely cold, especially the nameless wrinkled fellow who had the ghosts of children perennially around him. There was something about this one man, always propped in a doorway, which both troubled and fascinated her. It seemed horribly unnatural for someone so cared for by children, albeit spirit children, to remain in such dreadful conditions on the streets of Chicago. Thankfully, the ring of little ghosts never seemed interested enough in Suzanne to tag along after her, although they always acknowledged the charity from her and others with silent cheers and merriment. Bending down now, Suzanne handed the man a twenty, and the children bounced and danced around him like playful mist-colored kittens.

The solid bodies flowing around her as she continued to walk consisted of bundled-up, humorless pedestrians in drab colors dodging unpredictable cab drivers. But at least there were no gossips or busybodies on the streets of Chicago—no one cared what you did or what sort of southern pedigree you had. No one knew that your eccentric grandmother was a mystic, your father an alcoholic, or if you could see ghosts. No one noticed how nice you were or weren't, or where you were going. No one chatted ad nauseam about whether or not the Confederate flag should fly on state capitol grounds or stowed away in a museum. There was no discussion about the degree and provenance of southern pride. No little old ladies insisting you behave like a lady or say "yes, ma'am." And she'd never seen any gum-smacking young ones with big hair who said, "Hey, suga." No one ever said, "Hey, how ya doing?" to everyone coming within shouting distance. Hell, the people on the streets of Chicago didn't even make eye contact with one another, even though most of them were probably friendly, loving Midwesterners. Everyone just innately knew, for safety or just-can't-be-bothered reasons, to put on their citified game face or a mask of indifference.

Suzanne chuckled to herself. Most southerners would consider this aspect of Chicagoans' behavior intolerable rudeness. She wasn't being critical of their response; she loved them for it. There was a tremendous amount of goodness at the base of those southerners' opinions. They simply had no context or disposition for the range and scope of lifestyles found in a big city. They would be equally horrified to know she not only didn't mind any of these mores and nonexistent courtesies, but rather, she relished the break from the overly attentive folderol of southern dictates and fanfare. Suzanne found she rather favored the anonymity that Chicago's relative indifference afforded her. What a beautiful thing it was to walk in pure, unobserved freedom. It contributed in part to the magic and manna her world had become in Chicago, and she adored all aspects of it—the energy, beat and vitality of the glittering and surprisingly clean city, at least by the great blue of Lake Michigan. For now, however, all of that would remain her own fascinating secret.

As she passed restaurants, some of the best shopping in the world, and pedestrians who paid her absolutely no mind whatsoever, Suzanne remembered there was only one thing she disliked about this city. No, not the miserable weather; it was a cliché to detest Chicago's absurdly long and cold winters. It was this: She hated being so far away—eight hundred fifty-one miles to be exact—from her horse, Misty; her family; and of course, Hitchcock Woods.

Back at the office, Suzanne was resigned to the obvious fact that Jill was not going to show up, so she worked until about ten o'clock that evening, tweaking the PowerPoint presentation and printing the booklets herself; she didn't trust anyone else other than Jill or herself to get them right.

She sat at her desk exhausted, after thinking and doing too much, with an undertone of worry about Jill and her inexplicable absence. Picking up her phone, she tried Jill's cell again. The voice mail was full. She wondered if she should call Jill's friends and family, but realized though Jill had worked with her for two years, she knew little about Jill's personal life, a condition that would've been an unforgivable sin in the South. Suzanne didn't even know the names of Jill's parents. If the office had been magically transported to South Carolina, and they were in the midst of southern ways and customs, she would have the full genealogies of all Jill's family members by now. She'd make sure to find out after the presentation.

Suzanne's cell rang, relieving her of her mental burden for the moment. "Hello?"

"What's keeping you so late?" said Dan, sounding annoyed. "I need you to come home right now." They didn't yet live together, but he sometimes acted like it.

Suzanne exhaled audibly. "Listen, Dan, you know I have an important presentation tomorrow, and I said I'd probably be working late tonight. So just go to sleep. Okay?" She said it nicely, her southern accent exaggerated, but as soon as it was out of her mouth, she felt a stab of aggravation—both her own and his.

"I just want to be with you." His voice melted into something softer. "I need you, baby."

"Oh, good grief." Her lips tightened. If she weren't so tired, she might've laughed or come back at him with a crude joke. But in that moment, she was just sick to death of all the relationships she'd had with men, of the weight and expectation of them. She rubbed the nape of her neck. "I'm not finished. So please, don't wait up. Bye," she said, pushing the off button.

Laying her cell on the desk, she made an updated backup file of the presentation on the server, slipped into her suit jacket and sneakers, and went out of the office to the hall bathroom. She immediately smelled the offensive odors she'd encountered that morning, only now they had intensified and were impossible to ignore. She looked down the long hall and saw a man wearing a baggy coverall pushing a cleaning-supplies cart. He had on thick horn-rimmed glasses and wore yellow rubber gloves like her mother used to don on the rare occasions she washed dishes. His black, shoulder-length, unruly hair was topped with a Cubs baseball cap pulled low, obscuring his face.

"Excuse me, sir? Are you working on getting rid of the smell? I hope?"

Without looking directly at her, he nodded and, incredibly, pulled out a can of disinfectant spray.

She stepped toward him. "Is there anything else you can do? I've got an important presentation here in the morning, and the office can't smell like a dirty barn."

As if to avoid her, the guy quickly moved out of sight, pushing his cart around the corner. She heard it crash into a wall, causing her to drop her bathroom key card on the floor.

Great, the guy's not only incompetent, he's probably drunk. And a little scary, she thought, remembering it was late and she was alone. As she exhaled, she saw her breath fog in the air. She felt a painful twinge in her right shoulder. She looked up. There at the other end of the hall was a young boy, incandescent and as unnatural in this environment as the barn smells. He was waving at her. *Damn.* She'd never seen a ghost in her office building before.

"No, just don't," she said as his apparition faded into the shadows.

Hurriedly, she picked up the key card and swiped it over the digital lock, moving as quickly as she could. After finishing, she cautiously poked her head out of the bathroom door, looking both ways before proceeding. Her sigh of relief did not condense into abnormally cold air. *Okay, good.* The ghost and janitor were gone, but not the bad overpowering smell. *Two out of three...* Suzanne raced back toward her office, key card readied, suddenly feeling like she should've taken her cell with her. As soon as she reached her desk, she'd call housekeeping about getting rid of the smell.

But as she turned the second corner, she was grabbed from behind, her mouth covered. The last thing she saw was the hideous yellow rubber glove.

Chapter 7

"How did you say you got out of the locked closet?" Agent Griffin asked.

"Someone unlocked it," Suzanne said bluntly.

"Can you describe the person who let you and Ms. O'Neill out?"

"I know this sounds funny, but there wasn't anyone there, or at least I didn't see anyone, once the door opened. The clock was ticking...I went back to get Jill. It wasn't easy to drag her out. Then...I was a little preoccupied, trying to get us out of the building...before a bomb killed us."

"Don't you think the person who let you out would have at least said something, Ms. Clayborn?"

"Probably, but maybe that person just wanted to get out fast too. The alarms were blaring after all." She pulled her limp hair up to cool her neck. She'd left out the part about sensing the remorse of one of the watchers, the one who might've ended up letting them out. She also didn't mention seeing the boy ghost. Until now, she hadn't thought ghosts could move tangible things like keys, locks and doors. But maybe the one she'd seen had actually helped her get out—or not. But she wasn't about to mention anything about her psychic abilities to Special Agent Boyd Griffin. He seemed wary enough of her as it was.

"You said that when you woke up in the closet, you were on a cushioned mat and there was a pillow under your head."

"Yes." She scraped her itching, chapped hands on her pants.

"Doesn't it strike you as odd that someone would tie you up and leave you to die but, in the meantime, try to make you feel comfortable on a mat with a pillow, while you did not find Ms. O'Neill in a similar situation?"

"Yes, it does. But the whole thing seems odd. I don't know anyone who'd want to hurt Jill, but not me. Wait. That didn't come out right. I don't know anyone who would do any of this," she said, feeling her stomach lurch.

"You said your cell phone was on your person?"
"Yes."

"Ms. O'Neill's cell phone was found in the lobby trash. No prints."

"That's weird," Suzanne said, growing more confused.

Griffin nodded. "Are you aware that no other explosives were found in the Americos Building? Only on the fifty-second floor, where *you* work."

"Oh, no. I didn't know it was confirmed," she responded. "But obviously, I'm not the only person to work on the fifty-second floor." She hated that her words sounded defensive.

"The countdown did not start until after *you* became conscious. Do you think that was a coincidence?"

"I have to assume someone…was watching remotely, since there was a video camera and it was on." Her hands burned as she remembered feeling watched.

"Why do you think someone would want you to believe you were about to get blown up? But then give you a relatively easy way out?"

"Relatively easy?" Her heart was racing. "I don't know. Maybe they got some sort of weird satisfaction out of scaring the crap out of two women."

"Or just you," Griffin said, looking her straight in the eyes.

"What's that supposed to mean?" She held her palms up.

Ignoring her question, Griffin looked down at his notes and continued with a calm, assertive voice: "You claim that a cleaning employee locked you in the closet."

"I said that's what I've deduced because I saw the cleaning guy was wearing yellow rubber gloves. I was grabbed from behind after I came out of the hall bathroom. The yellow gloves were all that I remember seeing before blacking out. It's also how I was able to tell Dan that I thought we were on the fifty-second floor."

"Suzanne, you didn't tell me you were on the fifty-second floor," Dan said.

"I didn't?" She put her hands to her temples, trying to remember.

"No, you said you thought you were in the Americos Building when we got cut off. Of course, I relayed what you said to 911, but the operator told me the fire alarms in the building had already been activated."

"That doesn't make any sense."

"I'll rephrase my earlier question," Griffin said. "Why do you think someone would want you to believe you were about to get blown up? But then, possibly be the one to pull the alarms and let you out in time?"

"To scare us to death?" She shook her head. "Have you talked to the building's HR about the cleaning staff?"

"Yes. One of the recent hires on the cleaning and maintenance staff matched the description of the suspect you and Ms. O'Neill provided the police. The suspect listed his name as John Johns on his job application and he was mute."

"Mute?" She scrunched up her nose.

"Unable to speak. Do you know a John Johns who is mute?"

"Of course not!" She didn't like the way this conversation was going. "Why didn't someone else find Jill during the day?"

"Another member of the custodial staff reported being unable to get into that particular closet the day before, but our main suspect informed HR, in writing, that he'd already fixed the lock and taken care of the floor's cleaning. That turned out to be only partially true. Because he hadn't fixed the lock, but rather changed the whole doorknob out and presumably possessed the only key."

"So the SOB's handy," Suzanne mumbled.

Griffin continued: "A few of the security cameras were taped over, so we don't have a clear photo of him other than the one for his security badge and one in the elevator, taken the night before Ms. O'Neill's assault. Do you recognize him?" He held up the photos.

Suzanne looked at the photos, but the man had shoulder-length black hair covering most of his face, just as it had when she'd seen him in person in the hall. "No, but how could anyone tell? The man's face is covered." She noted that his nose was long and his skin was tan, but both looked fake.

"Have you ever let someone into the building late at night, Ms. Clayborn?" Griffin asked, abruptly changing the line of questioning.

"Just once. A boyfriend."

"Wait a minute, you've never let me into that building at night," Dan objected.

"It was before we met, Dan."

Dan crossed his bulky arms and jutted his chin forward, but remained quiet.

"We'll need his name and contact information," Griffin said.

"Sure, but I'm confident John had nothing to do with this," she said. She gasped with the realization that his and the bomber's moniker were the same.

Griffin and McMann looked at each other.

"I'm sure that's just a coincidence," Suzanne said, holding up her palms again. "John Reynolds is a shorter guy, probably five-foot-ten at the most, and definitely not handy with stuff like changing doorknobs or cleaning. He works for our sister public relations company, located over in One Illinois." She referred to an adjacent office building. "He's an account guy and supersmart with computers and digital media." She exhaled. "But if John had done this, he sure wouldn't have been stupid enough to use his real name." She rolled her eyes.

"Have you ever had any interactions with environmental activists, Ms. Clayborn?" Griffin asked.

"No," she said, exhaling again. "But I'm sure you already know that Climate Change activists have been protesting over several recent ocean-liner oil leaks with demonstrations in front of the Americos Building, and our PR people would be involved with that."

"Do you think John Reynolds would have had any direct interactions or conversations with environmental activists?" Griffin asked, ignoring her comment.

"It's possible," she said, again feeling nervous about Griffin's line of questioning and how it might tie to her. "As I said, PR gets involved when there are environmental protests."

Griffin made a note before continuing. "Our team has evidence of a man matching the description of the main suspect purchasing a doorknob at a hardware store next to the First Class Horse Carriage Company," Griffin said, still looking down at his notes. "Given the ingredients of the bomb, it appears the suspect had a second job there."

"At a horse carriage company?" she asked, shocked at this news and unable to ignore yet another connection to her: her equestrian background. Her stomach was in knots.

"We have reason to believe that our suspect stole ammonium nitrate from First Class Horse Carriage to make his fertilizer bomb."

"How convenient," she said sarcastically, shrugging.

"You're familiar with ammonium nitrate, then," Griffin said, with no expression.

But she felt his genuine inner surprise. "I'm aware that it turns horse manure into a suitable fertilizer for gardening and that farmers in South Carolina use small fertilizer bombs all the time. They mix ammonium nitrate powder with manure and fuel, to remove things like tree stumps and large root systems."

"Interesting," Griffin said. McCann typed. "That's exactly what the suspect did. He mixed ammonium nitrate powder with manure and fuel to make his fertilizer bomb." Griffin paused, as if for effect, before continuing. "First Class Carriage also reported that our suspect was mute, but he had substantial knowledge of horses and was quite good with their care. Not surprisingly, he hasn't returned to either place since the bombing event."

"I see," she said. "And he was employed at the carriage company for the same period of time as in the Americos Building?"

"Affirmative—for exactly two weeks," Griffin said. "Ms. Clayborn, do you think your former, um, friend, John Reynolds, would know how to use ammonium nitrate to make a fertilizer bomb?"

"No." She looked at Griffin as though he had lost his mind. McCann simply continued recording her answers with a neutral expression on his face.

"Have you ever discussed or shared your knowledge of ammonium nitrate and fertilizer bombs with Mr. Reynolds or anyone else in Chicago?"

"No, but for the record, I personally do not know how to make a fertilizer bomb with ammonium nitrate. As I said, I'm aware that it's done. I've never made one myself."

Griffin continued. "Are you certain you've never talked to or gotten into an argument with someone from an environmental group about climate change or the recent oil spills?"

"No, at least not to my knowledge. But everyone at the agency is familiar with eco-terrorism," she said, meaning acts of violence committed with explosives and illegal firearms in support of environmental causes. "Why do you keep insinuating the main suspect is connected to me?" It felt like her blood pressure was spiking. She was so done with trying to answer any more of his ridiculous questions.

"We're looking at all the angles, trying to follow the evidence," Griffin said, unperturbed.

"Let me just tell you this: I don't know any environmental activists. And I sure as hell haven't talked to one. I don't know anyone mute or anyone who'd be capable of doing any of this." But as soon as she said it, she had a flash of something on the night in question. Something had been muttered, soft and low, just as she was grabbed and her mouth covered. It might've been "Shoe, Sue or Suze." *No... It was "sorry, Suze." Oh my God. He knew my name and obviously wasn't mute.*

As this realization took hold, she was struck with the thought that she did know someone who had a working knowledge of ammonium nitrate, fertilizer bombs and horses: her own messed-up father. His family had long been in the peach-farming business, and he was an expert equestrian. He knew how to turn horse manure into a useful fertilizer with ammonium nitrate. He also knew how to make a fertilizer bomb with it. And had done it many times. He knew how to take care of horses. He was of similar six-foot or so height to the janitor. But she didn't want to mention these galloping thoughts to Griffin, nor did she care to mention that her father had accidentally shot her with a Colt .45, nearly killing her, when she was thirteen.

Sure, her father was handy but only with woodworking tools. He went by his initials, JJ, although his name wasn't John Johns. And he could get drunk enough to get involved with something this stupid and outrageous. Perhaps to scare her into coming back home to South Carolina.

Suzanne shook her head, immediately dismissing her thoughts as the paranoid product of a traumatized, tired mind and an exhausted body—and a childhood wound she'd tried hard to forget. She really wasn't at all sure the guy who grabbed her had said anything. After all, she'd been caught off-guard. He'd drugged her. She might have dreamt it. She was still confused. None of this had anything to do with her or her father. He loved her. He'd never do anything to hurt her—at least not intentionally.

"Did you say something?" Griffin stared at her with raised eyebrows.

"No, no, I was just trying to remember…but my head's still in a fog." She took a breath. "Agent Griffin, isn't it obvious that this cleaning guy, this bomber wannabe, and possible accomplices, is just some kind of wacko…perhaps wanting to emulate Timothy McVeigh, but didn't have the guts to actually kill someone? Or, the suspect may be part of some extreme protest group, or as you suggested, an environmental group trying to make a statement about Americos' recent oil leaks by scaring key people who work on Americos' ad team—not just me personally. It even makes sense that the eco-terrorists would use fertilizer and Americos gasoline to make a bomb in this case. Which means Jill and I were simply in the wrong place at the wrong time. Can we just finish this now? I'm so exhausted, I may pass out at any moment."

"We're almost done," Griffin said.

Both men were taking notes, Griffin on paper, McMann on the tablet.

She let go of her breath, feeling nauseated and hoping she wouldn't throw up. "Listen, since my office was damaged, I'm assuming I won't be able to return to work for a while. And, after this, um, conversation, I'm actually scared to be there or even stay in town right now, especially after you just made it sound like I might've been specifically targeted. Given all that, I want to go somewhere safe and recuperate from this mess until you make some arrests," she said. "I want to recover in my hometown in South Carolina, at my parents' house. I hope you don't have a problem with that." She wanted to cry, but the tears felt stuck, like they were encased in a scab of her past. "I'm sure my family's attorney will back me up if I want to leave," she said for emphasis.

"We can't stop you from leaving," Griffin said. "But we'll need your contact info."

"Fine," Suzanne said, standing up and walking to a side table. She grabbed a pad and pencil. "This is where I'll be as soon as I can make the arrangements to get there," she said, handing him the paper. "You have my cell number. Is there anything else? I'd appreciate it if you left now so I can make plans and start to get over this."

"We're done, for now," Griffin said, rising. "Thank you for your cooperation," he added in his softest voice of the evening.

Closing the tablet case, McCann stood up, joining Griffin at the door. "We hope you'll be able to recover quickly with your family," McCann said, finally making a comment.

"Thank you," she said, shutting the door behind them.

Chapter 8

Suzanne trudged into the kitchen and opened the refrigerator. "That was so stressful," she said, pulling out a wedge of Brie. "They made it sound like I'm being targeted, or I'm at fault somehow."

"I am surprised you know about ammonium nitrate and fertilizer bombs," Dan said, following her. He smiled as his eyebrows rose over his intense eyes.

Suzanne forced a smile. "Yep, I'm just full of surprises, aren't I?" she said, not feeling good-humored or like trying to explain herself further. She took a large bite out of the cheese, not bothering with a knife and plate as she sat at her little kitchen table.

"I didn't mean anything by that," he said. He approached and began giving her a neck massage. "I know you're smart about a lot of things. I wouldn't be with you otherwise."

She exhaled heavily, staring at the Brie in her trembling hands. "As I told the agents, I plan to go back home for a while. I need to feel safe again. I hope you don't mind either."

"You don't have to go. I'll keep you from harm, and I need you here with me, baby," he said, continuing with the neck massage. He spoke softly, but his touch was heavy-handed. A strand of her hair caught in his Rolex watchband.

"Ow," she said, pulling away. "And please don't call me baby."

"Oh, come on," Dan said.

"Sorry, I don't mean to be rude. But I'm so bone tired that I can't relax." She ate the remainder of the cheese.

"I know how to make you relax," he said coaxingly, rubbing her arms.

"Please, Dan, I need to call my parents again and my grandmother." She pulled away. "I also need to take a long, hot bath and…just go to bed."

"I'm good with that," he said suggestively.

She let out a whoosh of air. "Dan, I appreciate your being with me at the hospital and while the agents were here. But right now, I need some time alone to figure out how to process this and survive. And to make the calls. Can you give me a frickin' break?"

"Well, that's some thanks," he said. "I'm only trying to help." His voice softened as he added, "I just want to love you, baby, to help you relax. You shouldn't be alone right now. I can help make you feel better. I want to—"

Did he not hear what I just said? "Listen, this should go without saying, but I've just been through one of the greatest traumas a person can go through, and you're only thinking about—Please, can you just go home to your place tonight?"

He glared at her.

"And can you leave your key? Mine got blown up."

"You know, sometimes, you can be a real..." he started, slamming his key on the table. "Call me when you can be friendly and want some company."

Oh dear God. She shook her head as he stormed out of her condo. *How did my terrifying days become about him?*

Suzanne dead-bolted the door and armed her security system before dropping onto the sofa and clicking the TV remote. She wanted some background noise but didn't feel able to handle the local Chicago news broadcasts, with their endless stories of city violence and mayhem, not to mention the coverage of her and the explosion. She quickly turned the channel to something benign, and what had become a daily wind-down obsession anyway: the classic movie station. She rarely consumed anything else on TV, except for a few sitcom reruns. She favored online media sources for headline news, but right now, she didn't want to take in any of it.

She scrolled through the Recents list on her phone and hit her parents' home number. Just like before, there was no answer. She ended the call before it went into voice mail. She tried both of their cells again. Nothing. Frustrated, she sat a few minutes wondering how they could not know what had happened by now. She knew they watched the news. She called again, this time leaving messages, saying she was okay and planned to fly home soon. Finally, she rang up Gran, who answered immediately in her usual sweet voice.

"Oh, thank you, Jesus, someone is home!" Suzanne cried. "Gran, have you seen the news about the explosion in Chicago?"

"No, dear, I've been out in the fields today," she said. Gran lived on a massive peach orchard in Greenfield, South Carolina. "And you know how I loathe network news."

After she filled in her grandmother, Suzanne said, "I want to come home."

"Of course. I'm here for you, Suzanne."

"Thanks, Gran. I'm going to make airline reservations now, and I'll let you know as soon as I've finalized an itinerary."

"I'm so grateful you're okay and coming home," Henrietta said before promising to track down her son and daughter-in-law.

As soon as she hung up, it dinged. It was a reporter from ABC 7 Chicago.

"Listen, I'm trying to recover here," Suzanne said, hitting end. It dinged again. CBS. Exasperated, she shut down her phone.

After taking a bath and getting in comfortable pajamas, she flipped open her laptop to book a flight, her mind racing with the need to track down her father as soon as possible. She pushed the keys, but they weren't responding. She tried to restart the laptop as the light bulb in the lamp burned out. The TV screen filled with static.

"Well, isn't this just great timing," she said, breathing out the familiar misty clouds and seeing shadowy movement in her peripheral vision.

Closest to her was a blurred apparition of a boy, a woman stood behind him with her hands on his shoulders, perhaps his mother. He might've been the boy ghost she'd seen in the Americos Building the night of her assault. *He feels the same.* Each ghost had its own energy signature and could leave traces of itself like a cold, dusty fingerprint. But she was in no mood to examine this one more closely.

"Just go away. I don't want to know who you are or what you want right now." The boy and woman looked more sad than scary. Just as she was about to feel sorry for them, other entities crowded around them, appearing as black orbs floating like eclipses on small moons.

She'd never seen this many dark spirits crammed into her condo before. It felt like a thousand eyeballs were on her, studying her, searching her for fears and vulnerabilities like she was some sort of psychic Internet. *God, I hate when they do that.* She stood up. "Enough!" she shouted, stamping her foot. She pointed toward the door. "I'm claiming my space. Now go!"

They disappeared at once, but she knew it would be a temporary acquiescence. Once they made an entrance to a place, it was difficult to eradicate them completely—which meant she couldn't wait to get back to the one place she truly felt safe, where ghosts were not allowed.

Chapter 9

When Chicagoans, or anyone unfamiliar with the horse town of Aiken, South Carolina, first heard the words "Hitchcock Woods," they probably thought of something mysterious or related to the late movie director and master of suspense Alfred Hitchcock. Suzanne knew the Woods held a secret or two, but they were related to the sacred aspects of her childhood and had nothing to do with the filmmaker.

Hitchcock Woods was a massive, 2,100-acre forest preserve, located right smack-dab in the middle of Aiken proper. It contained a lush and verdant canopy of pines and hardwoods, which provided shade for some seventy miles of interlacing trails for horses, hounds, joggers and walkers. But above all, it was a horse lover's utopia, richly steeped in equine tradition, tack and the patinas of saddle leather for more than two centuries.

The Woods was named after its founder, Thomas Hitchcock, who was one of the leading American polo players in the latter part of the nineteenth century and a hall-of-fame horse trainer known as the father of American steeplechase horse racing. An early settler of Aiken, Hitchcock also was considered one of the founders of what was called "Aiken's Winter Colony," comprised of his fabulously rich snowbird friends wanting to escape the Northeast's cold. Meanwhile, a major rail line built in the mid-1800s ran through town, bringing visitors seeking a "healing place," for which Aiken was becoming known, for diseases like malaria and tuberculosis. Many of the early settlers' historic Victorian homes still stood throughout Aiken, as proud and well maintained as any Revolutionary War statue, marking a notable era in Aiken's past. Of course, Suzanne knew well that the Woods continued the tradition, as her true "healing place."

Unlike other mild-weather equestrian locations, the acreage that ultimately became Hitchcock Woods was imbedded with a rare geological feature that was also a highly coveted feature: white sand—miles and miles of it—considered one of the best horse-riding surface materials to be found anywhere in the world. Most people didn't know how all of that lovely sand, as fine as that found on any Carolina beach, came to be deposited in the Woods, especially since Aiken was located more than a

hundred and thirty miles inland. But it was neither
trucked in nor a supernatural occurrence; the lands had
simply been part of ancient coastlines some twenty
million years ago.

Truly, the most mysterious aspect of Hitchcock
Woods was the one only Suzanne was privy to—ghosts
were unable to cross over or remain within its boundaries.
Sometimes she wondered why that was the case,
especially since there was an area located near the middle
of the Woods many people considered an ancient Native
American mound—just the sort of place one might
expect to find spirits lingering. Yet Suzanne had never
seen a ghost near or by the old burial ground. Nor had
she been witness to any along the Woods' periphery,
where there were a few cemetery plots. Did ghosts ever
try to get into Hitchcock Woods, like kids sneaking into a
concert, only to be escorted out by some benevolent
force? Or were the Woods so dynamically alive that
ghosts couldn't survive in them?

There was no one to answer such questions and
speculations except the local ghosts outside of the
Woods, but they never gave Suzanne a straight answer. So
she chose to believe Hitchcock Woods was just too
sacred and lively for ghosts, due in part to the annual
Blessing of the Hounds, held there every Thanksgiving
morning. During the ceremony, hundreds of spectators
and riders gathered at the Memorial Gate entrance for the

blessing, officiated by a local priest, and they would pray
for the safety, good sport, and successful beginning of the
traditional foxhunting season, although real foxes did not
die in the event. Instead, raucous hounds followed a fox
scent that had been dragged across the land, creating an
invisible but malodorous trail to chase. Green-frocked
riders and others followed, joining in on the chase or
jumping over the horse fences made of logs and wooden
planks. Some of the jumps were named "Aikens," after
the town.

Hitchcock Woods breathed even as a horse
breathed, in stillness or enthusiasm, projecting strength
and grace, under the tender care of its foundation's
members and those who loved it the most. The Woods
had changed little through the years, unlike Suzanne. She
came to ride, of course, but now, treks in Hitchcock
Woods had more to do with recapturing the freedom and
sanctuary she had felt there as a girl—the girl she'd been
before she was shot in the back—before ghosts had
entered her outside world and spoiled her fields of vision.
She remembered how nurturing the Woods felt then, how
it seemed to love and mentor her, encouraging her to ride
better, jump higher and dream bigger. The Woods later
fired up her ambition to become an accomplished writer,
unafraid of ghosts, caprioling in a world-famous
advertising agency in a big city. Up until now, she hadn't
known the Woods could call her back home from such

dreams. But the Woods was wise and knew her well. Suzanne needed now more than ever before the healing, clarity and renewal that only its forested boundaries could provide. And the Woods was more than happy to oblige.

After three haunted days, two sleepless nights, and one make-up visit from a sheepish Dan, which left her feeling more drained than appeased, Suzanne was finally headed to Chicago's O'Hare International Airport. Following the flight, a cab driver dropped her off at a sprawling ranch-style brick house in Aiken. It was the home in which she was raised and her parents still lived. Bordering on Hitchcock Woods, it sat on three rolling acres with a small duck pond and gentle waves of land that looked like they had been cut out of the Woods' sylvan hemline.

She was arriving at a time in late March when the bloodred azaleas were in full bloom under a parasol of pines giving birth to a monsoon of pollen. Ancient wisteria vines, contorted up and over the front porch long ago, were now draping a fragrant curtain of purple over the entrance, like ripening grapes heavy in the fields. The window glass was disturbingly dark, a black eye over a lifeless interior.

Neither one of her parents had answered their phones or returned her calls since the bomb incident in Chicago. Typically, she wouldn't be alarmed by the lack of communication with her eccentric mother and father.

They were notorious for flying out of the country or taking off to Florida at the drop of a hat without telling her or even explaining to the domestic help anything about their travel plans. She'd not talked with her mother in weeks, and she couldn't remember when she'd last communicated with her dad. A month maybe? She felt a stab of guilt that made her stomach hurt.

After the cabbie drove away, she fetched the spare house key her mother kept under a planter. Stepping through the front door, key in hand, she called out into a darkened entry, "Hello? Anyone home?" Obviously not, but she searched the rooms anyway, flipping light switches on as she traveled the long stretch of the five-bedroom ranch house.

At the end of the long hall, she stopped to take in a deep breath. *How could they not know by now?* And where the heck was Della, their full-time cook and housekeeper? Suzanne's heart raced faster with the horrible thought that something awful could've happened to all of them too. Hurriedly, she backtracked to her father's study to use the house phone, since she'd left her cell in her bag on the porch. As she punched in her mother's number, she noticed two stacks of old, unopened letters on her father's desk. Next to them was a yellowed, maybe decades old, typewritten, short manuscript, *The Secrets of Bears Repeating*, written by her grandmother Henrietta. The manuscript surprised Suzanne; she thought she'd been aware of all of her grandmother's writings.

Voice mail full. Returning the phone to its charging stand, she thumbed through the six-inch stacks of unopened envelopes, also written by her grandmother. All were addressed to her father, with postmark dates going back many years. Suzanne had always believed that her father and Gran maintained a close and amiable relationship. These sealed, old letters didn't make any sense. What if they offered some insight about why her father was an alcoholic and chronic liar, irresponsible and unpredictable? She had her suspicions, but there was probably a lot she didn't know about their complicated history.

Man, I'd like to open these. Instead, she picked up the manuscript and became even more curious.

The Secrets of Bears Repeating
By Henrietta S. Clayborn

Preface

Through my experiences with an Apache medicine man named Bears Repeating, my own research and metaphysical channeling experiences, I have learned some ancient spiritual truths and healing methods, universal in nature, that are worth repeating and sharing with you now.

If something within starts to resonate, rest assured you too are ready to regain this ancient wisdom.

I say "regain" because this knowledge has been lovingly built into you by your Creator but is lying dormant and suppressed, waiting for you to reclaim it with your presence, awakening awareness and reintegration.

I wish we didn't need to relearn these universal truths; life would be easier if they had been taught to us in our childhoods and throughout our lives. But that is not where we are in our personal and collective evolution. Meanwhile, humanity has been intentionally deceived and manipulated by negative forces that work to keep us in the dark about our true divine identities and power. But that will change!

If you are willing and open to internalize this information and believe in yourself now with pure intentions, you will remember the truth about who you are, although it may not be all at once, as everyone's awakening to true freedom is a process and personal journey. But ultimately, if you choose wisely, you will learn how to create healing, wholeness, and happiness for yourself—everything you want in life.

It is actually a simple process that begins with—

Suzanne jumped when the phone rang. "Hello?"

"Suzanne, is that you?" Henrietta asked. "You didn't answer your cell phone, so I thought I'd try this one."

Suzanne, still shaking, breathed out with relief.

"Are you okay, dear?"

"Oh, Gran. The phone just startled me, and I'm already jittery..." Her shoulder started to throb, and she felt the scar on her back vibrating. She snapped her eyes to some movement in the shadowed corner of the room. "I just arrived and haven't even brought my bags in yet."

"Well, then, you'll be happy to hear that I've finally gotten ahold of your parents."

"Are they all right? Why haven't they returned any of my calls? Where's Della?" she said as the pulsating in her right shoulder continued.

"Not to worry, all are fine, but both of your parents are pretty far away. Your mother's been on a Mediterranean cruise with her girlfriends. That's why she couldn't be reached initially or call you back."

"Oh, thank God."

"I found out she's already on a plane back, because another friend contacted her before I could and told her what had happened. Your father's apparently been in a Florida rehab again, although he hadn't mentioned going to me. But at least he knows when he should go. I'm grateful for that."

"Me too," Suzanne said. "How long's he been there?"

"For the past month. That's why your mama felt she could leave, I suppose. They gave Della the time off, so I called her and asked if she could stock the kitchen for you. She said she would but had a few more personal things to take care of before your parents return, so she might not be there when you arrived."

"I can't tell you how relieved I am to hear everyone's okay," Suzanne said, exhaling loudly, with a hint of white haze in it. "How did you find out about Dad?" she asked, knowing cell phones weren't allowed in rehab.

"By luck, he just called because he wanted me to check on the horses, to make sure the barn hands were taking care of them. He was calling on a borrowed phone because he said he lost his cell phone, or was it his data? Anyway, after I filled him in about your situation, he asked me to tell you he's thrilled and relieved you're home, and he'll be back tomorrow or soon thereafter. He'll be driving up."

"Thank God! I've been so worried."

"In the meantime, will you come out here for a visit, then?" Henrietta asked.

"Yes. I'll be out to see you, probably this evening, if that's okay," Suzanne said. "Gran, as I said, I just walked in, and I desperately need to see Misty." She rubbed her right shoulder, trying to get it to calm down.

"Of course, I understand. Give her a check and a ride. And I already know you'll take a look at the others, as your dad asked. Can't wait to see you, Peaches," Henrietta said, using one of the family's pet names for her. "Love you."

"Me too, Gran! I won't be too long." Satisfied that everyone was safe and on their way back home, Suzanne wanted to ask Gran about the letters and the secret manuscript. But she decided to wait until she could do it in person. "Bye for now."

Looking down again at the words *The Secrets of Bears Repeating*, Suzanne's breath created a milk-white cloud and the hair on her arms stood up. Of course, she knew the ghost was in the corner, having detected him as soon as she'd answered the phone. But since she was ignoring him, and he obviously knew it, he was now accelerating the energy needed to get her direct attention. *I hate when they do that*, she thought.

The ghost looked like a young boy, perhaps ten or eleven years old, very similar to the one she'd seen once, maybe twice, in Chicago. Was he the same? She wasn't sure. The energy signature of this one was indistinct, as his translucent image faded in and out of the shadows. There was no mother with him this time, either. Assuming he was the same, Suzanne wondered why and how he had traveled with her from Chicago, like a ghostly stowaway. Up until now, she'd never encountered something like that.

"Yeah, I see you there," Suzanne said. "I know you're there. But I don't have time to talk with you right now." The throbbing continued, as she rubbed her shoulder. "Maybe later. Okay?" She let out a breath when the pain subsided.

Ghosts had haunted Suzanne from the moment she awoke in the hospital after being shot by her father. The shooting wasn't intentional, just a terrible accident, but the scars it left didn't know the difference. Sometimes, in moments of weakness or emotional overload, she didn't know the difference either.

Her father had been drunk and decided to try out his brand-new Colt .45 in the backyard. Meanwhile, unbeknownst to him, Suzanne had declined to go shopping with her mother and was playing behind the storage shed, feeding the ducks. His shot missed the target on the shed door, went straight through, and struck her in the back. The bullet missed her spine and lung but shattered her right shoulder blade. Della saw the whole thing from the kitchen window and, fortunately, was able to call 911 in a matter of seconds. In the meantime, Della applied pressure to the bleeding wound while Suzanne's father, wailing pitifully, stumbled about drunkenly. Even with Della's heroic efforts, Suzanne lost a tremendous

amount of blood. She went into cardiac arrest just as
paramedics arrived in time to save her life. Her near-death
experience lasted perhaps for only a few seconds or
maybe longer; she wasn't really sure. But afterward, the
ghosts began their long, unhurried soliloquies and tried to
use her to complete their unfinished business. It was as if
her suspended moments in spirit had opened up some
kind of psychic doorway in Suzanne's soul, and she was
unable to close it—though she'd tried many times.

As a young teen, she was scared to death of the
ghosts. She was too afraid to look at or be alone with
them in the dark. It was an inescapable nightmare, like
being locked in a room that's on fire. She begged her
mother to take her to shrinks, priests, psychics,
hypnotists—anyone who might fix her and make her
right again. She prayed over and over: *Please, God, make me
normal again.* Eventually, she resigned herself to simply
tolerate their appearances. That was, until she figured out
there were holy reprieves, or "healing places," in both
Hitchcock Woods and a few locales in Chicago. These
discoveries made her deliriously happy.

Her near-death experience also had turned her
into something the psychic world called an empath,
meaning she could clairvoyantly feel the emotions of
other people, including those of ghosts. It was almost as
bad as seeing and hearing them. Being a strong empath
came with a whole host of problems, like making the

heavy violence of some contemporary movies, shows and TV news downright impossible to watch. She absorbed the negative emotions of those who created and performed in negative broadcasts. Hence, her attraction to classic movies and only the sweet, funny sitcom reruns that were safe enough to entertain but not overwhelm her heightened sensitivities.

Sometimes, when she didn't see the ghosts, she could feel their presence in tangible ways. There was no rhyme or reason for the way they appeared, although she suspected it had more to do with their abilities than hers. She didn't know how ghosts could change the energy in, on or around her, but they could and she tried to decode it. When the temperature suddenly dropped around her, for example, it meant she was in the baleful gaze of a ghost. Her right shoulder might hurt; the scar on her back could vibrate. Her arms might tingle and her breath would turn white. Sometimes, when she successfully ignored the ghosts, they'd go away, perhaps knowing that she wasn't the right person to help with their particular issue. But if they thought she could be useful, they'd continue to pester her with annoying sensations, going to great lengths to gain her attention and advocacy. Like this persistent boy ghost, for instance.

She stared at *The Secrets of Bears Repeating*, wanting to at least skim it, but her mind was on her horse, Misty, and she couldn't wait to see her.

Leaving the manuscript and boy for now, Suzanne ran out to the front porch, returned the key to its hiding place, brought in her bags and locked the door. In her childhood bedroom, she pulled out one of the many riding outfits she kept in the closet, while the boy ghost fixated on her from outside the window. "Hey, no Peeping Toms," she said, pulling the drapes closed. Once in her riding breeches, shirt and boots, she popped into the pantry to gather some carrots and peppermints, knowing Della always kept an ample supply on hand. With the treats in her pockets, she walked briskly on a pea gravel path to the barn some fifty yards down a medium incline from the back of the main house. She grew more excited with each step.

The stable doors were wide open and several fans were blowing loudly. Randy Mackenzie, the family's barn manager, was there along with a groom, Brad Johnson. Randy was in the first crosstie stall, brushing the underside of Cole, her father's magnificent black thoroughbred stallion. Brad was grooming Juice, a flashy chestnut thoroughbred-quarter horse cross her father used as a polo pony. With the fans making a racket, neither human noticed her approach, but the horses did, and nickered a greeting.

Randy turned. "Wow! Whoa, hey, Suzanne! Thank God you're all right, and you're home!" He spread his arms out to her.

She'd seen Randy about eight months ago, and although she knew he'd filled out as an adult, she still thought of him as the skinny, rangy, timid, freckle-faced boy he'd been in grade school. Even so, his chest was now broad and he had defined biceps. He was tan and his wavy, strawberry-blond hair, just over his ears, was sun-kissed and beautiful.

"Hey, Randy!" Standing on her tippy toes, she returned the embrace of her long-time friend. He had the smell of a good barn: oiled leather, horses and sweet hay. "You look healthy."

"I've been working out some," he said, casting his eyes down with a blush. "You look great, as usual."

"Thank you."

"Hey, Suzanne, welcome home," said Brad, waving from the next stall.

She nearly gasped when she saw that he was wearing glasses and a Cubs baseball cap.

"Hey," she said, wondering if she should be suspicious of Brad, then, just as quickly, dismissing the idea. Brad was from a long line of outstanding polo players but had lacked the athleticism to play past junior high school. His ambition unrealized, Brad had turned into a pudgy, pasty-faced, worried-looking guy, but had made a surprisingly committed polo pony groom. He was the primary caretaker of Juice and was the person who regularly exercised him. Suzanne had seen Brad pretending to play polo while riding Juice, much like someone listening to a favorite tune will play an air guitar. "How've you been, Brad?" she asked.

"I'm good. Staying busy."

"I'm kind of taken 'back by your cap," she added. "I'm shocked that you're a Cubs fan." She felt her hands sweating, her heart pounding.

"I'm not," Brad said. "They suck. My uncle gave it to me. He's given me a number of them."

"Your uncle who lives in Chicago?" she asked, her voice uneven.

"Yeah, good memory," he said, appearing oblivious to her qualms. "Uncle Tim was a great polo player. He's in finance now."

"Have you been there, I mean recently, to visit him?" she asked, remembering what Detective Griffin had said about the bomber having a knowledge of horses and working at the horse carriage company.

"No. I haven't been there since last year's U.S. Open Polo Championship," Brad said with a grin. "Uncle Tim's in town, so I was wearing this one for him. He said he might stop by," Brad added. "Hey, I heard what happened to you in Chicago. I bet you're still freaked out. Oh geez, I probably shouldn't be wearing the hat." He pulled it off, revealing that his short, brown hair was prematurely receding.

"Yeah, way to remind her," Randy said, interrupting. He flashed Brad a stern look.

"How did y'all find out about what happened?" Suzanne asked, letting out a breath and rubbing her hands on her breeches before covering her churning stomach with them, to calm herself. "To me…in Chicago?" She was picking up disturbing vibes, and her shoulder hurt, though she was uncertain about what it meant. She looked around nervously.

"Uh, well, it's been on the news," Randy said, stepping in between Suzanne and Brad. "And it's all the gossip. No surprise there. And if that wasn't enough, your grandmother called not long ago. She wanted to check in on the horses for your dad." He smiled with a head tilt, like he always had. "But I told her we have it handled as usual, no problem," he said. "We cover for each other when necessary, so your parents never have to worry."

"Yeah," said Brad. "We cover for each other." He puckered his lips and rolled his eyes. He stood and she noted for the first time he was a little over six-feet tall.

But before she could worry further about him or try to decipher what Brad meant with his obvious sarcasm, a greeting whinny came from the other end of the barn, snapping Suzanne back to her main purpose. "Excuse me, guys. I've got to see my Misty!" She ran to her horse's stall. The mare's gray-white head was nodding up and down eagerly. Opening the stall door, Suzanne

hugged Misty's neck and kissed her peach-fuzzed muzzle.
"Oh, how I've missed you, my sweetie," Suzanne
murmured, holding the embrace to soak in the perfect
love and understanding that grows so naturally between a
girl and her horse. After a minute, the mare bent her
head, searching Suzanne's pockets. "You know I've treats
for you, don't you?" she said, pulling them out.

Misty was an Andalusian, an impressive horse
with a striking silvered white coat, thick white mane and a
trifecta of entwined whites, grays and browns in her tail.
She was both a strong and elegant jumper who also had a
showy rhythmical walk, high-stepping trot, and a smooth,
rocking canter. Her head was majestic and her eyes large
and kind. Even with Suzanne's long absences, Misty's
temperament was infinitely loving, never "marish," a
slang term they used to describe a cranky mare showing
impatience or general grumpiness.

Randy led Cole back into the adjacent stall, while
Misty put her head on Suzanne's shoulder and nuzzled
her ear, something the horse always did when Suzanne
haltered her. It was a sign she wanted Suzanne to massage
her face. Despite Suzanne's time away, the ritual
continued. Suzanne closed her eyes as she rubbed,
warming two hearts while dissolving the anxiousness
she'd felt earlier.

"Have the police caught the people who did this to you?" Brad asked, returning her attention to the unfortunate events that brought her home.

"No, not that I've heard, anyway," she said, attaching a short lead rope to Misty's halter. They walked out of the stall and into the crosstie area. "I hope they do soon though," she said, thinking of her own unfinished business with the Americos Oil ad campaign.

"Well, I for one am really glad you're home. That's all that matters," Randy said, as he exited Cole's stall. "Is there anything I can do for you?"

"Yes, as a matter of fact, you can help me tack up Misty," she said with a broad smile—until she caught the unmistakable image of the boy ghost, who was obviously following her and wanting something from her. He peered obliquely over a stall door. "A ride in Hitchcock Woods cannot come soon enough!" she shouted, but at the same time, she felt an unexpected sorrow for the ghost. She'd give him a chance to explain himself later.

"My pleasure," Randy said with enthusiasm. He started to brush Misty's coat, readying it for her English saddle.

As Suzanne rubbed Misty's ears and watched Randy work, she remembered how painfully shy he'd been when they first met. It was rumored that his mother had become a drug addict after her much-older husband, Randy's father, had died. His father had been as old as

her grandmother. Sadly, there was also talk that Randy's
mother might have been a prostitute; she'd died from an
accidental overdose when Randy was in the tenth grade.
After that, he and his kid brother, Jimmy, had to move
two hours away to Spartanburg, South Carolina, to live
with their only relative, their aunt Jane, who was a
domestic live-in for a family with a hundred acres of
farmland and a stable of horses. It was while living on the
Spartanburg farm that Randy finished high school and
learned about horse care and training.

Even before she knew about the sad story of
Randy's parents, Suzanne had sensed that he was an
underdog who had great potential but was in desperate
need of a hero. Their friendship was sealed through a
trauma bond that started the day she found Randy stuffed
in a locker in their junior high school hallway. He was
crying pitifully, arms cut and bleeding, and unable to get
out. Other students stood, stared and did nothing. Some
even snickered. The memory of his pain and their cruelty
still haunted her. She'd wept as she helped him out of the
locker, knowing his sweet soul had been terribly
wounded. And as she walked with him to the nurse's
office, she'd made a vow. She'd use whatever was
necessary, be it her feistiness, status or popularity, to
guard him and others from a bully-infested school. It
worked to keep the meanest kids away from him,
although after the locker incident, she noticed there were

many days he simply withdrew emotionally, even from her. He also started to skip class more frequently, claiming illness. When in school, he'd follow in her wake to the point everyone started calling Randy her shadow. She didn't mind; at least she could keep him safe.

When he'd moved to Spartanburg, she'd prayed that he'd be okay, hating that he was so far away from her. So it was a relief when he returned to Aiken the summer before she left for Northwestern, interested in a job with horses. Apparently, his brother, Jimmy, had remained in Spartanburg. It was around that time Suzanne found out their deceased father, Craig Mackenzie, had once been a friend and employee of her grandmother. So with that connection and the fact she'd always held a fondness for Randy, she talked her parents into hiring him as a barn hand and letting him live in the apartment above the stables. This decision turned out to be lucky for them all, for it soon became apparent that Randy had the whisperer's gift with horses. She knew there was something special about him! He also quickly grew into a terrific barn manager and one of the best trainers in the area.

"Hey, Suzanne, did I tell you that I've decided to follow in your footsteps and major in journalism?" Randy asked, bringing her back to the present. He finished securing Misty's bridle.

"No, you didn't, but it'd be a shame if someone as gifted as you didn't work with horses anymore." Suzanne led her mare out of the crosstie to the outside courtyard.

"Oh, I'd never do that. It's just, well, I'd like to have a career that would allow me to write about horses. Maybe even produce some how-to videos using my knowledge of horses, as I get older. I like the technical aspects of producing videos, too, and I'm better at it than you might think."

"Oh, I've no doubt." She smiled. *He's trying to please me, like he's always done.* He was one of the few who'd never called her Suzy Q, because he knew how much she detested that nickname. "Sounds perfect," she said. "Are you taking classes now?"

"A few here and there, mostly online. I've learned a lot that way. But to finish, I have to wait until my brother Jimmy graduates, since I'm paying his college tuition."

"That's awfully good of you, Randy."

"I realize it's late for me, going back to college and all, but I wanted to wait until Jimmy was more settled. He still needs me." He turned his head slightly before looking down.

Suzanne noticed something had changed in his expression, but she couldn't quite feel what it was about. It felt off somehow. "You're different when you talk about Jimmy," she said.

"Well," he said, rubbing his nose. "Jimmy's been in and out of the juvenile system for years, but I was finally able to get him to go to the University of South Carolina's Aiken campus. I don't mind paying for his tuition and room and board, if it keeps him from trouble." He rubbed a foot on the pea gravel. "He can't really help it. Our childhood was worse on him. But like I've said, he wouldn't cause problems here. He loves the horses as much as I do."

"He's lucky to have you, Randy," she said. She felt a new, suffocating sadness about him, despite his smiles—it was one that still clung to him like tangled plastic wrap.

"Can I give you a leg up?" Randy held his hands out.

"Yes, please!" She pulled her left knee up and waited for his help. He held her leg with one hand below her knee, the other near her ankle, and as she pushed off with her right leg, he lifted her left. In an instant, she was gracefully sitting astride.

"This beautiful girl sure has missed you," Randy said. "Like everybody else 'round here, I reckon." He tapped her boot. "Stirrups the right length?"

"Perfect." As he ran a practiced hand between Misty and her girth, checking it for the right tightness, she turned and noticed a book about Alfred Hitchcock sitting on top of a couple of other older books on one of the concrete benches.

"Hey, are those yours?" she asked, pointing.

"Nah...they're Jimmy's. He must've left them. He had a class...the history of film or theater, something like that. And we found these in the vintage bookstore on Laurens."

Suzanne raised her eyebrows before Randy replied a little too defensively, "Aw, come on. Your mama said it'd be okay if Jimmy came over occasionally. He'd never cause problems here, I promise."

She heard Brad let out a gruff breath. She looked over at him, but he was looking down at his task, shaking his head with a smirk on his face.

"I wasn't being accusatory. I'm sure it's fine that Jimmy visits you; he's your family. And this is your home," Suzanne said. "It just struck me as funny, a book about Hitchcock is sitting next to Hitchcock Woods."

"Ha, I get it," Randy said. "That is kind of funny." He bent down. "I better put 'em away 'fore they get messed up."

It wasn't really funny, Suzanne admitted, but she realized she was laughing for the first time in more than a week as Misty stepped onto Clayborn Cut, a short trail that led into the rich green and brown colonnades of the Woods. At the damp intersection of the Cut and Doll Lane, pines and oaks were draped in Spanish moss like miniature gray shawls, splattering the sunlight into a kaleidoscope of shapes. The familiar sights and the rub of leather on Misty made Suzanne giddy with happiness, as did the piquant nip of muscadine berries, some fallen from their vined clusters bordering on the curved trails of horses.

A quarter mile in, they crossed the Sand River. It looked exactly like what its name implied: a dry run of white sand some twenty-to-fifty-feet wide that wound gracefully through the Woods. Rains, however, could turn Sand River into treacherous terrain with fast-moving water runoff. A sign posted on a nearby tree warned: "Danger: Quicksand after Heavy Rain." But there was no such threat on its sturdy, dry surface today, although a humid musk of its hazardous potential often clung to the air.

Just past Sand River was Devil's Backbone, one of the main trails leading to her favorite "healing place" in the world: the inner Horse Show Ring. For new visitors to Hitchcock Woods, this acre-size clearing of unexpected grassland, designated with a post-and-rail wooden fence, had a surprise factor akin to discovering a fabulous tree house in the middle of a jungle trek. Perhaps adding to the magical feel of the ring was its location in the heart of the wooded preserve. And it was just east of a gentle slope of earth some believed was an ancient Native American mound but was now named, rather unsuitably Suzanne thought, Bluebird Hill.

Suzanne rode to the northern side of the ring, dismounted near some picnic tables, and sat on a bench, letting Misty graze. On quiet days like this, just being in the Woods at the inner Horse Show Ring helped diffuse any tension she might have brought in with her. Breathing in the tranquility, steeped in equine tradition and Indigenous American history, she remembered a meditation her grandmother had taught her. Henrietta had once lived on the Medichero Apache Reservation in New Mexico, where her grandfather had served as a physician and medical researcher.

Standing up, arms stretched high toward the heavens, Suzanne closed her eyes and imagined her soul's light moving down through her feet and into the ground, spreading like roots of slender pines before sending it back up her spine and out through her limbs, toward the golden sun. "Ahh," she said aloud before sitting back on the bench to relax and breathe deeply, eyes closed and palms turned up on her thighs.

After a few minutes, her eyes flew open and hot tears rushed to the surface. All she could do was let them rise and fall, shoulders heaving. She wept until she could weep no more.

During the catharsis, Misty came to her side, gently rubbing Suzanne's ear with a gentle caress, like she'd done so many times before. Suzanne pressed her tearstained cheek to Misty's chiseled one, and it was a deep comfort. She only looked up when she heard the scolding of an eastern fox squirrel, squawking away at her, as if to reprimand her for not coming back home more often. The squirrel was right. How could she argue?

For Suzanne, the Woods possessed a special nurturing power, awesome and quiet, that was able to draw an assemblage of friends, neighbors and varied strangers, bonding them together at the level of heart, horse and hound like no other place on earth. Even the forest's subcultures held her respect and fascination with their vast mini-universes, pulsating with life. The fuzzy caterpillars were already nesting in their massive weblike tree tents, as silent as seeds sprouting, dreaming of their aerial futures. Carolina lizards were guarding their stands of shrubs from the moist bunkers of leaf mold and fallen bracken. Honeybees worked on the pollen of azaleas under nutrient-rich pine needles, swaying and green. The staccato knocks of the pileated woodpecker mixed with the intermittent calls of cardinals and blue jays, while the lulling songs of warblers carried weightlessly on an ethereal stream of a humid wind.

Playfully, she conjured up in her mind's eye the tinkling laughter of invisible wood nymphs, prancing along beach-colored trails, unseen by joggers, walkers and prized thoroughbreds. There were no limits to the rhythms and cadences of her imagination in this favored spot, held gently between the sublime coos of mourning doves and the sedating drone of cicadas.

And then it hit her—her prayer had been answered! The one she'd frantically made from the darkness of a cleaning supply closet on the fifty-second floor of the Americos Building—and in this moment, in this place of light and truth, she knew she was blessed, and she sent up a spontaneous, silent prayer of gratitude to the divine Creator who'd made her, horses like Misty and the loving embrace of Hitchcock Woods.

With tears falling, she cried aloud: "Dear God! Thank you!"

Chapter 10

Hearing a soft nicker in the distance, Suzanne turned and was startled to see a paint horse standing some forty feet away on the path between her and Bluebird Hill. She squinted, trying to see if she recognized the paint's rider, but the late-afternoon's still-bright sun was settled directly behind his head.

Closer now, the paint finally stepped into the shade of pines. The rider's face was now obscured by greened shadow.

"Hey, how ya doing?" she said, blinking hard, trying to make out his identity.

"I'm just hunky-dory, how 'bout you?" came the reply in a deep southern drawl.

It took a moment for Suzanne's vision to recover from the glare and clear, but she discerned that the paint also held the features of a mustang, a mix of breeds not often seen in Hitchcock Woods. Just as unusual was its rider. He was riding bareback, and he was wearing preppy madras shorts, a pink polo shirt and Top Sider deck shoes with no socks. Suzanne guessed him to be about twenty years old. He was handsome, with a dark tan and stylish sunglasses, and he wore his black hair pulled up into a man bun. She knew most everyone who rode in the Woods, and they knew her as a native daughter. But she didn't recognize him, and she felt her pulse accelerate. Should she be afraid of him?

He gracefully dismounted his horse, sliding off to one side, before rambling over, standing between his horse and Misty. He removed his sunglasses and smiled broadly, revealing an unexpected kindness that was palpable, the type to which animals are magnetically drawn. Sure enough, Misty moved next to him, softly questing his pockets. He petted her warmly and, like a proper southern gentleman, offered her and his horse each a peppermint.

There was no need to fear him. He had the shining eyes of an old soul, and she felt there was nothing he didn't know, though he was just a young man standing between two mint-nibbling horses in Hitchcock Woods. She felt her heart smile.

Just as Suzanne was about to introduce herself and comment on his horse's breed, she heard the rumbling thud of hooves on sandy ground traveling at breakneck speed toward them. She jumped up to take hold of Misty's reins, as the stranger mounted his horse behind her. From the Devil's Backbone Trail, Randy thundered up on her father's black stallion and stopped abruptly in front of the bench.

"Hey, Suze," Randy said breathlessly. "Sorry to bother you here, but your mama just got home and sent me out here to fetch you."

"Oh, okay, thanks. I'm really glad to know she's back." Suzanne turned, looking west, barely catching the young man and his paint as they disappeared over the crest of Bluebird Hill. She wondered why he'd left so quickly and without saying a word. "Randy, did you see that guy on the paint mustang who just took off?"

"Nah. But I'd love to see a paint mustang."

"That's weird," she said.

"Yeah, you don't see many mustang crosses in the Woods."

"No, I mean, it's weird you didn't see them. They were right here a minute ago. You should've seen them," she said, but realized the stranger had emitted a vibration that was different than anything she'd felt before. She searched her body and emotions for further answers, while noting she had no throbs, pains or milk-colored breaths. *At least he didn't have ghost energy, thank God.* But why hadn't Randy seen them? Maybe he just wasn't paying attention when he rode in—or maybe the stress of recent events was making her hallucinate. "We should get going," she said, climbing into the saddle, as an unsettling feeling returned to her stomach.

Back at the barn, Randy offered to put Misty away. "You better go find your mama, quick like. She's anxious to see you."

"I want to put Misty up first; Mama won't mind," Suzanne said, taking her time.

"Yeah, sure," he said with a grin. "I'll just help, then." In a smooth nearly seamless motion, he replaced Misty's bridle with a halter, and clipped her into the crossties, while Suzanne grabbed the curry comb for Misty's sweat marks.

It wasn't that Suzanne didn't want to see her mother, but knowing her mother was safely back home, Suzanne just wanted a few more minutes with Misty— and to gear herself up for what was sure to be one of Lita's inevitable, high-octane entrances.

As if reading her thoughts, Randy said, "You know, my mother was a bit over the top, too."

"I know, Randy. I love Mama, but sometimes—"

"At least your mother never put your life in danger. I think your mom's the greatest."

"Oh, Randy," she said, trying to think of some consoling words, but when she turned, he was already heading to the tack room, carrying Misty's saddle.

"Suzy Q, Suzy Q! My baby, Suzy Q! There you are!" squealed Lita Clayborn, as she ran into the barn. Her hair was bigger and blonder than ever, her tan was darker than usual and her face was covered in full cake makeup. She sported her usual style of clothes: perpetually florid and sprightly sensual. Today, she was dressed in a low-cut, flowered, silk blouse tucked snugly into a size-six blue-jean miniskirt along with her trademark stiletto heels. Suzanne never could figure out how her mother managed to negotiate pea gravel paths and dirt floors in those things without falling or breaking an ankle.

"Is my Suzy Q all right?" Lita said, hugging and shaking her and talking at the same time. Before Suzanne could squeak out any words, she allowed herself to be enfolded in the safety and comfort of her mother's exuberant embrace.

"Yeah, Mama. I'm okay. Just a little tired."

"I'm exhausted from my flight too. But that's neither here nor there," Lita drawled. "My Suzy Q is more important. Come on up to the house, my baby girl, and tell your mama all about what happened in that awful Chicago. And we'll see if good ole Della came in yesterday to leave us anything tasty for supper."

"Yeah, Gran said she called Della to stock the kitchen. But I'm not at all hungry, Mama."

"Well, I'm starving! But first, let me look at you." She held Suzanne at arm's length while looking her up and down. "You're a little pale, sugar. No, I wasn't going to say too thin, 'cause I know that comes naturally, and it's a beautiful look on you. But your natural blonde hair is too limp and there's too much red in the brown eyes I love," she said with a tsk, looking deep in Suzanne's eyes with her matching almond-shaped ones. "This thing that happened in Chicago, I hope it means you're all done with that place now," she said, prattling on without taking breaths or allowing space for Suzanne to reply.

"I just came—" Suzanne started.

"Be that as it may, I want you to know I cut my cruise short. And let me just tell you something: it was not easy to get a flight out of Mykonos at the last second. That's a Greek island, so gorgeous. But I did it, baby, and I mean the second I heard about your accident."

"It wasn't exactly an accident," Suzanne said without expression.

"Oh, whatever. It's just so good to have you back home for some good ole southern mama loving and Della's cooking." Lita chuckled, hugging Suzanne again.

"Thanks, Mama. I was wondering where you were." Her voice cracked. "I was worried."

"Oh, sugar, it's just that I'd given everybody strict orders not to call unless there was an emergency! This was an emergency, of course." She drew back. "But truthfully, I was ignoring my cell. And that thing really didn't work out in the middle of the Mediterranean, anyway. So Lucille did have trouble tracking me down. You can thank her for finally getting through to the captain of the ship."

"I'll be sure to do that," Suzanne said, for once grateful for Aiken's gossip circuit and the persistence of Lucille, one of its prime members.

"Hey, why don't you come back with me? We could finish my girls' trip, and it'd get your mind off that Chicago thing." Like many lifelong southerners, and despite traveling to exotic locales on a cruise ship, Lita had trouble imagining the specific details of events that happened in big northern cities like Chicago and New York.

"Sorry, Mama, but I'll need to return to work as soon as the office is back in order." She felt a twinge in her abdomen but chose to ignore it. "In the meantime, I just wanted to recover here, see y'all, of course, and ride Misty. I'm sorry to have interrupted your cruise."

"You didn't say how I looked. Don't you think I'm looking younger than the last time you saw me?" She turned around, holding her hands in the air. "And even after being on planes for more than twenty dang hours?"

Suzanne tried to answer, but her mother continued without taking a breath. "Everybody tells me all the time I don't look my age at all. You know I'm almost sixty. What do you think?"

"I'm thinking you don't need to fish for a compliment. You get them almost nonstop," Suzanne said, shaking her head. "Besides, fifty-five is hardly almost sixty." She mocked her mom with a sideways smile.

Lita narrowed her eyes and pouted.

"Oh, Mama, you know you look good. Prettiest mama around at forty, fifty-five, or sixty."

"There's my Suzy Q. Thanks, hon." She paused momentarily to study Suzanne's face, perhaps searching it for sincerity, before smiling. "You're so cute, Suzy Q, I could just eat you up with a spoon!" She gave Suzanne a pinch on the cheek.

Suzanne rolled her eyes. *Is it any wonder I have to be the serious one in this family?*

"Come on, let's see what Della's made for us," Lita said, pulling on Suzanne's hand.

As they entered the kitchen, Suzanne sucked in her breath at the sight of the yellow rubber gloves next to the sink. "Mama, are those your rubber gloves?"

"Lawd, no. Della must've left them out," she said, shoes clacking as she walked over to the sink. "I turned her onto using them. Saves the manicure!" Lita wiggled her fingers. "But I swear. Della's now got herself a million pairs of them things." Lita picked up the gloves as she would a dead fish. "Eww, these ones stink to high heaven," she said, promptly dropping them into the trashcan and washing her hands.

As Suzanne tried to forget the last time she saw yellow rubber gloves, the telephone rang.

Lita slid over to answer. "Well, hey, Trish, how ya doing, hon?...Oh yes, I just got back! And yes, my Suzy Q is here, and she looks as beautiful as ever...Yeah, she's okay, but tired, I'm sure you can imagine. Just needs a little of her mama's loving and Della's good cooking. Ha!" She paused to listen. "Uh-oh. You don't say. Oh my lawd! Well, I know it's not Christian and all, but I can't say that I care what happened to that fella. I'm just sorry for my Suzy Q. She shouldn't have to hear about this kind of stuff right now, just as she's getting home after her tragic accident, I mean, the bomb thing, you know, that thing in Chicago...Yes, ma'am, you better believe it. Well...okeydokey. See you later, hon. Thanks, bye-bye."

Suzanne stood next to her mother. "What is it? What should I not hear?"

"You know that awful professor Bobby Lindley? The one you had the trouble with?"

"Mama, obviously I know who he is."

"Well, they found him dead this morning. He apparently fell down the steps in his own dadburn house and broke his own dadburn neck, and I mean literally." Lita shook her head.

"Oh my God. That's terrible!" Suzanne said, exhaling. "I've got mixed emotions about him, too," she said, remembering her terrible lapse in dating judgment.

"Well, you heard what I said to Trish. I don't like to talk badly about the dead. So I'll just have to drop it."

Even though her empath antenna had been up and nagging at her as soon as she met the professor at a party, Suzanne had made the mistake of flirting with him, even going out on a date with him during the busy summer after her senior year in high school. It hadn't seemed like a big deal. But to him, it was a different story. And she should have listened to her little voice's warning and avoided him straightaway. It was an error she would unfortunately repeat.

After the date, which had been awkward and icky, she ignored his follow-up calls. Refusing to take the hint, he started to stalk her and leave disturbing "anonymous" texts and handwritten messages for her that she knew were from him. Thankfully, the pestering eventually ended, although she'd get a text from him every now and then, which she also ignored. Not long ago, Suzanne had heard that he'd been suspected of being one of those creepy clowns, the kind of weirdos who try to lure kids to play in the woods near apartment complexes, although she didn't know if he'd ever been arrested for it. She had blocked him on her phone and from all social media.

"Let's talk about something else," Lita said, peering into the refrigerator.

"Gladly," Suzanne mumbled. Thinking of the professor made her recall Detective Griffin asking if she knew anyone who might want to hurt her. She had said no but had forgotten about Bobby. He was dead now, so the issue was moot. "Do you think Bobby's death was an accident or…?"

"I've no idea, but Trish said the police are investigating it."

"Wow," Suzanne said. They both stood still in a rare silence for a few moments.

"Hey, looky here," Lita said, changing the subject back to food. "Della made us some fried chicken and okra. Yay! Now let's see what else? Oh, wait a minute, hold on. Stop the presses," she said, pausing for dramatic effect. "A real big craving for wine just flung up on me," she said, pulling out a chilled bottle of Chardonnay. "Hey, let's have a glass or two, eat this fine dinner and watch a movie together. Just you and me, baby, until I pass out from jet lag." She took in a deep breath. "Don't worry. It can be something light, maybe on the Hallmark channel." Lita smiled widely, her voice playful.

"Ha ha. Very funny." Of course, her mother knew all about Suzanne's empathic sensitivity to the violence on TV and in movies. Suzanne crossed her arms.

"I'm just teasing you, hon. I like Hallmark too!" Lita laughed with a snort before turning serious. "We'll just forget about that yucky professor. May God have mercy on his soul. And let's not dwell on this Chicago stuff anymore either."

"I hate to tell you this, Mama, but I promised Gran I'd go see her this evening. Would you mind?" Suzanne smiled, but now she felt bad about leaving her mother.

"Oh, please don't go right now, Suzy girl. Can't you wait until tomorrow morning? Henrietta will forgive you, hon," Lita whined, facing her with a pout. "I've missed you, and I think I deserve most of your time, especially since I rushed home from the Mediterranean and all." She hugged Suzanne.

"Yes, you did. And I appreciate it," Suzanne said. It was true. She hadn't spent quality time with her mother in a long while. Maybe it'd do them both some good. "Okay, Mama. I'll just give Gran a call and let her know, then," Suzanne said, remembering the manuscript. She wanted to finish reading it before she saw her grandmother and her father got back, anyway. "When do you think Dad'll be home?"

"He's driving up from Florida, so maybe tomorrow. That is, if he don't get sidetracked again."

Lita pursed her lips, and Suzanne swallowed another rising discomfort about her father.

Chapter 11

By the time her mother let her slip away to bed, after a couple glasses of wine on top of the day's travel, Suzanne couldn't keep her eyes open one minute longer, much less read Gran's pages. She drifted off as soon as her head hit the pillow.

She awoke the next morning to a check-in phone call from Dan. Before saying good-bye, she promised to make a decision soon about when she would return to Chicago. After a shower, Suzanne went straight to her father's study, only to find Gran's manuscript and letters missing from his desktop. Was he already home? She tiptoed down the hall to her parents' closed bedroom door, opened it, and peeked in. Her mother was sleeping on one side of the king-size bed; the other side was still pulled up, undisturbed. How strange that her mother would have removed documents that had nothing to do with her after Suzanne had gone to bed. She wondered where her mom put them and was more curious than ever about the old manuscript.

Well, I might as well hear it all directly from the horse's mouth, Suzanne thought.

After writing her mother a note about borrowing her red BMW convertible, Suzanne grabbed a coffee and set off on the twenty-five-mile drive to the estate of her paternal ancestors, located on a sprawling peach farm in Greenfield, South Carolina.

She drove up the circular drive at the neoclassical-style, white mansion, surprised to see her grandmother sitting in a rocking chair on the immense veranda, snapping green beans into a brown paper bag. Gran was an organic gardener and marvelous cook, and stubbornly independent, always refusing kitchen help, unlike many wealthy women.

Henrietta Clayborn hopped up with remarkable agility for a woman in her eighties. "Hey! Welcome home, Suzanne dear!" she shouted, waving. She wore a sleeveless white blouse, khaki pants and a pair of white tennis shoes. Her once-blond hair was platinum and styled into a neat bob. Animals always hung around her, and several calico kittens pulled on her shoelaces even now. Two spaniel mixes, no doubt from the local shelter, sat up, barked, and stood protectively.

Someone might have mistaken Gran for the late Doris Day had it not been for the amount and type of Bohemian jewelry she wore, even over her classic, conservative garment choices. Her wrists were stacked with beaded bracelets made of quartz, amethyst and other healing crystals. A large turquoise stone from New Mexico anchored a multicolored gemstone necklace. Her fingers sparkled with large diamonds, emeralds and gold.

"Hey, Gran, don't you think you may be overdoing the jewelry just a tad for the task of snapping string beans?" Suzanne said, hugging her.

"Nah," Henrietta said. "I just love the energy of all my crystals and precious stones." She pulled back and placed her hands akimbo. "Also, I enjoy making a vibrational fashion statement," she said, giggling.

"You're funny," Suzanne said, hugging her again.

"I'm so happy to see you." Henrietta smoothed back Suzanne's hair, her bracelets jingling as she moved. "I knew you'd come back, no matter what happened, safe and sound." The spaniels rubbed on both of them.

"How'd you know that, Gran?" Suzanne saw her reflection in her grandmother's still-bright-blue eyes.

"I believed it to be true. And then, I felt it to be so." She patted her heart.

Suzanne affectionately touched her grandmother's cheek. There was an intuitive golden essence about her grandmother that even others could sense. It bubbled out of her like a natural spring.

"Come in and tell me all about what happened in Chicago," Henrietta said, carrying her green beans.

"You probably already know that, too, don't you?" Suzanne smiled, picking up and hugging the kittens.

"Well, Lucille did call to give me all the gossip, if that's what you mean." She looked back at Suzanne with a knowing smile. "And don't forget, you gave me the gist over the phone when you called. Later, I read more about it on the Internet, of course."

"I see," Suzanne said with a sideways grin. "You're a smart old bird."

Henrietta nodded with a smile. "Let's go to the kitchen, Peaches." They entered through the twelve-foot-high front door. "I'd like to hear your point of view."

The dogs ran ahead as they moved through the home, originally built in the early 1800s. It was mostly furnished with period and family pieces that had changed little through the decades. But Henrietta had the kitchen expanded and completely modernized, keeping it well maintained and up-to-date. The cabinets were white; the walls golden; and the counters were topped with slabs of rare quartz crystal. Stainless steel appliances included a huge farmhouse kitchen sink with a spring spout faucet, large professional-grade ovens, stove and two tremendous double-door refrigerator-freezers.

Henrietta pulled out a tall pitcher of iced tea and a plate of mini-sandwiches she'd made earlier, placing them on the large distressed-wood kitchen table. Suzanne put the kittens down on the floor next to some feather toys.

"The police haven't arrested anyone yet," Suzanne said, sitting at the table after giving her grandmother a summary of the events of the past week.

"They will, all in good time," Henrietta said.

"They made it seem like the bomber guy, or guys, is someone I might know." Suzanne wrinkled her nose before taking a bite of a cucumber and cream cheese sandwich. "This is delicious, Gran. And hits the spot," she said. "I forgot to eat breakfast."

"Well, do you have any idea about who the bomber might be?" Henrietta's right eyebrow arched up as she took a sip of ice tea.

Suzanne stirred in the padded wooden chair, took a deep breath, frowned, and said, "Gran, I have to ask you something. Do you think Dad could've been involved in something like this?"

Henrietta leaned back in the chair and let out a deep belly laugh.

"I'll take that as a no. I know how ridiculous it sounds. But I just want to make sure I'm not going crazy."

"Well now, wait a minute," Henrietta said, between breaths. "Do I think JJ is capable of coming up with a harebrained scheme to get you to come back home from Chicago…a scheme that might have gone all wrong?" She was still half laughing. "Yes." She held up a finger, calming down. "But, and in all seriousness, do I think JJ would've intentionally put you and others in danger in a terrible, premeditated crime? The answer is a definite no."

"Sorry, my head's still in a mess from this whole ordeal."

"You know, Suzanne, you could use this disruption in your life to your benefit. It's often the case that the trauma, pain and challenges in our lives are the very things we need the most to propel us forward, as transformational fuel, so to speak, to connect us to the truth of God's power within us…to navigate us toward our life's authentic missions." She spoke with the wise words of a shaman. "Instead of letting something like this break you down, use it to change your course for the better. Keep your face turned to the light."

Padding over to a kitchen desk nook Henrietta said, "In truth, we're the ones attracting what we want, need or believe on a subconscious level, in effect to stop us from living in a certain way that is not in our highest good and also to redirect us to the right path." She pulled two books down from the shelf and returned to the kitchen table. "Here, these might give you some insight about what's going on in your head." One was *The Law of Attraction* by Esther and Jerry Hicks. The other book was *The Power of Now* by Eckhart Tolle.

"Thanks, Gran, for the advice and books. I'll read them. But I can't imagine what I'm thinking that would've attracted these frightening circumstances into my life," Suzanne said, already knowing some of the basics described in *The Law of Attraction*.

A colony of sparrows was making a ruckus in the shrubbery outside the picture window, and Henrietta got up for a closer look. After a few seconds, with her back to her granddaughter, she said: "Suzanne, I've watched you struggle with the trauma of being shot when you were a girl. I've seen you wrestling with ghosts and wanting to escape from your psychic gifts that came to you by way of what you think was a tragic accident. I know that you've felt like a prisoner of the fates," she said as the sparrows continued their boisterous chorus. Henrietta turned to face her. "But Suzanne, you are not a sparrow, nor are you a pretty songbird in a cage." She paused. "My dear granddaughter, you are an eagle!"

Suzanne's eyes widened and she leaned forward, lured by the mention of an eagle and its magic she'd known.

She had been with her friend Clair and Clair's parents on their ski boat on Lake Thurmond the summer just before the shooting accident. It was a carefree time, before ghosts had complicated her young life. She recalled the feel of sunshine, her skin pink to the touch but not yet sunburned, a warm can of Coke, the crisp water, her mood as buoyant as her ski vest. Her legs tingled as though fish were nibbling on them as she waited to be pulled up on the slalom ski, gripping the rope bar, as Clair's father yelled, "Are you ready?" She'd nodded, tilting back, her right foot booted in rubber, her left stuffed up as far as possible in the rear toe strap. She'd flexed her muscles and held her breath, then felt the sudden drag, the rising, the pop-up, in balance, in control, the wind on her unstoppable grin, and the pride of getting up on one ski her very first try—just as a bald eagle swooped in, flying low over the water's surface not more than fifty feet away, unexpectedly, miraculously.

Given her excitement and focus to remain on the wake and not fall, she might not have noticed it. But how big and close the eagle was to her! Its great beak driving, wingtips skimming, its body smooth and aerodynamic over brown-blue water, parallel in speed, as if it wanted to ride shotgun with her on her thrill ride, even for only a few seconds, before soaring up and away. It was a breathtaking moment in the middle of another breathtaking moment. Yet, to her utter disbelief, when she'd gotten back in the boat, she discovered that neither Clair nor her parents had seen it. But she knew it had happened. She knew what she'd witnessed. The magnificent bird had shown up like magic, a surprise celebration, a talisman—but perhaps for her eyes only. And that made her feel as special and golden as the girl who'd gotten up on a slalom ski the first time she tried it.

Now, she looked at her grandmother feeling that same sense of portentous awe. "What do you mean, that *I'm* the eagle?"

Henrietta turned back to the window with a finger to her chin, as if pondering how to explain. But in the next second, she gasped. Her hands flew to her heart. Her giggling grew louder. And Gran's enthusiastic laughs were hard to ignore.

"What, what?" Suzanne said, jumping up.

"This is just so perfect, Suzanne." She clapped and pointed. "Look!"

Suzanne almost couldn't believe it—there in the sky was a bald eagle flying above the western orchards. It was a half-mile or more away in the distance, but there was no mistaking its massive, brown wingspan and white head and tail.

"Incredible," Suzanne said, taking in a deep breath and shaking her head. "How'd you do that? Conjure up an eagle, just like that?" She snapped her fingers.

"Not me! Spirit sent this special communication, this impeccable timing, just for you, my dear Suzanne."

"What do you think it means?"

"The Apache say if the eagle shows up in your life, you're being called by the Great Spirit to rise higher, to walk a sacred path of beauty and honor, to be a messenger for the Great Spirit. With eagle vision, you can fly above the shadows of your past with an open heart and soul. It's the spirit animal at the very top of the totem and therefore the one that offers the greatest perspective for healing, wisdom and self-power."

"Wow," Suzanne said, remembering her previous eagle encounter. She'd had her near-death experience only a month later.

"But I think it means exactly what I was trying to say a while ago. You were given special psychic gifts, including eagle vision. And it's high time you started using them for the higher good, including yours."

"Gran, if I have eagle vision, why do I fall for men who are all wrong for me? They start out great, wonderful and charming. But then they end up being selfish jerks, some are narcissists. Why am I not able to pick up on that right away?"

"Maybe you did pick up on it, only you weren't paying attention."

"Of course, you're right," Suzanne said, shaking her head.

"On the bright side, I've found that narcissists have at least one admirable, very important trait for us."

"And what, pray tell, could that be?"

"They're actually very good at finding and befriending true empaths. It's like an affirmation of this ability of ours." She patted Suzanne on the arm.

Suzanne felt the truth in her observation but asked, "How do you know that?"

"Let's just say I've had my own issues with a narcissist. So I've studied it. There's actually a symbiotic relationship that exists between the empath and the narcissist. And it's quite fascinating!"

Suzanne's eyes widened. "You're kidding, right?"

"Not at all. The empath picks up on and feels deeply the soul pain in the narcissist and wants to help ease it. The narcissist wants and needs to feel what the empath feels and be what the empath is but, because of his or her soul damage, has lost the ability to do it. The attraction is quite natural."

"Very interesting," Suzanne said, nodding. "That actually makes sense."

"Feeling emotion is a big part of what makes humans unique, divine even—and this is energy the narcissists are after and want to take, desperately so. Which is why they become very good at rooting out empaths, like pigs to truffles."

Suzanne laughed and shook her head. "That's funny. Sadly true, but funny."

"It's easy for the empath to fall for the narcissist who's mastered a technique called 'the love bomb'; that is to say, they've learned how to lavish the empath with good emotion—but the narcissist is simply mirroring back the best of what's in the empath, which makes it almost impossible to resist."

"Hmm."

"Even so, the empath may feel something's off in that, until there's some triggering event, like when you want to break off the relationship. That's when he'll show you his true character; that's when he can hurt you. Or at least, that's when he'll try to hurt you as much as possible."

Suzanne nodded, sensing her grandmother was speaking more about her own experience than Suzanne's.

"Relating this back to eagle vision," Henrietta said, "it's useful to remember that having a natural ability and mastering it are two different things. With intention and concentrated practice, however, eagle vision, as well as the other abilities you possess, can be strengthened."

Suzanne smiled, feeling grateful that her grandmother had hit on and answered the very question that had always baffled her. Finally, there was a reasonable explanation as to why she'd had trouble with narcissistic men. It's seemed so obvious now.

Her grandmother added: "Empaths will have their run-ins with narcissists, no question about it. Fortunately, at some point, as soon as we become aware of their MO, like magic, we no longer need to attract their traumas or dramas in our life."

"Thank you for that, Gran. It helps me more than you know. But," she said, shaking her head. "I still don't know how to make sense of being locked in a dark closet with a ticking bomb. I'm not seeing the big picture of that."

"Give it some space. Pay attention to special occurrences like this. They come, in many cases, to provide confirmations and answers to your prayers."

"I definitely noticed that I made it out of that closet and back here alive—a prayer answered, for sure."

"Excellent. So now, take the time to go for long rides in the Woods, to meditate, be still and to breathe. Listen for your own inner answers." She patted her heart.

"But, Gran, I don't plan to stay that long. I've got an important presentation to get back to in Chicago. And after that, assuming all goes well, my team and I'll be producing the new campaign, meaning that I'll need to be on location."

Her grandmother smiled and cocked her head.

"I know that look. Okay, I'll try to meditate more, at least until I have to go back to Chicago. I know I need to do that anyway, for my own sanity," she said as the phone rang.

"Excuse me, Peaches," Henrietta said, moving to answer it. "Oh hey, Lucille. Say what? Yes, you heard right. My granddaughter is not only in town, but she's also visiting with me at this very second. You do? What?" Gran paused to listen. "Oh dear. She'll want to know about that." She listened some more. "Actually no, I don't think that," her grandmother said, sighing. "Please let me know about the arrangements when you know what they are. And pass along our prayers to the families involved. Yes, thank you. Good-bye."

"What was that all about? Was she telling you about Bobby Lindley?"

"No, no. Suzanne, dear." Henrietta picked up Suzanne's hand before continuing. "It was about your friend Tomás Sanchez. He's dead. They found him in the Vaughns' stables, apparently kicked to death by a horse."

"What? That doesn't sound right. No, that can't be," Suzanne said, almost shouting. She stood up and paced.

An Argentine polo player, Tomás Sanchez was an expert equestrian who was hired to play on a team sponsored by the Vaughns, a prominent Aiken family. He lived on their estate in a carriage house. Tomás was the complete opposite of Bobby Lindley. But they shared at least one thing in common: Suzanne had dated both of them.

"Gran, that's the second death involving a man once close to me since I got home yesterday. Do you think that's just a coincidence?"

"Lucille asked me that as well," she said, looking down before meeting Suzanne's eyes, which were full of tears. "I said no...because my wise Apache friend once told me that there're no such things as coincidences." She paused for a second before continuing. "Only synchronicities."

"You're talking about your friend from the New Mexico reservation where you lived with my grandfather, aren't you?"

Henrietta smiled. "Yes, Bears Repeating was his Apache name."

That reminded Suzanne that she'd come here to visit and ask about the unopened letters and the manuscript she'd found on her father's desk. "I want to hear more about Bears Repeating, but right now, I have to look into what really happened to Tomás. It just doesn't make sense."

"You mean with the synchronicity and timing of it?"

"No, I meant it doesn't make sense that Tomás was kicked to death by a horse. There's no way it's true. Tomás was too much of a professional for that to happen," Suzanne said with furrowed eyebrows. "There's got to be another explanation."

"It can happen," Henrietta said. "Remember that Australian wild animal guy who was killed by a stingray? You know, the Crocodile Hunter? Steve um…"

"Yes, Steve Irwin. I remember. It was a freak accident for someone as skilled as he was to be killed by something not usually considered highly dangerous. It was an awful tragedy for animal lovers. But, Gran, I've been home for one day, and two guys I once dated are now dead. And that's after my almost being blown to bits. Are these things synchronicities? What do they mean? What am I to make of it all?"

"My dear Suzanne, when you start waking up to the truth of your inner powers, things can get interesting, even dicey, before you've mastered the eagle vision, before you can see the good in it from a higher perspective. You must try not to focus on or become embroiled in the negative dramas unfolding."

"How can I not get involved any more than I am?" Suzanne slumped, with a feeling of nausea taking root. She pressed her palm to her stomach.

"Someone once said that difficult horses have the most to teach, the most to give you," Henrietta said. "Old fears and false beliefs are like that too. They're brought to the surface of our consciousness so we can see them. This may sound incredible, but it's done intentionally by you, from your subconscious, so you can see what you need to release and what needs to go from your life. Even so, while these hidden things are being presented, they can sometimes feel and look like a nightmare."

"Nightmare is right," Suzanne said, grimacing. The two places she called home were both filled with terror. *How am I to let go of that?*

Chapter 12

Reeling from the news of Tomás, Suzanne left her grandmother's home and drove directly over to the Vaughn estate in Aiken's historic district. Situated on a four-acre wooded parcel near the Winthrop Polo Field, Aiken Training Track and Whitney Polo Field, the Vaughns' massive two-story redbrick, colonial-style mansion wasn't far from Hitchcock Woods. Suzanne had ridden Misty over to their home many times and had it clocked at about twelve minutes, even with the one stoplight in between. In Aiken, equestrians had their own rider-height buttons on stoplight poles, and horses had perpetual right of way. She didn't even have to dismount to cross the busy street.

A well-fleshed African American woman in her fifties with tightly cropped salt-and-pepper hair, shrewd eyes and a pretty, round face opened the door. She wore a royal blue tunic blouse over black leggings and patent leather sandals. A large silver cross pendant on a long chain hung over her ample bosom, dancing as she moved.

"Well, looky at what we're havin' right cheer," the older woman said with a lyrical, drawling, smooth-as-silk voice. Her smile was broad with deep dimples and large, bright-white teeth. "It's our Suzanne girl, come home from the big city." She held out her expansive arms.

"Hey, Emma. I was hoping you'd be here. How are you?" Suzanne said, embracing the large, beaming woman she'd known since junior high school.

Emma's full cheeks held a hint of pink sheen. "Now, where else I gonna be? I'm doing jest fine. Thank ya. Good to see ya, child."

"Thanks," Suzanne said before pausing. "Um, is Nick here?" She knew that Nick had moved back into the childhood home he and his brother inherited several years ago. She was glad that he'd continued employing Emma. Suzanne loved and missed her.

"He's out back with the horses," Emma said. "I bet you've heard about Tomás."

"Yes, ma'am, and I wanted to express my condolences," Suzanne said, her eyes downcast and misting over.

"It's a real shame about that young man. Such a shame," Emma said, shaking her head. "Honey, you wanna come on in here and wait in some good bought air while I go and fetch Nick?"

"Oh no, that's okay; I don't want to be a bother," she said, wiping her eyes. "I can walk around back and find him." She smiled weakly.

"I reckon you can do jest that," said Emma, who was well aware that Suzanne and Nick had been high school sweethearts and that they'd spent a great deal of time together in the Vaughns' home and with their horses. "Well, go on, then."

"Thanks, Emma," Suzanne said as the door closed. She walked toward the Vaughns' stables, navigating around a giant magnolia tree and two great live oaks toward a pea gravel path. It led to the mansion's matching redbrick barn with eight stalls, white sliding doors and a carriage apartment where Tomás had lived.

A brief search found Nick in one of the stalls with a pitchfork in his hands, mucking out the manure. *How strange,* she thought. She'd never known Nick to do the menial chores of the polo pony business. But before she could say hello, Suzanne's sinuses were inflamed with the vapors of ammonium nitrate. Instantly, the memory of being locked in the closet in the Americos Building came back to her. She sucked in air, fighting for oxygen, but it was like taking in exhaust fumes. She coughed violently.

"Oh my God, Suze!" Nick's blue eyes registered alarm, but it looked like he had been crying. "You scared the hell out of me." He wiped the moisture from his face, smearing dirt on a cheek that held more than a day's worth of black stubble.

"So-sorry about that," Suzanne sputtered, her hand on her chest, struggling to regain her composure. "I didn't mean to surprise you like that. The smells sort of got to me for a minute. Finally catching her breath, she rubbed her face with the inside of her shirttail, accidentally revealing her midriff. She watched Nick's gaze fall and linger there. He'd once said it was one of her best features. She jerked her shirt down and cleared her throat, feeling the flush of embarrassment on her cheeks.

"Ever think about giving a guy a heads-up phone call?" He combed back his brown hair with his fingers. A natural athlete, Nick had been a homegrown polo success and was popular in school. Even with the sweat, tears and tousled hair, he was as ruggedly handsome as ever.

"You didn't hear I was back home?" she asked.

He shrugged. "I just wasn't expecting to see you here right now, that's all." Uncharacteristically, his eyes darted nervously toward the door as though someone might catch them together.

"I, um, well, I just heard about Tomás," she said. "And since arriving back home yesterday, I wanted to... Regardless of what's happened between us and him in the past...um...I wanted to, as strange as it may sound, to

express my condolences. I know y'all cared about him."
She rubbed her sore hands together.

He shook his head. "It's funny. After you and I
broke up, I was mad as hell at you both. I couldn't believe
y'all dated. And then you were gone to Chicago. But I got
over it."

"You shouldn't have made fun of my
grandmother," she said. While they'd been dating in high
school, when she'd trusted him, Suzanne had shared with
him some of her grandmother's history on the Apache
reservation and the metaphysical beliefs she'd developed
because of her experiences there. Later, in an argument
over her leaving, Nick had used that information to hurt
her.

"I'm glad you're leaving," she remembered him
saying. "I don't want to date someone who has a witch
for a grandmother anyway. She might put a spell on me."

"Mocking Gran was a deal breaker," she said.
"Gran's hardly a witch. In fact, quite the opposite. She's a
wise, gifted woman who's been able to help a lot of
people."

"I know." He looked down at the ground, before
blurting, "But Tomás wasn't your type at all. He had a
bad-boy reputation from the get-go."

"So did you," she said, with a half smile.

"You weren't his only roll in the hay, you know."
His comment carried the sting of a well-placed crop.

Given the circumstances, she decided to let it go. "Touché."

After breaking up with Nick at the end of their senior year, Suzanne had casually dated other guys, including Bobby and Tomás—not necessarily to make Nick mad, but she enjoyed that it did. She was leaving that fall for Northwestern's Medill School of Journalism, in Evanston, Illinois, on a half scholarship she didn't really need and a self-dare she did: to go after a big-city career outside the longitudes and latitudes of a southern haunting.

Tomás was tall, dark and handsome, with a muscular, sculpted body and a sexy accent. He had an uncanny way of synthesizing with his polo pony that was both uncommonly graceful and divinely masculine. He was irresistible to watch, and he knew it. At the time, and especially after the blowup with Nick and the awkward situation with Bobby, Tomás was exactly the distraction she needed until her departure. He played around with everyone but knew how to make Suzanne feel as though she were the most important person in the room. He'd fill her text messages with hearts and smiley faces. He flattered and charmed her. It was easy to have a last-minute fling with him. Unfortunately, it didn't end well either.

"I'll at least admit that you're right about something," Nick said.

"Oh?" Her eyebrows shot up.

"I did care about Tomás, and of course, I forgave him, especially after you left for Chicago. But I've got to tell you: I've never seen somebody as mad as he was when you broke up with him. There was a lot of name-calling and trash talk."

"Yeah, he was a lot madder than I thought he'd be. He wanted to lock me down, even though he made it obvious he was still playing the field. His reaction to my leaving was really over-the-top."

"I guess he thought *he* could stop you from leaving, like I..." He coughed over his words.

"I'm sorry. I didn't mean to hurt him or...anyone," she said. "I was focused on my future, and I had good reasons for choosing Northwestern and following through with it. At least your friendship with Tomás wasn't impacted too badly by it."

"Not at all. In fact, if anything, it became something stronger. It went way beyond the girls we dated...or traded." He looked up. "No offense." He grinned, and it was as devilish as she remembered.

"Yeah, sure." She pursed her lips, taking the jab with good humor.

"I came to trust him, implicitly, as a teammate and friend." He paused before adding, "Even though he got into trouble with that little girl and all." He looked down with reddened cheeks.

"What do you mean by 'that little girl'?" she said, frowning and crossing her arms.

"I thought maybe you would have heard. Some thirteen-year-old accused Tomás of raping her."

"What? A thirteen-year-old girl? Oh my God." She turned around, hating what she was hearing. "No, I didn't hear about it."

"It couldn't be proven one way or the other, but I didn't believe it for a second."

"Why?"

"Girls of all ages were always throwing themselves at Tomás. You of all people should know that," he teased. "He liked them pretty, of course. But he'd never had an interest in underage girls—at least, none that I was aware of. He swore he didn't do it."

"Maybe he was just being friendly, and she got the wrong idea?" Suzanne wanted to give Tomás the benefit of the doubt. "Or maybe we didn't know him as well as we thought."

"I decided to believe him. So we helped him get out of it," he said. She assumed that Nick was including his brother, Bruce, who was also on their polo team. "But I'm afraid it was starting to become a pattern. I mean, there were accusations by other underage girls. Tomás denied them all."

"Why would so many girls accuse Tomás if it wasn't true?" Suzanne said. He had come across as vain, shallow, fun, but harmless. Now, and especially in light of his excessive anger over her departure, she wondered if he'd been just another narcissist looking to be validated, feeding on the attention from her as well as others, no matter how young.

"He claimed that someone was trying to frame him," Nick said. "We wanted to take his word for it, even though his polo game had started to suffer, especially this last year. We hadn't been winning, and he was uncharacteristically nervous. His lack of focus was taking its toll on everyone else. But it wouldn't mean…this…he wouldn't die like this…"

"Tomás was a highly-rated polo player, and obviously he knew horses," Suzanne said. "He wasn't the sort of guy who'd just let a pony kick him to death, lack of focus or not."

"Agreed," Nick said, his voice almost a whisper. "So, what I've been feeling…I mean, what I've been thinking is maybe someone else, like maybe someone's father, started believing the accusations." He stepped closer to her.

"That could be it," she said, looking into his eyes. "What do the police think?" she asked, not yet pulling back into her personal space.

"They're still investigating," he said, shrugging.

"I'm guessing it happened in Duchess's stall?" She motioned toward the yellow caution tape draped over that door's grillwork.

He nodded and they walked over. She peered over the tape. It reminded her of the tape and events in Chicago. Nick was standing close behind her as she took in the crime scene. His breath on her neck made her own quicken.

He put down the pitchfork he'd been holding, and she turned toward him. "There was an imprint of a horseshoe on Tomás's forehead," he said. "It's definitely what killed him. We found him lying here in Duchess's stall. But I don't see how she could've done it."

"Do you mind if I take a look at her hooves," she asked, feeling that there might be something wrong with the horse's shoes.

He licked his lips and stared at hers. "We moved her to stall eight, over there," he said, nodding.

Suzanne knew the agile thoroughbred and that she'd been trained to pick up her feet when asked. She patted the pony's forehead. "Hey, girl, let me see your back feet." With fearless expertise, Suzanne stood next to the pony's hip, facing backward. She placed her left hand on the top of Duchess's hindquarters and slid it down the exterior side of the rear leg. From this safety position, Suzanne picked up the hind foot, pulling up the toe and resting the hoof on her thigh so she could examine the shoe. "Oh, you're using Circle Forge now?" she said, referring to a brand of horseshoe.

"No, that's not right. Let me see!" He lightly brushed up against her right arm, also unconcerned about Duchess kicking him.

"Circle Forge Polo, clear as day," she said.

"Our farrier mentioned wanting to try them, but I didn't think he'd already put them on her," he said with annoyance. "I thought she was still wearing Blue Gems. We've used them for years."

"This may explain why she might've kicked; maybe the Circle Forge shoes aren't as comfortable," Suzanne offered.

"I wouldn't think so." He shook his head. "In any event, after the police did their forensics, I had our vet draw a blood panel on her and give her a thorough exam, just to make sure there wasn't a medical reason for her alleged kick. I'll be damned if I let a good pony be put down for something that wasn't her fault," he said, looking down.

"Or maybe she didn't do at all. You should have the police and coroner check Tomás's face for a logo."

Each looked straight into the other's eyes before Nick turned abruptly. But she'd felt his emotion rising before seeing his tears, though he tried to hide them from her.

She let go of Duchess's foot gently, letting the mare lower her hoof to the ground, and followed him. "Oh, Nick," she said, touching his shoulder. He turned and she hugged him with a deep sense of condolence. There was something about the death of a friend and possible horse abuse that made even ardent enemies call a truce and find common ground, at least momentarily. "Putting her down would be wrong on so many levels," she added.

He bent his head down and brushed her cheek before kissing her on the lips.

She promptly pulled away. "Way to ruin it."

"Sorry, Suze. But come on. I know you still have feelings for the ole Saint Nick." The devilish grin was back.

Sorry, Suze, she repeated in her head.

"Well, well, well. Isn't this a cozy little reunion?" Pamela Brooks drawled loudly, hands on her hips. Pam was a brunette with shoulder-length hair and an hourglass figure, accentuated with form-fitting riding breeches and a low-cut shirt that revealed an ample cleavage.

"It's not what you think, Pam," Suzanne said, turning to discreetly wipe off her mouth. She had heard Nick and Pam were an item.

"Oh? And what am I thinking?" Pam's left eyebrow was raised, her eyes narrowed. Her face was a study in contrast—anger laced with her cloyingly sweet, pageant-perfected smile.

"Look, I only came over here to express my condolences to Nick about Tomás," said Suzanne.

"How gracious and neighborly of you," Pam said, her voice lilting with sarcasm. She suddenly shook her head and said, "I'm sorry, I'm being rude. It's good to see you back in town, Suzy Q." She used the despised nickname in the cool way Suzanne remembered so well. Pam stuck her hand through Nick's forearm, staking her claim on him.

"Yeah, you too, Bam-Bam," Suzanne replied, mocking her with the name Pam had earned when they took lessons together in riding school—she'd always used her crop too hard on her horse. "Well, I'd better get going."

"Wait," Nick said, moving past Pam and grabbing Suzanne's arm. "Listen, I'm sorry, Suzanne. I mean about everything," he said, seemingly referring to their past and with genuine sincerity. "I heard about the bomb scare in Chicago and what happened to Bobby Lindley, too. I thought Bobby was a dick, and he was accused of some bizarre things." Nick didn't need to elaborate.

"Thanks," Suzanne said, pulling away.

"But at least it's given you a good excuse to come home." He touched her arm again, gently this time, but an emotional charge passed between them, so palpable even Pam felt it. Her mouth dropped open. "I bet Misty's happy," he added with a soft smile.

Suzanne nodded, but she was trembling, so taken aback by his unexpected apologies and the old sexual tension, undeniable, still simmering below the surface.

"I gotta go," she said, sprinting back to her mother's car as a rush of paranoia hit her. Something wasn't quite right about how Nick had immediately associated the recent tragedies with her return to Aiken. Her little inner voice was screaming at her, but with so much emotion and tension running through her, she had no idea what it was trying to say.

Chapter 13

That night, Suzanne dreamt of getting shot in the back again, only without the sudden knock to the ground. There was no searing heat on a shoulder blade shattering, overwhelming her small frame, nor were there any painful remnants scorching her trust in the one person she loved best. Dreamland performed its magic, bringing the surreal to life with a fantasy of her swimming and swaying blissfully, without direction, like a glob of lava floating in a lamp of oozy liquid light. Soon she was dancing and soaring, a shimmering bubble in flight, when she was seized with an epiphany—she had died, but she wasn't dead. The shot to the back and loss of blood had killed her, but she was still alive! There was no fear of death in this un-haunted place. That stirring thought jolted her awake.

No, no, no. Not yet. She closed her eyes, trying to withdraw back into the womb of sleep's comfort. But the morning light wasn't going to let it happen. So she decided to replace the feeling of the dream with an early morning jaunt with Misty.

Once outside, she spotted what looked like a dark gray Honda that had been modified with darkened windows and a black spoiler slowly pulling out from behind the barn. It was as out of place as an alien spacecraft, having been altered hideously into some other vehicular species. As she neared, it abruptly zipped out of the driveway. She wondered if its driver might be Jimmy, paying a visit to his brother.

Yet Randy wasn't in the barn, and neither was Brad. Suzanne tacked up Misty on her own before steering her over veiny roots encrusted in a pale, loamed incline, toward the trails of Hitchcock. After an hour of riding and jumping, she ended up at her usual spot near the interior Horse Show Ring.

With elbows on knees, Suzanne sat on the picnic bench trying to process what had happened to her and to Bobby and Tomás, and to see it all with new eyes—with what her grandmother had called eagle vision. She let her mind drift through and over the wooded acreage, envisioning the surf of pines as they swayed on the rise and fall of unseen winds, until she felt something change in the air. Her pulse quickening, the silence lengthened until it became all-powerful. Suddenly, it was like being pummeled by invisible waves, throwing and tossing her until she wasn't sure which way was up. She shook her head to clear it.

A *ca-reeeeeek* came from behind. She flinched and whipped around. But the only movement was a white-tailed deer chewing leisurely on a bit of greens. She let out a breath. *Get a grip, Suze.* She reminded herself that no matter what happened in the outside world, the Woods would remain both her truest friend and an inviolable place of peace, free of ghosts. Intuitively, she knew that the fears and confusion she felt lurked within her, not in Hitchcock Woods. It was up to her to discover the way to let go of them.

As she turned back toward the ring, two jumper riders on chestnut thoroughbreds passed on the other side of the show ring. She recognized the riders, longtime neighbors, even though they wore helmets and were about a hundred feet away. She waved, and they returned her greeting without stopping, cantering toward Bluebird Hill and beyond. She heard them jumping over the logs and brush fences of the adjacent landscape. Their sounds faded away as they traveled deeper into the Woods, probably to Ridge Mile Track.

She heard the whinny of the mustang-paint before seeing it and the young man on its bare back.

"Hey, how ya doing?" she said as they trotted near and stopped in front of her.

"Just fine and dandy," he said in his rich southern drawl. He wore lime-green cotton slacks and a hot-pink polo shirt. Just as he did the first time they met, he wore his hair in a bun, but today, he'd added a cross-body man purse.

"Excellent," she said, smiling.

"Do you mind if I sit down?" he asked, pointing to the space beside her. He and his horse created an uncommon distraction that was both unthreatening and entertaining.

She smiled. "Not at all. Help yourself." She noted that his shirt featured the iconic bright-yellow US map insignia of the Augusta National Golf Club.

"Have you seen the Masters?" she asked. Given Aiken's close proximity to Augusta, it wasn't unusual to see this type of golf shirt worn year-round.

"Oh yes, many times," he said, extracting two water bottles from his bag. "Do you need some?" He held out a full bottle that held no label. His bottle looked exactly the same, except it was already half-empty.

"Sure," she said. "Thanks." She turned the sealed top, snapping it open, and took a sip.

"Ah, what a glorious morning!" He pulled off his sunglasses and hung them over his shirt collar.

"Yes, it is," she said. "Your horse—he looks like a mustang-paint cross. Am I right?" She grinned, knowing that she was.

"Good eye! He is indeed. His name is Raziel," he said, finishing his water bottle. "After the archangel." He put the cap on and returned the bottle to his bag.

"Oh? I've never heard of an archangel named Raziel." She took another sip and set her bottle down on the bench.

"Ah, but he's a great one! *Raziel* means 'secrets of God.' He's full of wisdom and good humor, much like a guru." The reflections in the young man's brown eyes glittered and danced.

"Are you speaking of your horse or the archangel?"

"Ha, I suppose both." He chuckled, and Suzanne noticed for the first time that his coloring and features might be those of a Native American.

"Do you ride often?" she asked, although she was dying to ask where he was from. But Chicago had taught her to be mindful of questions that sounded too southern…or racist.

"Yes, I grew up with horses. I love them all, but I must say that Raziel has become a very special friend to me."

"What brings you to Hitchcock Woods?"

"Raziel likes to ride in here because it's a vortex with high levels of good Indian spiritual energy."

She searched his face to see if he was joking, but his expression was neutral—pleasant and unreadable. "I've heard this area of the Woods is associated with Indigenous American legends, although I've never heard it described in exactly that way," she said, grinning and turning her head slightly.

He nodded. "I also come to meditate and contemplate all that Raziel has shared about the Great Spirit's secrets of life."

"Are you saying that you know the secrets of God?"

"Yes," he said. "I am."

"And Raziel, the horse, communicated these mysteries to you?" She was uncertain about his level of seriousness because the emotional feedback she was getting felt neutral and she had no discomfort.

"The secrets of life shouldn't be mysteries at all, but rather taught to children and young adults before this world talks them out of them. We should teach children about the Great Spirit's universal principles of love and heart consciousness and how to take care of our landscapes."

"Wow." She looked at him. "My grandmother says stuff like that all the time."

"I hope you're listening to her." He looked straight into her eyes. "So now I'll ask you," he said, turning back to face the ring. "What brings you here today?"

"I'm trying to get past a bomb-and-kidnapping incident that happened to me in Chicago last week, and then there are two people I know, I mean, *knew* here in Aiken, who've died since I got back in town, just two days ago." She blushed, surprised that she'd so easily blurted out her troubles to this young stranger. She was equally surprised that it felt good to do so.

"Ah. The Woods," he said. "It's very good about helping us to let go, and heal."

"Yes, you're right," she said, accidently knocking her bottle to the ground. She leaned over and returned it to the bench.

"All that comes up in your life that is dark is coming up for you to address and release, to surrender and transform into something lighter, something better," he said. "It has to do with becoming conscious of your shadow, the fears and limitations you've put upon yourself or have allowed others to put upon you. Usually you have to dig deep into the subconscious to identify these false constructions. Other times, and in your case, it sounds like the specifics are being presented to you— almost like a nightmare."

Suzanne's mouth dropped open. *Fears presented as nightmares—he used the same words as Gran did only yesterday!* Most people in the South, or anywhere in her experience for that matter, just didn't talk like that. *Other than Gran, of course.*

"A nightmare is right." She wasn't sure if she said it out loud or not.

He turned toward his horse and laughed. "Raziel says, to get over your nightmare, you need to wake up and apply the Great Spirit's secrets of life to your situation."

As she was about to ask what *that* meant, the trails trembled. She looked toward Devil's Backbone. Randy was once again galloping in on Cole.

"I'll be seeing you," the young man said, promptly jumping on Raziel.

"Wait! I didn't catch your name!" But he was already disappearing over the knoll.

Randy stopped Cole abruptly in front of her. "There're some investigators up at the house. They asked if I could find you and bring you home," Randy said, breathless.

Exhaling, she turned to grab the water bottle before leaving, but it wasn't there. She looked on the ground. It wasn't there either.

"That's so strange." She put her fingers to her furrowed brow, still looking around.

"Not really. I seem to be doing a lot of this lately. Right?" Randy chuckled. "Actually, it was Della who asked me to come out to find you. I figured you'd be here."

"I don't suppose you saw that guy riding the mustang-paint this time?"

"Oh, yeah, I saw them. They were taking off just as I rounded the corner."

"Well, that's a relief," she said, feeling an unnatural twinge in her left shoulder, the good one. It could've meant nothing—or it could've been the signaling of something new. But in that raw and confusing moment, the new sensation was as indecipherable as an unknown ancient language.

Chapter 14

While Randy attended to Misty, Suzanne walked to the house, shaking more by the minute. She feared what might be waiting for her, that the authorities might try to tie her to the local deaths. It was probably a silly thought, but she steeled herself as she entered the kitchen.

Della was serving coffee and cookies to a man and woman, both in navy suits, as though she were using southern courtesies to corral them and prevent them from snooping. *God bless her!* A white woman of fifty-two with a strong presence and sturdy, nearly six-foot frame, Della had a matching personality and brown eyes that were both astute and distrustful. No one could mess with her, and that thought made Suzanne smile.

"Hello, I'm Suzanne Clayborn," she said, holding out her hand.

"I'm Mark Rhodes," said a stocky African American man who looked to be in his forties. He got up from the kitchen table and stepped toward her. "And this is my associate Barbara Jones." The short, white woman had acne scars, short curly brown hair and silver wire-rimmed glasses.

"Sorry, my hands are chapped," Suzanne said, reaching out. "It's not contagious. Just a sensitivity to something." *To stress*, she thought, catching another pair of yellow rubber gloves sitting next to the sink.

"No worries," Jones said, returning Suzanne's handshake. "We're here about the bomb incident at the Americos Building in Chicago…on behalf of Americos Oil's insurance company," she said. "I hope you don't mind our visit and a few questions."

"Oh," she said, surprised. *Insurance investigators.* "Listen, as I told the police and agents in Chicago, I don't know anyone who could've been involved with bombs, kidnapping or hurting me or my colleague Jill." Suzanne cringed at how defensive she sounded.

"Be that as it may, we just have a few questions. First, do you happen to know the whereabouts of someone named Jefferson Clayborn Junior?" Rhodes said, looking down at cell phone notes. "Who goes by the initials JJ?"

"Why in the world would you want to talk to my father?"

"Thank you for confirming his identity, Ms. Clayborn. Do you have any idea where your father might be?" Rhodes asked.

"He's on his way back from—" She stopped herself. These two weren't police officers after all. "Listen, I don't mean to be rude. But I don't have to answer your questions. And I'd rather not." She started to herd them to the door.

"Wait. You may be interested in why Mr. Clayborn's name was flagged for us," Jones said.

"Well, you're right. I don't understand why insurance investigators would want to know about my father," Suzanne said, crossing her arms.

"He's been missing from a south Florida rehabilitation center for the last couple of weeks," Rhodes said.

"What?" Her mouth was hanging open.

"I can see that information surprises you," Jones said. "Given his relationship to you and his criminal record, we would like to interview him in connection with this case."

"My father has nothing to do with this case. He's on his way back home now from Florida, not Chicago," she said, forgetting to self-edit. "But he can get easily diverted." *Damn, why am I saying that?*

"How is he usually, uh, diverted, as you say?" Rhodes asked, this time less accusatory.

"It's very likely he got sidetracked with the polo pony clubs and sales in Palm City, near the rehab in Boynton Beach, for example," she said. "He's done it many times before."

Daddy could have just as easily gotten lost in the casinos, Suzanne thought, but decided it unwise to point out this particular pattern of his behavior. He had a short attention span and might bounce around town for days without so much as a phone call. Her father was traveling on an endless road of addictions, trying to escape the ghosts of his own.

"I see," said Jones, sitting back down at the kitchen table to type notes into a computer tablet.

"I really don't see how you could think my father had anything to do with the Americos Building incident. Is that really all you've got?" she said, her stomach twisting. *Yes, the thought crossed my mind, but I was traumatized. They're not.*

"Given your experience as an equestrian, it's highly likely that you knew what you were smelling on the fifty-second floor," Rhodes said.

He's fishing for more information. "Of course I recognized the smell of horse fertilizer. That's why I called out to the cleaning guy that night. The police know this. I'm sure it's in the report and you know this as well."

"In addition to being on the custodial and maintenance staff at the Americos Building, the suspect had been hired as a barn hand at First Class Horse Carriage. Your father is an expert equestrian and has a family background in farming," Jones stated.

"Yes, but my father has never had a real job in his life. He wouldn't know the first thing about how to even apply for one, much less two. Also, and this is perhaps the most important point: my father would never put my life in danger like that."

"I agree it would be strange for a father to intentionally put his daughter in this sort of dangerous position. But he has a history of drunkenness and DUIs. He shot and nearly killed you when you were young."

"It was an accident." She breathed hard through her nose, crossing her arms.

"So it was ruled," Rhodes said, looking down at his notes.

"Let me point out something else that would eliminate my father as a suspect: the bomb guy was much younger."

"He wore a disguise."

"Yes, but clearly, he also had an expert understanding of electronics and computers," Suzanne said. Her voice was more defiant now. "He set up complicated spy equipment, a video camera and countdown device. My father barely understands how to use a cell phone, much less rig it to detonate a bomb. He has no idea how to go online or even how to download an app."

"I see," Rhodes said, as Jones recorded notes on her tablet.

"And as far as me knowing someone with horse knowledge, well, that's practically everyone here in Aiken, and probably at least a few people who work in the Americos Building."

Both Rhodes and Jones nodded. "If you hear from your father, will you please have him call us?" Jones said, rising and handing Suzanne two business cards.

"Sure," she said, stuffing them in her back pocket. *But I've got to talk to him first.*

Chapter 15

Suzanne's whole body was tense, and her aching head was letting her know it. She'd tried to sound convincing in her arguments regarding her father, but in truth, she wasn't sure about anything. Her father was such a mixed bag.

She didn't want to think any more about the insurance investigators as she walked to the barn, relaxing the closer she got. "Hello, my sweeties," she said. The horses' heads were already sticking into the aisle over the yokes of their stall doors. She turned her head sharply, detecting some movement in the shadows near Cole's stall.

"Well, hey, girlie girl. How about a kiss and hug for your good ole daddy?" JJ said as he ambled toward her with arms open.

"Oh, Dad, you scared me," she said, hugging his neck.

"I came as soon as I heard about what happened in Chicago, sweetheart," he said, kissing her forehead. "Damn, Suze, sorry you went through that. Are you all right?"

"Yes, but there's a lot of strange things going on."

"Yeah, your grandmother filled me in," he said.

"She doesn't know about this. Just a minute ago, we had some insurance investigators here from Chicago asking about you leaving rehab early. And let me just say, the police will probably be here to question you as well. They actually thought you might have had something to do with the bomb incident in Chicago." She looked at him directly, putting a palm over her throat. "You didn't, did you, Dad?"

"What? That's crazy talk," he said, dismissing her comment with a wave of his hand.

"Please tell me where you've been, then," she said, crossing her arms.

"Well, I was scheduled in for rehab for a bit and had a bunch of doctors looking at me, up one side and down the other. Only, after a few days, I couldn't stand it anymore. It was just a nuisance and a big waste of time. So I went fishing."

"You've got to be kidding!" She threw up her hands.

"Well, that's the low-down truth," he said with a dimpled grin. "Since your mama was on the cruise, I left and went to our condo at the beach." He looked up. "I just wanted to be by myself for a while anyway. I've had a lot on my mind." He paused. "But, Suzanne, baby, you know I wouldn't have done anything intentionally to hurt you. You know that, darlin'. Please tell me you believe me." His eyes softened.

"Of course I do, Dad!"

"There's my Suzy cutie. Hey, let's go up to the house. I can't wait to see your mama."

"Dad, I think you should call the investigators and get that out of the way. Here's their contact information." She handed him the two business cards. "I was about to go for another ride."

"You're going out now, just when I got home to see you?" he said, his voice tinged with disappointment. "I don't give a damn about the stupid insurance investigators. It's not like they're the police." He threw the cards in the air.

"It's been such a trying day." She bent down to pick them up. "But I'll go up to the house with you now, if you want. How come you're in the barn?" she asked.

"I just wanted to pop in and make sure the boys were taking good care of the horses in my absence, especially my Cole." The giant thoroughbred, hanging his head over the stall door, looked adoringly at JJ. "The boys aren't here right now. But the horses look good; I'm satisfied." He patted Cole's face. "See ya soon, boy."

She wondered where Randy had gone, but said, "We're all making sure they're being taken care of properly."

JJ put his arm around Suzanne's shoulders. "There's my good girl. Come on, let's go find your mama, Suzy Q," he said.

She acquiesced, like everyone else did with JJ, and they walked out.

The locals believed that JJ was special and unique, a demigod, despite the Clayborn family's tragic past, which included his father dying when JJ was only two—not to mention his mother's eccentricities and dabbling in metaphysical subjects. A golden-haired toddler, JJ had grown into a beautiful, high-spirited boy in love with the rhythms and cadences of expensive thoroughbreds. He was noted for having high intelligence, a flamboyant charm and a dimpled smile. His eyes were pale blue, his skin rosy. The cute, round features of his young teens transformed into something delicate and aristocratic as he aged into adulthood and at just over six feet, his frame became lean and muscular. He was naturally gifted in polo, the town's obsession, and an expert equestrian. Most women rushed to please him, begging him to dance with them, trying to win his favor and sizable trust fund. The gossip circles suggested these women actually wept in utter shock and dismay when JJ chose Lita Newton as his wife.

But for all of his God-given gifts and projected self-confidence, JJ was moody and unpredictable. In the last ten years, as his middle-aged body started to fail him as a polo player, he'd become a sloppy alcoholic. He was blessed with masculine beauty his whole life, yet he might go days without bathing. It was an exasperating mystery to most why he did what he did, choosing to sabotage the good in his life.

But Suzanne had a theory: his problems were because of the pestering ghosts.

Unlike her ghosts that came after a near-death experience, JJ's ghosts were murmuring voices, faceless and nameless, tormenting him in his dreams in the dead of night. She suspected his haunts were the result of a childhood trauma, of losing his father at such a tender age. When his ghosts came, he would cling to Lita. He claimed she had the power to banish them, being too vibrant and alive for ghosts to tolerate. How could he have chosen a more perfect and powerful wife?

As Suzanne and JJ entered the back door to the house, Lita was coming out of the bedroom, still in her flowing nightgown, despite it being past noon, her eyelids sooty from yesterday's makeup. She ran into JJ's arms and they kissed like long-lost lovers.

"Hey, cut it out," Suzanne said, blushing and shaking her head. "I was going for a ride, Dad, but you said you wanted me here. I'm here."

"Okay, okay," he said, pulling back but keeping one arm around Lita. "I just missed this gorgeous woman." He squeezed her waist.

Lita squealed and beamed with joy. "Let me grab some coffee, and we'll catch up," she said, twirling off in her silken slippers.

Coffee cups in hand, they gathered in the family room and Suzanne recounted the stories of the fertilizer bombing and the deaths of two men she had previously dated. Suddenly, a mallard with a dozen babies waddled in through the back door, which had been accidentally left ajar.

"Oh lawd!" Lita shouted, jumping up. "Get those ducks out of here!"

When JJ got up to chase them, the babies darted around the room, the mama quacking in angry protest. Lita ran behind JJ, holding down the sides of her swirling nightgown, as if she feared an attack on her ankles. The comic display further panicked the poor ducklings, who sought refuge under the leather sofa.

Suzanne got on her hands and knees, trying to reach them, while Lita picked up the phone and, absurdly, called 911.

"This is Lita Clayborn. We've a whole mess of ducks in the house, and we need help," Lita said loudly, over all the quacking and squeaking. "No, I'm not drunk, and I take offense at that accusation."

As Lita slammed down the phone, Della calmly came into the room with a broom and shooed the babies out from under the sofa and into a corner, gently picking each one up and putting it in her apron. The ducklings safely contained, she carried them outside toward the pond as the mama duck quacked away, but followed in her wake. Returning and closing the door, Della padded over to the phone.

"Hello, 911? This here is Della Brown at the Clayborn's residence. Yes, ma'am, we got that duck problem taken care of. You can cancel our call. It was made by mistake. Thank y'all very much." Hanging up, she returned to the kitchen without comment, a grin or even looking around at anyone's stunned face.

"Way to go, Della! I think you just saved us from getting a big fat fine," JJ said, clapping, as he busted out laughing. "Now, those ducks coming up from the pond and right in the door, that's what I call a grand homecoming for us, right, Suze?"

"Typical insanity," Suzanne said, shaking her head and rolling her eyes. *As usual, no one in this family takes anything seriously.*

"Hey, Suze, come check out my new sound system. It's first-class," he said, opening a door of the full-wall cabinet he'd built. "And I've missed playing my favorite tunes on it since I've been out of town." He picked up a rather complicated-looking remote and pushed a button, selecting "My Girl" by the Temptations from a playlist he had titled *My Favorite Beach Music*. "Now that my girl's home, I've got sunshine on a cloudy day," he sang, using the song's lyrics, while moving his feet to its three-beat rhythm. "Come on, let's shag," he said with a chuckle, referring to the South's iconic dance.

"Oh, Dad," she said, brushing him away. "Did you install this system yourself?"

"Sure, it wasn't that tough," he said, putting his hand out to Lita. "I can focus on stuff like that when I want to."

Suzanne shook her head. "I've never known you to be able to figure out electronics," she said with a deep frown and arms crossed.

"You're right. I was just kidding. I focused on it by calling an outfit in town who did this top-notch job." He chuckled again as he turned to Lita with effortless grace.

Relieved, Suzanne got up, but felt a warm sensation in her good shoulder again. "Do you mind if I go riding now?"

They ignored her as they continued to kiss and dance, acting like shameless adolescents with their usual short attention spans. Suzanne slipped out the door, finally, to return to the Woods and get the horse therapy she so desperately needed.

Chapter 16

Randy was muttering something to himself in the stall with the Clayborn's senior bay quarter horse, Barnie.

"Hey, where you been?" Suzanne asked, standing at the stall door.

"Oh, hey. Um…I had to get some salve for poor ole Barnie's horsefly bites," Randy said, crouching near the gentle gelding's forelegs. "Also, had to pick up a new security camera and a new router for the wireless system that's been on the blink, for your mama. Don't worry; I've already fixed it, in case you need to use it. I'll replace the security camera a little later," he said, sounding more like a handy man rather than a barn hand. Before I left, my brother showed up, needing some money. So I also had to go to the ATM."

"You don't have to tell me every little thing you did."

"Well, you asked," he said, turning toward her with a sideways grin.

"I guess you're right," she said, laughing. "Hey, I'm in desperate need of a ride, but please, don't stop what you're doing. I actually want to tack up Misty myself," she said. Like all "barn girls," Suzanne loved everything about the equipment and process. To her, the smell of oil-softened leather and sweet hay was better than any aromatherapy. And she'd take dusty boots over her designer pumps or her mother's fancy stilettos any day. But then, barn girls were taught from a young age to always keep their heels down—in the stirrups.

She settled into the saddle with reins in hand, feeling the tension already starting to melt off. "See you later," she said, with a flick of her hand. Randy gave her a backhanded wave as he continued with Barnie's treatment.

As she rode down Clayborn Cut, Suzanne thought about how Randy had seen the preppy Native American when she was last in the Woods, confirming at least the young man wasn't a ghost. *Thank goodness!* But the missing water bottle continued to gnaw at her. She hoped to find the stranger in the Woods again and was on the lookout. She was in high spirits when she caught sight of him on foot next to Raziel, near Kalmia Trail. She dismounted at the picnic tables as they approached.

"I'm surprised you're still in the Woods," she said when he came close. She brushed the pollen off the bench before removing her riding gloves.

"Actually, like you, I took a midday break. I hope all went well with your meeting."

"Not really, but I don't want to talk about it. I was surprised to see you walking over there and not riding." She took in the sweet sight of Kalmia flowers exploding in pink clusters along the trail's edge.

"Well, Raziel was keen to find a treasure there," he said, pointing. "I was helping him look."

"And did y'all find it?" she asked, half smiling, trying not to mock.

"Indeed we have," he said. He handed her an ancient arrowhead.

She gasped in wonder as she fingered its flinty surface, getting an image in her mind's eye of a young man with a face not unlike the one before her, but who was dressed in leathers as he roved the Woods carrying a handmade bow and quiver of arrows. "You're right, you did find a treasure."

He smiled and patted Raziel's forehead.

"Hey, before we get interrupted again, I want to ask your name," she said. "Mine is Suzanne Clayborn." She held out her hand. His handshake felt like silk on her dry, peeling palm. "Sorry, my hands are chapped." She rubbed them together. At least his hands felt real. She wondered how to ask if he'd taken back the water bottle before he'd dashed off before.

"It's a pleasure to officially meet you, Suzanne Clayborn. May I suggest creating a salve for your hands by mixing a couple drops of lavender and myrrh essential oils with fractionated coconut oil? Apply it to your hands when needed, but especially in the evenings before sleeping. They should heal soon thereafter."

"Thanks for the advice. I'll give it a try. About your name…"

"Some call me JB, and it suits me for now." He bowed with his palms together like a prayer.

"Well okay, JB," she said, accepting it with a chuckle, especially since her father introduced himself in almost the exact the same way, without a last name and even with a slight bow of the head. "It's nice to meet you too, and finally get a name."

He scratched Raziel's ears.

"So now that we're formally introduced, JB," she said, recalling their previous conversation, "I'm curious about what you…and um…" She paused to look at his horse and smiled. "Raziel said…to get past my nightmare, I needed to apply some sort of secrets to my situation. What did you mean by that?"

"Are you asking for guidance?"

"I was thinking more of another perspective. But, sure, I guess you could call it that."

He smiled as he let go of Raziel's reins and sat next to her on the bench. His horse stepped toward Misty and they stared at JB and Suzanne, the horses standing side by side, as if they were about to watch a human movie.

"Do you hear that?" He was looking toward the ring.

"Hear what?"

"To listen and learn you must be still."

She attuned her ears to the quietude around them. There were no stray conversations coming from unseen equestrians on nearby trails. City noises were nonexistent. No leaf blowers in distant yards, and no roars of airplane engines in the skies. She was audience only to the symphony of nature: the fluted songs of the wood thrush, the occasional percussion of a woodpecker, the droning hymns of cicadas, the light play of leaves strummed by an invisible warm breeze.

JB closed his eyes and held out his arms, like he was about to conduct an orchestra. In the next moment, as his hands danced, the varying instruments of the Woods banded together, harmonizing and amplifying, as though someone had turned up the volume on a giant speaker.

Suzanne's mouth dropped open. Her heartbeat accelerated with inexplicable excitement.

"That comes from the inner power, the breath of silence," he said, opening his eyes wide.

"Wow" was all she could say.

"Let us listen to hear!" He closed his eyes again.

She nodded, and they simply sat with straight spines on the bench next to each other without speaking. At last, she turned to ask a question but had to refrain. He was performing a mudra meditation, a hand position with the tip of his thumb touching the tip of his index finger, palms up on the thighs of his lime-green pants.

She'd often seen her grandmother unexpectedly drop into a meditative state, so his pose was not alien to her. Out of respect, she remained mute, letting her eyes graze on the sweet grasses and foam-colored trails, thinking of how nimble Indigenous tribesmen, who once sought the healing magic of a waterless sand river, had dropped their arrowheads for lucky treasure hunters of the future to find.

After a while, with his eyes still closed, JB began to speak. "You are like a star in the morning."

"Thank you?" She wasn't sure if he was flirting or being poetic.

"I will give you a reading now."

"A reading? Are you a psychic?"

He opened his eyes and as he turned toward her, his face beamed. "Not exactly, but I am in receipt of some guidance to pass along to you," he said.

She felt a warming in her good shoulder that moved toward her heart, silently conveying a sense of safety that also came to her when she was being present in Hitchcock Woods. "Well, okay. I'd love to hear it."

With head tilting up and eyes again closed, JB began speaking in his southern baritone as though channeling from a higher, unseen dimension: "Suzanne Clayborn, you are a spiritual being born with luminous sensitivities made more powerful by your brief moment in Spirit. You glow with joy and empathy, resonating strongly with horses and nature, but without proper boundaries and a golden neutrality, you are merely an emotional sponge cake. This can make you physically ill at times and an energy vampire's favorite dessert. Consequently, you've attracted a lot of broken people and chaos."

Whoa. She felt her stomach flip. *How does he know that?*

"You're able to perceive beings and entities on various vibrational planes because in death you were alive, and your subconscious located in the heart now holds the belief of this as a possibility. Bear in mind that new higher energies are incoming to Mother Earth now, amplifying everyone's soul senses, including yours."

"What?" She was trying to follow.

"Yes, everyone has extrasensory perception, although these abilities may not be known or developed

in a person. You don't have to have a near-death
experience to have them. As I was saying, new higher
energies are coming into this world right now. They may
be perceived as positive and uplifting, but also intense as
they stir up old, detrimental energies, trauma wounds
from the past, and false programs in need of release. You
must not ignore them. You must not run from them. You
must let them go in a state of peace and non-
resistance...or you'll endure more suffering."

"More? What're you saying?" Her palms were
burning as she held them up.

"My dear Suzanne, it's essential, even in the midst
of the most chaotic and emotional of situations, for you
to get quiet and retreat into golden silence, into a space of
noninterference and inner wisdom, where you can be
neutral, free and able to listen for and sense inner truths,
and gain clarity, just as the masters know and practice,
and as we're demonstrating today. This will help prepare
you for what is, and what is to come," he said, pausing to
breathe in and out in a deliberate way. "And it will protect
you from having a negative charge."

She relaxed a little at the soothing words that
were also used by her grandmother.

"There's more to your soul's senses than just *seeing*
what you refer to as ghosts. You pick up information
from touch, just as you did with the arrowhead a moment
ago."

She gasped. She had in fact done that. *How did he know?*

Without waiting for her to comment, he continued: "Expand your soul's senses by knowing you can taste and absorb the essence of nature's wisdom through the blessing of food. You can receive ethereal messages from smelling the landscape's aromas. You can hear vibrations. You have a natural rapport with spiritual intelligence and can converse without talking."

"I've never thought of the soul as having its own set of senses." She looked up. "I've probably done all those things and felt them without consciously understanding their significance."

"Generally speaking, most people don't understand that the soul, body and emotions speak a language, and empaths are natural interpreters of that language."

"Oh!" Suzanne felt her heart confirming his statement with its warm, confident tones.

"The guidance for you is that you stop seeking answers to life's problems out there somewhere." After he inhaled and exhaled another several times, he spoke again. "It's time for you to take the reins of your life, to gain insights from within by expanding your soul's senses, and then sharing the wisdom with the world. This is the goal of your soul."

Suzanne was surprised to feel a trust in him and how his words were taking hold of her. Now she wondered if he could give her a greater understanding about the ghosts she saw.

Returning to his pose with closed eyes, incredibly, he answered without her asking aloud. "Ghosts and higher spiritual beings unseen by most humans are on different rungs of the vibrational ladder. Someone with your clairvoyant bandwidth and vision, however, can easily learn to discern the differences. And you should learn, instead of trying to ignore them. Your body and emotions are speaking to you all the time, but you're not listening. Your soul's senses are trying to tell you a story, but all too often, you choose to close the book before the story's finished."

"How do you know I do that?" she whispered.

"Granted, there are times to detach for your own protection," he went on. "For example, in the present, you mustn't allow yourself to get entangled in the negative dramas unfolding around you, although you can safely observe and be a neutral witness to them. For there will be more."

"More of what?"

"There's a high probability that two more people close to you will pass into Spirit within a week's time or soon thereafter."

"What?"

"And there's also a high possibility that one of those persons will be you."

"What?" Suzanne repeated, sucking in her breath. "I thought you said I could protect myself."

"Indeed."

"How?"

"Call for protection in your meditations, imagine a gold bubble around you, and believe it in your heart. It's also useful to remember that what you focus on is what you get, so think carefully about what you want for yourself. As long as you don't know what your soul wants, life will continue to give you situations to help you decide and cause you to choose."

"I don't understand."

"You will. As you become more adept in your abilities. You'll know in your 'knower' that you know," he said and smiled.

She put her hands on her head. "But you're saying two others I know will die, and one might be me. By next Wednesday!" She waved her arms around.

With eyes still shut, he added, "Or soon thereafter."

"This all sounds like some kind of weird riddle. Not exactly the guidance I was looking for!"

"Please bear in mind: These are probabilities. Not certainties."

"So what am I supposed to do with ...with your

probabilities?" She didn't know how she could handle it all—the bomb, the ex-boyfriends' deaths, and now more would die. Ignoring it all sounded like a perfectly good idea—running away, even better.

She paced, tears falling, rubbing her hands together. They were stinging, her wrists ached, and the pain traveled up her spine, lodging in between her shoulders. *What a fitting metaphor of my life!* She was standing in excruciating pain between her good and bad shoulders.

"Seek your answers and protection in the forest preserves of meditation, expand your soul's senses, listen, and then follow the inner guidance received. You may be able to affect the probability of these so-called deaths based on the choices and actions you and others make."

Her head felt like it might explode, and her ears seemed to be on fire. She placed her palms on her forehead and breathed hard. "Do you mean I or someone else could stop them?" She looked up.

Incredibly, he pressed his palms prayerfully and said, "Namaste," effectively ending his apocalyptic reading with a respectful bow of the head.

Just as she was about to demand more of an explanation, the Woods erupted in activity with a cavalry of neighbors driving horse carriages coming from the South Boundary side.

One of the carriages, driven by a neighbor, Jean Sellars, came up seemingly out of nowhere.

"Welcome home, Suzanne," said the woman, fully accoutered in carriage driver attire and smiling wide. "It's wonderful to see you! We were all so worried about what's been going on with you in Chicago."

"Thank you, Mrs. Sellars." She wiped her face, sat on her now trembling hands and forced a smile.

"I'm real interested in hearing all about your adventures in Chicago," Mrs. Sellars said, making an overture of concern. "Perhaps over some tea soon. Have you been riding long this afternoon?"

"No, ma'am. Just came out here to chill out a little," she said, relieved that Mrs. Sellars wouldn't be pressing her about events right now and didn't seem to notice her agitation.

"I shall let you get back to it, then. Precious is anxious to rejoin the others," she said, referring to her horse. She pulled the reins to the side. "I'll be sure to pass on your good news to the others. Tally-ho," she said, departing with a light snap of her whip.

Suzanne wasn't sure to what good news Mrs. Sellars referred. Maybe she meant that it was good news Suzanne was still alive and back in town. But how strange that she didn't even look at or acknowledge JB. He too had remained quiet during the brief exchange. She shook her head. "I should've introduced you. That was rude of me. Sorry about that. I'm just so stunned by all that you've said, I'm not even sure I heard what *she* said."

"Not to worry. She was obviously in a hurried state of mind. I must go now, too," JB said, climbing on Raziel's back.

"Wa-wait," she sputtered. "What am I supposed to do with...with all you've told me?"

"Just remember to pay attention to the feelings and guidance you receive from within. That is important for you to learn." He thumped his chest with his fist before turning to ride off.

In the tense silence, she watched him round the path's corner toward Bluebird Hill. She turned back and saw something on the bench that made her gasp. *The missing water bottle!* The one with no label and only a few sips taken out of it. Had JB put it back without her noticing? Or had it reappeared out of thin air?

She stood in awestruck silence, now feeling the energy of the arrowhead as if it were growing hot in her pocket. *I should give it back to him,* she thought, pulling it out, knowing it was just an excuse to follow him, that she'd move fast and hard, and couldn't help it, like a moth to flame. With a sense of panic, she galloped Misty to the middle of Bluebird Hill, where it intersected with three other trail spokes. Unclear which path he'd taken, she halted and hopped off, examining the sand. Carriage wheel tracks headed down Lover's Lane, but there were no fresh hoofprints behind them. She turned north to inspect the two other trail entrances. No new single hoofprints there either. Suzanne stilled herself to listen for movement, her heart pounding, adrenaline shooting through her veins, and had a terrible thought: a ghost might've just violated the inviolable.

Yet she'd had no chilled breath, no hair standing on end. No creepy, crawly skin. His hands had felt solid and real. She exhaled heavily. She now wondered if Randy had lied to her about seeing JB before, just to please her.

Ignoring the lack of hoofprints and the magical water bottle for a moment, she thought it could be possible that JB was simply a true psychic medium. She'd been to a couple of psychics after the shooting accident, and like JB, they'd told her things they couldn't possibly have known. They too had given her tips for handling incoming negative energies, which turned out to be useful. *Which means I probably shouldn't just dismiss JB's predictions too quickly.*

She climbed into the saddle, her thoughts more tangled up than ever with emotions. "Let's go, girl," she said, leaning forward and gently squeezing with her calves, commanding her mare to gallop hard up The Manage, a trail leading to Ridge Mile Track. She intended to exorcise the demons and release the mounting tension by jumping a few fences. She needed to fly—and scream.

Chapter 17

Like everything else in the Woods, Ridge Mile
Track was inherently organic in construction with rough-
hewn timbered beams forming rustic steeplechase
obstacles. The riding surface of the oval track was part
grass and part sand. It encircled a loosely forested area
that also held a number of log jumps. Thomas Hitchcock
had originally installed it in the 1920s for training young
steeplechasers.

As Misty flew over the wooden obstacles,
Suzanne's mind continued racing with troubling thoughts.
*Maybe JB could predict when others would die because he was the
one who murdered the first two!* She stopped to listen to her
body. *No.* JB didn't have the vibe of a psychopath, but his
vibe wasn't normal either. *Was he a true psychic medium?* She
got the feeling he was, and yet she sensed there was so
much more to know about his abilities. On the other

hand, he could've done a background check on her or heard about the local deaths and her ghost-seeing abilities through Aiken's gossip vine.

Nevertheless, she'd definitely sensed that she should take his warnings seriously. The tears fell again as she continued with another round of unanswerable questions. *Does "close to me" mean another old boyfriend, a childhood friend or someone in my family? If two more people close to me die, how might one of them be me? If I don't die, does that mean someone else is condemned?* Suzanne cried harder, hating that on top of everything else going on, JB's riddle was so morbid and seemingly unsolvable yet she felt it also rang true.

Her cell phone pinged and vibrated. She halted Misty and wiped her face with her gloved hand before answering.

"Hi, Suzanne." Clyde, her boss, was at the other end of the line. "I realize you're trying to recover from the bombing, but we're getting pressure from Americos to move forward with the presentation as soon as possible."

"Of course, I understand," she said, trying to stifle her heavy breathing.

He informed her that the files had been recovered and materials recreated. The firm was using a temporary open space on the third floor until the office was repaired. And the presentation was rescheduled for the end of next week—next Friday.

What?

"I'm sure you'll want to fly back to town for it, at least by next Wednesday, to get prepared. After all, it's mainly your creative," Clyde said.

"Thanks Clyde, but I have to confess that this ordeal has shaken me to the core," she said, speaking with a nasal voice from crying.

"I'm so sorry, Suzanne. We can talk about more time off, after the presentation."

"Have you heard any more from the police about a possible arrest?"

"No, they seem to be at a dead end, although I've been told that Americos' insurance company has hired private investigators to help out."

I'm well aware of that, she thought, but kept it to herself. "How's Jill? I wanted to call her, but her number's still not—"

"Actually, she's back at work as of today," he said with a tone that implied Suzanne should be back, too.

"Already? I must say, I'm surprised. Happy but surprised."

"Also, the building's management has already installed new-and-improved security measures and technology. So, you have nothing to fear in coming back to work."

She decided not to tell Clyde that she was now more worried about the upcoming deaths, predicted by a strange psychic dude in Hitchcock Woods. "That's reassuring, but..." For the first time since graduating from college, her career wasn't the most important thing in her life. "Is there any way you could do the presentation without me?" Suzanne tried, shocked at her own words. "I'm not quite ready to get back on the horse, so to speak, but I know I will be—after next week. If I could just have a little more time, it'd be much appreciated."

"You don't sound like yourself, Suzanne, and I know this has been traumatic." He paused, and Suzanne could feel his impatience. "I don't mean this to sound harsh, but Jill's back, and you're going to have to choose what you want," he said.

Choices—there it is again, she thought, remembering JB's words: *As long as you don't know what your soul wants, life will continue to give you situations to help you decide and cause you to choose.*

"The job is still yours, of course, but you've got to still want it," Clyde continued in her silence. "And, obviously, we assume you'll work with the same commitment and attitude you had before the incident. Be a good little soldier, Suzanne, and get back before the presentation."

Did he really just say, "Be a good little soldier"? She felt an unexpected anger rising. "I'm confident the team can present the campaign without me this once," she tried again.

"How about this?" he said. "Give it a couple more days and then call me with your decision. Okay?"

"Fair enough. I will. Thanks, Clyde. I'll call soon."

But she didn't see how she could. *Two other deaths, maybe mine, might occur by next Wednesday! How am I supposed to fly back to Chicago on that same day and prepare for a major presentation on Friday? How am I supposed to make a life decision and be a "good little soldier" with this terrifying deadline hanging over me? Holy crap…I might be dead by then!*

She rode Misty into the middle of Ridge Mile Track's interior forest, dismounted, and sat down on one of the pine logs. She looked up through an opening in the trees, watching clouds shapeshift into animal forms, thinking how her life was also shifting and changing into something completely unexpected.

Feeling tickles on her hands, Suzanne looked down only to see a colony of little black ants crawling all over them and her breeches. *Oh dear Lord!* She jumped up, brushing them off just as her cell phone rang. She bounced, swatted and shook. Finally free of the tiny crawlers, she saw the caller had been Dan. He'd sent texts every day and called her every morning, and she missed the one he'd made earlier. She took in a deep breath and hit the button to call him back.

After a brief catch-up and apologizing for not getting back to him sooner and not yet having a firm date for returning to Chicago, she took another deep breath and asked, "Dan, what do you think connects us? Do we share any values?"

"We're great in the sack."

She felt her heart sink. "Is that all that matters to you?" she asked, but already knew the answer.

"Um. No."

She could picture him with a puzzled look on his face and felt his irritation rising. But she wanted him to feel what she was feeling. "Can't you see I'm having a personal crisis? I'd like you to say something meaningful and real. Maybe empathize with what I'm going through."

"I'm sorry, Suzanne. Of course we share the same values. You're the most important person in my life. When are you coming back? I miss you. I need you. Is that what you want to hear?"

She shook her head. *He has no idea how I feel,* she thought. *But, then, how could he? He isn't empathic in the least.*

"No, Dan. That's not what I want to hear," she said. "But don't worry about it."

She sighed, knowing he wouldn't.

"Listen," she said, almost in a whisper. "There's so much going on here, I'm not sure when I can get back.

I'll let you know as soon as I figure it out. I'll talk with you soon, okay?"

It's over with him already, she thought, climbing in the saddle. *And he'll get really pissed.* She rode back hard, not caring, moving as fast as she could toward the only counsel she could trust, the only person she knew who could truly empathize and help her.

Chapter 18

"Gran, I'm so confused right now." They were sitting in white rockers on Henrietta's veranda. "I don't know what to do."

"Tell me about it, dear," Henrietta said.

"There's been a new development, and it's weighing heavily on me." She leaned over, combing her hair with her fingers. She sighed as she watched dozens of light strands fall onto the gray-painted planks. "I'm hoping you can help me see it better."

"I'll try."

"I'm supposed to go back to Chicago next week for what is probably the most important presentation of my career. But my life's been altered so much in such a short time that it's changed my thinking; it's changed my heart. My old life feels like an illusion, and I've lost my ambition for it. Chicago holds no appeal for me right now, including my boyfriend there, and that makes me sad. I want to cry about it. But I can't seem to do it."

"I'm sensing that," Henrietta said. "Is that what you meant by new development?"

"Yes and no. I should back up. I met the most unusual young man in Hitchcock Woods."

"And you're afraid to get involved with him with all that's happening?" She raised her eyebrows, looking as though she'd picked up on Suzanne's fears.

"Not exactly."

"What then?"

She hesitated, searching for the right words. "He says strange things, psychic things, deep and spiritual things. It's like he's a psychic medium. He speaks of probabilities and...prophesizes." She shook her head, not knowing where to begin or how to explain.

"He doesn't sound at all like your usual boyfriends."

"It's not like that. Not at all. He's actually younger than me, probably still in college, making what he said even more extraordinary. He dresses like a frat boy," she said with a frown. "Well, sort of." She shook her head at the memory of his man bun and purse. "He looks like he might be part Native American."

"How interesting! When you say that he prophesizes, what do mean by that?"

"He gave me some warnings that the probability was high…that two other people close to me would die by next Wednesday and one might be me."

"And you believed him?"

"I'm sensing I should, but it might be that I'm just still feeling my own paranoia after almost getting blown up," she said, pausing for a fraction of a second. "Now that I say this stuff out loud, it seems ludicrous to take him seriously." She was talking fast.

"Okay, just slow down, take a breath and start over. Try to interpret the meaning of what you're feeling, of what you're getting empathically."

"That's exactly what he said I should do!"

"How interesting," she repeated. "What specifically did he say?" She put her fingers to her chin.

"He first gave me what I'd call a psychic reading, full of insights and secrets about my life that he couldn't possibly know. He used many of the same words and phrases you use, like you just did, which was why I listened. He even gave me an essential oils recipe for my chapped hands," she said, wincing as she rubbed them.

"Let me take a look," Henrietta said, holding out her hands to Suzanne's raw, cracked ones. "Oh dear. Well, I'd say you'd benefit greatly from some lavender and coconut oil."

"That's exactly what he said! Only he suggested mixing myrrh and lavender with fractionated coconut oil."

"Oh! He's absolutely right!" Her eyes brightened and she smiled as if getting a subtle joke. "And you're in luck. I have all of those ingredients. Come with me," she said, walking inside, to the inventory of essential oils she kept in the kitchen.

After she helped Suzanne mix and apply them, Henrietta said, "Now where were we?" She motioned for them to sit at the kitchen table.

Suzanne rubbed her hands together. "Ah, that does feel good. Thanks," she said, pausing to gather her thoughts as she sat down. "He said that what I focus on is what I will get, so I'd better think carefully about what I want and choose wisely. He advised me, like you have, to seek answers within, with my psychic abilities, expand on them even, and not to get embroiled in the, quote, negative dramas unfolding around me, end quote, although I could safely be an observer and witness. And that as long as I don't know what my soul wants, life would continue to give me situations that cause me to choose—stuff like that."

Henrietta leaned forward and whispered, "I once had a friend like that."

"You're speaking about Bears Repeating, aren't you?"

"Yes, I am. How'd you know?"

"I found your manuscript."

"Oh, what perfect timing," Henrietta said with a giggle and clasp of hands.

Suzanne shook her head, realizing her grandmother wasn't at all alarmed about the potential deaths predicted by JB, as Suzanne had expected her to be. In fact, quite the opposite.

"May I ask how you came across *The Secrets of Bears Repeating?*"

"It was on Dad's desk. I didn't mean to be nosy, but just after I arrived from Chicago, I went into his study to use the phone, and there it was, along with stacks of unopened letters—all from you. Before I was able to read it, this boy ghost, who's been pestering me for a while, interfered with my focus. In any event, when I went back to Dad's study the next morning, both the manuscript and letters were gone. Mama must've moved them, probably to protect his privacy about such things, like she usually does."

"Not to worry, dear. I've been saving you a copy."

"Why didn't you give it to me before now?"

"As Bears Repeating and other gurus have said, 'When the student is ready, the teacher appears.'"

"Gran, I'm ready now. I need some answers, but I need them fast."

"Well then, I'll get it posthaste." Henrietta went to the metal cabinet next to her writing desk and withdrew a file. She returned with the pages in hand.

"That didn't take long," Suzanne said.

"Let's just say I've been anticipating your readiness." Henrietta smiled, giving Suzanne a stapled photocopy of the twenty-page document.

Suzanne exhaled with a halfhearted smile. "Thanks, Gran. I'll read it. But I'll probably have lots of questions."

Henrietta nodded. "I'm sure you will. You're a lot like me, more than my own children." A look of ancient pain crossed over Henrietta's blue eyes.

"You still worry about Dad, don't you? He's always been a mess, hasn't he?" She shook her head.

"A mother is always connected to her child, no matter how different, difficult or old. But you've sensed correctly. Yes, I still do worry about JJ. But at the same time, through the many ups and downs with him and this family, I believe he'll ultimately choose wisely for his highest good. I have faith. Knowing he's pulled out the old manuscript and the letters, these are encouraging signs. Thank you for telling me."

"There've been rumors about my great-grandfather being abusive and violent. Is that why Dad's an alcoholic and haunted? Is it genetic? Do I have those issues in my genes, too?"

"No, dear, you've wonderful gifts and abilities embedded in your DNA." She patted Suzanne's cheek.

"So what are in the letters you wrote Dad, anyway?" Suzanne asked.

"They were my attempts at explaining what happened to me and him early on. I was trying to teach him about the ancient healing secrets of God that I learned and later recorded in the manuscript. I sent similar letters to Frannie and Annie," Henrietta said, referring to her twin daughters, JJ's sisters. "The girls were and are more open about it and the past. They embraced both conventional and spirit medicine, just like their father had. And they seemed to have inherited his passion for medical research but knew they had to leave the South to pursue it. And, of course, they did. I'm so proud of them and what they've accomplished. Their father would've been delighted. And I love that they visit us from New York every three months, like clockwork."

"They like precision in their schedules, as well as with everything else."

Henrietta smiled and nodded. "My only regret with them is that they never found the right partners and had children. But not everyone is cut out for that sort of life."

"No, not everyone is."

"Yet the girls are happy in their life's work. They're following their bliss. That's all that matters."

"Yes, I believe you're right," Suzanne said, looking down at the manuscript. "Gran, do you really know the secrets of God?" Suzanne noted with surprise that it was the second time that week she'd asked this unusual question.

"Only the ones I'm supposed to know. And share. But JJ wasn't ready to accept any of it. He just wanted to run away. You're like him in that way. But it's okay. Everyone comes back to the truth eventually. It takes longer for some than others. And that's okay too."

"What exactly were you trying to show or tell him?"

"Through my mystical experiences and subsequent meditations, I came to know the secret to happiness is to recognize that God's greatest masterpiece is the one that emerges from within us, from our hearts. This is the first point in *The Secrets of Bears Repeating*. You'll read about why and how it's the number-one secret."

"I can't wait to read it. But Dad…he's just so screwed up; he's an alcoholic."

"Ultimately, I believe he'll make the right choices for himself. But it'll be in his time, not mine, and not yours. I love him enough to let him travel his own path, bumps and all, without judgment. He has to make his own life choices, just as you do. We have to let our children skin their knees. But we need to be there to kiss them, to love them and not judge them for falling down. They'll learn through experience like we all do."

"Hmm," Suzanne said. "You're so wise, Gran."

"I credit what I know to the Great Spirit and my Apache friends."

"You had so many dramatic, life-altering experiences on that reservation, didn't you?"

"Yes, we've spoken of the traumas, but there were many good times, much laughter and some miracles too," Henrietta said, getting up to retrieve a photo album marked 1958–59. She flipped it open. "Here's my beloved Jefferson, your grandfather," she said, pointing. "I still miss him so much," she said, her eyes getting misty briefly.

"I'm sure."

"You've seen some of these photos before, of course. But you may not have seen this one of my beautiful Apache friend Altie. She was married to Bears Repeating," Henrietta said, pulling out a small square photograph from its four corner tabs. Altie was sitting on the front steps of the doctor's cottage, where they'd lived on the reservation, holding a one-year-old JJ on her lap.

"Yes, Altie was beautiful," Suzanne said. "What was Bears Repeating's real name?"

"Joe Loco," Henrietta said with a belly laugh. "When I first met him, I honestly did think he was loco as in crazy." She made a circling motion with both forefingers at her temples. "But Loco is a real Apache name. Isn't that funny?" She giggled.

"Yes," Suzanne said, sharing in her grandmother's easy little laugh. "Do you have any photos of him?"

Henrietta nodded. "Just one," she said, flipping the pages of the album. "We didn't take many pictures back then, like we do now. I'm lucky to have the one. Ah, here he is," she said, pointing. It was a square four-by-four color photograph. It showed a man who looked to be in his early thirties, with his bangs combed high in a pompadour and side hair in long braids. He wore a lavender-colored shirt, dress jacket and dark sunglasses. He was standing in front of a blue-and-white teepee and holding a guitar.

"That's not at all how I pictured him."

"Joe Loco was a riot. He was a unique combination of Apache and Buddhist wisdom, Elvis fetish and a miracle-healing shaman who also held a doctorate in conventional Western medicine. He was way ahead of his time. My friendship with him and Altie helped me through some very challenging times. Their spirit medicine started me on my own spiritual journey. I am forever grateful to them."

"Why didn't you tell me these things a long time ago?"

"I've given you bits and pieces of my history with Bears Repeating, but perhaps you weren't ready to really hear them. Also, I've not shared the secrets publicly. It's not because I don't want to, but rather, I know that before a person has walked his or her own journey and is ready for a certain level of spiritual truth, the words will be misunderstood."

"Don't take this the wrong way, Gran, but do you think Joe Loco could be a ghost?" she asked, recognizing some physical similarities to JB, although they did not look exactly the same.

"My heavens, no," Henrietta said and paused as though trying to sense the truth of it. After a few moments, she looked straight into Suzanne's eyes. "No," she repeated. "He is most assuredly not an earth-bound ghost."

Suzanne let out a breath of relief. "Good!"

"Bears Repeating was not a confused soul, and he had no unfinished business," Henrietta said. "He lived an extraordinary life of helping people recover from trauma and other soul-loss issues. He was the only truly enlightened person I've ever had the honor and privilege of knowing in this life. I'm sure he ascended into heaven when he passed from his physical body. That was more than ten years ago. But sometimes, I've felt his presence. I know when he visits me."

"Do you see him?"

"No, I don't have the gift of clairvoyance as you do. For me, I can empathically sense his good energy just swoop in and visit sometimes. It may sound funny, but I can also feel his deep sense of humor. He reminds me to laugh. And then I do." She let go a stream of giggles and tears.

"I'm really glad to hear that," Suzanne said, joining in with Gran's laughter. "I was beginning to think JB, the guy I met in the Woods, might be your Joe Loco. You've no idea how relieved I am."

Henrietta slowed her giggling and wiped her eyes. "I'm well aware that you believe Hitchcock Woods doesn't allow ghosts."

"Guess it's just a coincidence that JB and Joe Loco have a lot in common."

"What makes you say that?"

"JB speaks like a guru, although he has a strong southern accent. Like Joe Loco, he has light-brown skin, shiny black hair and wears colorful clothing. Except his clothes are not Elvis style, but rather, as I mentioned before, those of a southern frat boy."

"I don't believe in coincidences," Henrietta said. "Perhaps he is *your* Joe Loco."

Suzanne tilted her head and smiled. "Perhaps."

"I would love to meet JB," Henrietta said.

"That might be fun. You guys could compare notes, so to speak. I'll see about setting up a meeting, Gran." Suzanne stood and stretched, feeling much better than when she'd arrived. "I better go; I've got to call

Clair. You remember my best friend from school, Clair Davidson? She's called me twice, and I owe her a visit. Thanks for my copy of *The Secrets of Bears Repeating*. I plan to read it soon," she said. "Thanks, too, for the medicine for my hands."

"Oh, here, take these with you," Henrietta said, handing over the bottles of essential oils.

Suzanne hugged her grandmother before leaving. Once again, Gran's inculcations and presence had regrounded her. As she drove back to Aiken, she also felt better about JB and his ominous riddle, though she did not know why.

Chapter 19

Suzanne's best friend, Clair Davidson, grew up in a large white Victorian house with navy shutters. It was set back a good quarter-acre off the busy South Boundary, an avenue that also intersected the main entrance of Hitchcock Woods. The Davidsons' yard was a landscape abloom in color and textured greens. A thicket of moss-covered live oaks, aged to gigantic proportions, lined their driveway. A coppice of dogwoods and a variety of azaleas were in full bloom and drew the attention of strollers, equestrians and garden club patrons every spring.

As she stood at the front door, on a porch flanked by trellises covered in bright-yellow roses, Suzanne let the memories of the Davidsons' merry home flood her mind. Clair and her siblings, sister Roz and brothers Matt and Jason, rode horses together and with their parents. They participated in competitions and volunteered for charities and political campaigns together, without any embarrassing dramas, angst or rivalries. Even now, with separate residences and families of their own, this house was a common meeting place. Their familial cohesiveness was how Suzanne envisioned true normalcy. Just knowing them and being in their home was all it took to fill her with instant happiness.

As she reached for the heavy brass doorknocker, Suzanne caught a glimpse of two five-foot, sheer, oval shapes flapping around like the gigantic wings of angry wasps. The rockers moved eerily, their wicker squeaking on the wooden planks. Suzanne's right shoulder throbbed and her stomach cramped as the shapes started to transition into human forms—an older woman who possessed a soul-chilling presence and the other, a grumpy old man with his face hidden by a gray shadow. Both were in the dress of a former era, perhaps the early 1900s, during Aiken's gilded age. In addition to Thomas Hitchcock, Aiken's Winter Colony of elite equestrians included well-known names such as W. C. Whitney, Vanderbilt, and even Evalyn Walsh McLean, the last personal owner of the infamous Hope Diamond.

But Suzanne had seen all the photos of the Winter Colony's founding members, and they didn't include these two unfriendly faces looking at her now.

She jumped when the door opened.

"There you are, girl. It's about time," said Clair, a petite brunette in khaki riding breeches and blue polo shirt. Her body was lean, compact and muscular, like that of a cheerleader. Though her nails were always immaculately kept, she liked them short and unpolished. Her hair was in a ponytail that bounced lightly as she moved.

"Oh my God, Clair," Suzanne said, running in and slamming the door. She hugged her friend with a desperate enthusiasm. "I'm so glad you're safe!"

"Whoa, Suze, of course I'm safe." Clair hugged her back. "I know that close call with a bomb in Chicago must've scared the crap out of you, but you look and feel stiff and you're acting paranoid...like you've seen a ghost." She smiled and squeezed Suzanne's hand.

"You have no idea how correct you are." Suzanne turned around, looking through the sidelights of the door.

"Hey, don't tell me you're seeing ghosts here, in our house."

"Not in here. Out there." Suzanne pointed to the porch.

"Well, I'll just tell them to scat." She opened the door again. "This is my space, ghosts, and you just get the hell out of here," Clair said, even though she was speaking of her parents' home. Unlike most people, Clair was not afraid to push envelopes—or the buttons of ghosts.

Suzanne peered out again, seeing that Clair's scatting had done little to shoo away the hovering apparitions. "Still there, but at least they're staying outside." Clair was the only friend who knew everything about her ghost-seeing ability and didn't think she was raving mad.

"Let's just ignore them, then," Clair said with a wave of her hand. "Come on. I'm about to make you a most delightful brunch."

They walked on shiny wood floors toward a bright kitchen with a color scheme of whites and yellows and wallpaper featuring illustrations of blue porcelain accents. On the kitchen table, Suzanne spotted something that made her gasp.

"Clair, why do you have one of those?" Suzanne pointed to a spirit game board.

"Oh, my niece Beth, you know Roz's girl, was here and had a sleepover with a bunch of other silly teenage girls last night. It's harmless," Clair said, waving her hands in dismissal.

"No, it's not. And it might explain why those two ghosts outside have been able to approach this usually happy home," Suzanne said, her hand over her throat.

"But they're not coming in." An uncommon doubt was creeping into Clair's voice.

"Just so you know, this thing can be like a welcome mat to them," Suzanne said, referring to the brown-lettered board.

"Geez, Suze, how could a game do that?"

"I wouldn't call it a game," Suzanne said. "Actually, the board itself is not the problem. It's the evoking of a communication with spirits that are quite often the dark, scary ones."

"That sounds wacky. How do you know that?" Clair said.

Suzanne stared at her friend. "Let's just say I've been told by those in the know of such things."

"You make an iron-clad argument." Clair crossed her arms. "How can I argue?"

"Your niece and her friends may have unknowingly invited in the darkness. Fortunately, you and your family have infused this home with so much love and light over the years, it's keeping the ghosts at bay. But that doesn't mean they'll stay put. So let's get rid of this thing."

"How do you suggest we do that?"

"Burn it?"

"No time like the present," Clair said, picking up the board.

"Don't forget the pointer thingy," Suzanne said.

"Follow me," Clair said, grabbing up the board's indicator. "We're going to kick some ghostly booty right now. She led Suzanne into the detached backyard garage next to the barn.

The hair on Suzanne's neck stood up straight as her eyes darted around. "They're still here, and they don't look happy."

With her usual efficiency, Clair pulled out a metal trashcan used for burning leaves and carried it into a clearing away from the barn. She threw the board and indicator in, squirted them with lighter fluid, and set them ablaze. "What should we do now?"

Suzanne nodded. "Better claim your space again."

"Okay, listen up, ghosts and foul creatures," Clair said, pointing her finger in the air. "In the name of Jesus and all that's good and holy, I am claiming my space, this home and grounds, for myself, my family, my horses and everyone nice who comes here. Dark entities must leave this instant. And I pray for our ongoing protection and the highest good of all."

Suzanne smiled as Clair used the words Gran had taught them both many years ago as the most powerful when dealing with possible dark energies. Her right shoulder and the hair on her neck started to relax. Looking around, she let out a huge breath. "Good job, Clair! They're gone!" She exhaled heavily.

"Yay!" Clair clapped before sliding her arm through Suzanne's. "Now how about that delightful brunch I promised you?"

"I'd love that."

"After our gallant deeds today, I think we've earned a reward. Ride after?" Clair said after returning to the kitchen. She turned on a Bose radio to an oldies station. The Bee Gees were crooning about how to mend a broken heart. Clair hummed along as she pulled two plates from the cupboard, setting the kitchen table.

"Boy, does my heart need that. There's nothing more I'd rather do than go for a ride with you. The ghosts being here, of all places, coupled with everything else that's going on...it's all just freaking me out," Suzanne said. She rubbed the back of her neck as she sat down.

"The ghost whisperer is freaked out? Well, what does that mean for the rest of us?" Clair said. She placed a broccoli and cheese quiche slice, croissant and fruit cup on each plate.

Suzanne plopped her chin in a palm. "Wait until I tell you about the warnings I've received from someone totally unexpected—in the Woods."

Chapter 20

Over brunch, Suzanne filled in Clair about the mysterious JB, the life-and-death riddle and how she still wasn't sure if he was real or an unusual type of ghost.

"Well, how about this? While we're on our ride, let's see if we can track this JB down together," Clair said. "If I can see him, you'll at least know that he's not a ghost."

"Great idea. I'll call Randy to get Misty tacked up now," Suzanne said, hitting her cell. After they cleared the table, Suzanne opened the front door and peeked out. "Hallelujah, still all clear."

"Yay! Things are looking up. I'll see you at the usual in about forty-five minutes," Clair said, referring to the place they'd been meeting in Hitchcock Woods since grade school.

Clair was waiting at Memorial Gate on her horse, Jif, when Suzanne and Misty joined them. They came from different directions, with Suzanne's ride being about twice the distance.

"Sorry for the wait," Suzanne said. "Hey, Jiffy, how ya doing, boy?" she said, greeting Clair's peanut butter–colored Hanoverian, a German warmblood used in sport riding and show jumping.

"He just took a couple of ribbons in Wellington," Clair said, meaning the Winter Equestrian Festival, a prestigious show in Florida.

Suzanne gave her a gloved thumbs-up. "Way to go, Jif!"

"Since you've been meeting this JB guy at the ring, let's try it first," Clair suggested, and they set off down the trail.

As they neared the ring area, Clair stopped long enough to say, "Dang, I forgot about the show preps." The Aiken Horse Show was an annual event where riders of all ages had been competing on grass and over indigenous wood fences in the Woods for more than a century. This year's show was starting tomorrow, Friday morning, and would run through the weekend. "I hope that doesn't mean a no-show for Mr. Fortuneteller."

"Come on, let's try Ridge Mile Track," shouted Suzanne, exerting leg pressure on Misty's barrel, moving the mare forward into a quicker pace. "Even if he's not there, we can jump off some nervous energy."

After a couple rounds over the track's obstacles, they slowed, and Clair trotted next to Suzanne. "I was thinking about something important we should do," Clair said.

"What's that?"

"Since the first two deaths were old boyfriends of yours, that might suggest a pattern."

"Not necessarily. It just means they were at one time close to me. It's just as likely they are a common denominator for someone other than me."

"True. But let's just say it does indicate a pattern related to you specifically—we should make a list of all the guys you've ever dated. And that might take us a while." Clair shot her an exaggerated grin.

"Ha, ha. Very funny."

"Do you think we should limit our list to your Aiken guys? Or should we consider the ones you've dated in Chicago?"

"I don't know." Suzanne let go of the reins and crossed her arms.

"Given the first two jerks to go, let's try to put the rest in order, from jerkiest at the top, down to the nicest. Then, we can see if there's some correlation with Bobby and Tomás and who might be the next to die."

"Good Lord, Clair, be serious. You're making it seem like a game." They stopped, dismounted, and walked toward the inner part of the track.

"I am being serious. Let's put Nick at the top of the list," Clair said without a hint of sarcasm.

Suzanne pursed her lips. "We don't have to worry about Nick."

"Oh?" They sat on a pine log. "How come?"

"I doubt Bam-Bam would leave him alone for more than five minutes."

"And she's got that crop, you know," Clair said with a giggle.

They both busted out laughing.

"God, I needed that," Suzanne said, catching her breath.

"Maybe it's Bam-Bam who's been terrorizing you. She hates you," Clair said.

They laughed again until tears ran down their cheeks. Finally calming down, Clair asked: "What about Randy?"

"I never dated Randy," Suzanne said, yanking her gloves off to scratch the palms of her still-scaly hands. "And you know he's gay."

"Yeah. But you two were pretty inseparable in school before he moved."

"And you know why: I had to protect him from bullies." She slapped her gloves on her knee.

"I never understood that. Why did you have to protect him?"

"It's hard to explain. Maybe because I don't have siblings and Randy's like a little brother to me. Maybe because he needed help and I could help him. Maybe because I love him. And I don't want anyone else to hurt him," Suzanne said, exhaling. "But no, we never dated. And never will."

"Ah, but does our killer know that?" Clair patted her temple with a forefinger.

Suzanne shrugged, with a feeling of anxiety in her gut. "I don't know what to think about that. Or if it even matters."

"Me neither. So…let's get back to our list. Who else did you date? John Taylor?"

"He moved to Florida."

"Was there anyone else?"

"Ray Brown, Chris Healy," Suzanne said, looking up.

"Geez. You did go out a lot," Clair teased.

"When you put them all in a list, it sort of looks that way," Suzanne said, looking down at her hands. "As far as I know, none of them live in Aiken anymore."

"Ray moved back last year," Clair said. "He's on the amateur polo circuit, so he's not around much."

"Does it really matter?"

"Any one of these guys could be either a killer or possible victim, for all we know," Clair said, shaking her head.

"I don't see how any of them could be a murderer," Suzanne said. "They do, however, deserve to be warned. We should give them all a heads-up to be careful."

"Yes, of course. So, let's review our list," Clair stated as she checked them off one at a time on her invisible notepad. "Bobby Lindley and Tomás Sanchez were the worst, with Nick Vaughn a close third," Clair said. "Two are dead."

"I once loved Nick," Suzanne said, sighing. "I mean really loved him like he was my soulmate or something. But as you know, he made me mad with his insults about Gran. But now, his presence reminds me that I always knew we were too impulsive and immature at the time for a true romance. We might be better at it now. I've seen him since I've been back in town. He's not really a jerk."

"I'm flat-out astonished at such an admission," Clair said, throwing her gloved hands in the air. "Do you hear yourself? Please tell me you are not getting back with Nick Vaughn. And, do you even trust the situation enough to be with any man right now?"

"No, I don't. The point I was trying to make is that I truly don't believe Nick would ever be capable of locking me in a closet with a ticking bomb or going around murdering guys from my past."

"Why did you just associate the Chicago crime with these local deaths?"

Suzanne gasped. "I don't know," she said, although her chest tightened at the thought.

"Well, it's hard to think about any of this happening, especially to you," Clair sighed and changed the subject. "Hey, I just heard that Bobby had been talking with the police about making a deal of some sort. I'm assuming you know about his clown routine."

"Yeah, what a creep he was."

"He was apparently out on bail at the time of his death."

"Wonder what kind of deal he could possibly make?" Suzanne pulled her gloves back on.

Clair shook her head and made a grimace. "I don't know, just thought I'd mention it. Might be relevant. Or not," she said. "How do you feel about it?"

"Honestly, I feel overwhelmed." She sighed and shook her head. "On top of the bomb scare in Chicago and the murders here, I've got a boss and a boyfriend in Chicago pressuring me to come back and perform by next week." She rolled her eyes at her own unintended pun. "I've got a mysterious psychic dude telling me there are two others close to me who are going to die by next week, one of whom might even be me. I'm seeing more

ghosts and in places they've never been before for me. If
I quit my job, the career I love is over."

"It's so crazy." Clair picked up her thrown gloves
and put them back on.

Suzanne looked up, seeing the paint-mustang in
the distance, at the eastern edge of the track. "Hey! There
he is! Over there." She pointed.

"Where? I don't see him," Clair said.

"Well, he's gone now."

"You mean gone, like in disappeared gone?" Clair
asked, her voice uneven.

"No! I meant he just rode down The Manage,"
Suzanne said. "Let's go!"

They ran to their horses.

Chapter 21

It was the only time Suzanne ever remembered being disappointed in Hitchcock Woods. They neither caught up with JB on The Manage nor saw him again even after riding all the trails surrounding it.

"Why don't we take up another hunt for JB after the show?" Clair offered.

Suzanne nodded as they cantered back in the direction of Memorial Gate.

Stopping at the turn for Travers Line, Suzanne said, "Thanks for everything, Clair. I'll keep you posted. In the meantime, I'll be locked in my bedroom until this nightmare of a deadline is over."

"Call me if you want some company or if you want to search again for JB."

"I will. But I wouldn't want to risk putting you in danger," Suzanne said before they parted. "Promise me you'll be careful."

Trotting back on Doll Lane, Suzanne considered her options. She could close herself up in her bedroom, as she'd sarcastically said to Clair, and wait it out until after next Wednesday. She could move in with Gran, who could protect her. Or she could just ignore it all, dismissing what JB had said as nonsense, and fly back to Chicago on Wednesday for next Friday's presentation. She blew out a deep breath of air and shook her head. *How did everything get so screwed up and out of control?*

Her stomach flipped and tightened in pain at the thought of trying to make a client presentation. And there weren't enough Brie sandwiches in the world that could calm it down. Clearly she was in no shape to do it—not now, not next week. Which meant going back to Chicago on Wednesday was out of the question. All she could do at this point was hope her job would still be there after things settled down. She might as well tell her boss now.

After an uncomfortable, but short, call to Clyde, she pointed Misty toward home, intending to drive over to the Vaughns' home immediately. She reasoned Nick was first on her list to warn, anyway.

From the Vaughns' driveway, she walked directly to the stables, feeling that Nick would be there, instead of in the main house. She spotted him in the tack room, crouched behind a rack full of saddles and blankets. His left arm was covered in blood, a trail of red visible on the concrete floor. He held a rifle in his right hand. And it was pointed directly at her heart.

"Nick! What're you doing!" she shouted, ducking behind the bottom half of the Dutch door.

"Someone just shot me in the yard," Nick yelled back. "What in the hell are *you* doing?"

She looked around as a terrifying paranoia swept through her. "I came to warn you that something bad might happen to you."

"You're a few minutes too late. Get in here now!" Nick shouted.

She dashed in, slammed shut both halves of the Dutch door, and dead-bolted them. She ran to his side.

"Your timing couldn't be worse," he said. "I ran in here for cover. It was closer than the house...and because I keep a loaded Winchester here in the tack room," he said, nodding at the rifle. "You're lucky I didn't blow your head off just now." He was positioned next to the window. He peeked out the window at the yard behind the main house. "I don't see anyone else right now."

"What happened?" she said in a strained whisper.

"Someone shot me!"

"Obviously. But who?"

"Don't know. I was feeding the hounds, and there was a shot out of nowhere, and then heat on my arm," Nick said.

The heat—she remembered it well.

"I realized I'd been hit by a bullet just as another one whizzed past my head. I ran in here and grabbed my rifle. And now here you are. You aren't going to kill me, are you, Suze?"

"Of course not!" She pressed her eyelids shut, then opened them, trying hard not to remember the pain of a bullet scorching through flesh. "As I said, I came to warn you."

"I haven't even had a chance to call 911," he said, speaking in a strained whisper.

"I'll do it." She pulled the phone from her back pocket, about to make the call, when Nick said, "Wait. I want to call Emma first and make sure she's okay up at the house."

"I still have her number." She hit it from her contacts list and held it up to his ear.

"Emma," he said. "It's me. Are you all right? Oh my God. I'm so relieved…Okay, good…Shoot anything that comes near you…Yeah, I got hit in the arm, but it's not too bad. I think we'll be fine here in the barn until an ambulance can get here…Yep, Suzanne's phone. She's here with me…Don't worry. It'll be okay. I've got my Winchester and it's loaded…Thanks."

He nodded to Suzanne and she hung up for him.

"Thank God Emma's fine. She's on the other line with 911 right now. She's got one of my guns out, and she knows how to use it. She said she doesn't see anyone around the barn or the dogs, and the ambulance is on the way."

"Let me look at your arm," Suzanne said. "But keep an eye out for anyone who might sneak up on us."

He pointed the rifle at the door. "I don't think it's as bad as it looks, or I wouldn't be able to move it."

"Let's be thankful the shooter was no marksman," she said.

"Actually, it sounded like a pistol, hard to control from a distance."

"Did you see anyone?"

"No. I was taken completely by surprise. But it had to have come from the west side of our house, next to the wooded area. Might've been an accident or some crazy kid with a new gun. Or it could have been someone trying to kill me." He paused and took a deep breath. "Like the others."

"I'm so afraid you're right," Suzanne said, tears spilling as quickly as Nick's blood.

"Do you have a first aid kit in here?" she asked, wiping her face. "We can at least try to stop the bleeding until the ambulance gets here."

He nodded toward the cabinets along the tack wall.

"Cover me, and I'll get it," she said, crawling over. She stood up to find the kit and spotted a bottle of Jack Daniel's. She grabbed both. "Here, swig this," she said. "We need to get your shirt off. Sorry, it'll hurt. Brace yourself." She unbuttoned his blood-covered white shirt and removed it. A piece of fabric was stuck to his wound, and he moaned when she tugged it free.

"Take another sip," she said, using gauze to apply a red-colored antiseptic to the top of his forearm. She placed a large bandage on it and tied the remains of his shirt around it for pressure, unable to resist admiring Nick's muscled chest and arms.

"I didn't see any bullet or fragments, just a big ole divot in your forearm," she said. "You're lucky it didn't hit your funny bone." She tried to smile.

He gave her a fake smile as he held the barrel of his gun next to her head. "Suze, don't take this the wrong way, but I think all the violence is about you, that it's somehow connected to you."

She nodded, grabbing the bottle and taking a gulp.

"Even so—and believe me, I don't have a death wish by any means—since you've come back, you're all I can think about. I know I should stay the hell away from you, and you me. But I don't want that."

She looked into his eyes and felt the truth of it but said, "I think you've had too much Jack." She took another drink. "And what about Pam?"

"I broke it off with her," he said, touching her hand, despite his wound.

Their eyes locked, but neither said another word.

Sirens pierced the stillness of the countryside, upsetting the horses in their stalls and echoing the wails of the hounds.

Through the commotion, Nick leaned over and gently kissed her on the lips, sweet and slow. She said nothing, and this time, she returned it in equal measure.

Chapter 22

The paramedics placed Nick on a stretcher, and as they lifted him, Suzanne touched him on the shoulder. "I'll check in on you later. They want to question me about this." She nodded over to the police who were waiting.

She trembled as she recounted the events Nick had relayed and she witnessed, all the while remembering other sessions of police questioning that she'd experienced. Afterward, she was told to expect yet another visit from police investigators. She drove back to her parents' home more shaken than ever, chastising herself for kissing Nick. *What am I doing? Getting back with him isn't smart, and I definitely shouldn't follow up with him at the hospital. It might get him killed.*

She wondered if Nick's shooting or him almost shooting her could be counted as part of the death toll in JB's riddle. But just as quickly, she dismissed the thought.

Think! Is there anything I can do to change the probability of JB's predictions? She sighed. At least she could mark Nick off the list of potential killers.

If I'm the reason these predicted deaths might happen, what if I take myself out of the equation? She could leave town, perhaps drive a circuitous route back to Chicago without anyone knowing her plans, including her. *Yes, that's it!* She'd withdraw a lot of cash from the ATM and use it to buy what she needed on the way back, so no one could trace her steps. She'd be like a spy escaping an enemy threat, plunging into crowds, remaining unseen through the masses, until the nightmare was over and the criminals were arrested.

But what if my scheme makes it worse? What if my leaving makes the murderer even more irate and irrational, and in retaliation, he starts to kill everyone close to me? Dear God!

There was only one person who might be able to shed some more light on the situation, and that was JB. She glanced at the time on her cell. It was already late afternoon, and she'd have to hurry before it got too dark.

To save time, Suzanne pulled her mother's car in front of the barn, instead of returning it to the garage, and hopped out. Despite being tired, she hastily threw on Misty's saddle before galloping the tangle of trails to what had become an accidental meeting place. Unfortunately, the horse show's work crews were still in and around the ring. She stopped for a breath, relieved to see that they were in the process of departing. But the sun was moving fast, the light starting to fade.

Please be here.

Eugene, a red-faced foreman dressed in brown work clothes, told her that there might've been someone fitting the description of JB and a paint-mustang who rode in the direction of Bluebird Hill perhaps an hour ago. But he wasn't at all sure about it.

"Thanks anyway," Suzanne said, pulling out her cell. It was nearly six thirty. She had less than an hour to find him and get back before it got too dark. She traveled past Bluebird Hill and toward Ridge Mile Track, sweat drenching her hairline and shirt. *So little time!*

In vain, she backtracked to the ring, now deserted and deadly quiet. She stopped to listen and feel the ground for the throb of hooves, but heard only the evening songs of cicadas. The hour was too late for him, or anyone, to be there.

If and when I find him again, I'll quiz him until I get some solid answers. There was no more time for subtleties, southern courtesies and cryptic readings.

A noise behind startled her, and she whipped around only to see a raccoon tiptoeing through the dimming undergrowth toward his nocturnal labors. All around were shadows and the incandescent crosses of dogwood tree blooms under dense stands of pines swaying in eerie silhouettes against the sunset. If she didn't turn for home this instant, she'd be trapped in the dark and have to feel her way out. She'd been caught in the Woods after sunset many times, and on those nights of slow and cautious travel, unseen mosquitoes stung her all the way home. *Not fun or smart*, she thought.

Thunder rumbled in the near distance as she approached Sand River. Dismounting, she palmed its surface, only to be reminded that wet sand might not be the only potential danger. Someone who wanted to kill her might be lurking. The sand was dry and safe enough to cross. *But how could I've been so careless to be alone without a weapon?*

The sound of slow-moving hooves on the trail ahead sent chills down her spine. When she looked up, she saw the whites of a mammoth stallion's eyes.

"You're a great horsewoman, but I was getting a little worried about you," JJ said.

"Oh, thank goodness, it's you, Daddy." She usually didn't refer to him as a child would, like many in the South did even in their elder years. But it popped out of her at times. And she knew he preferred it.

"Don't worry. I've got what you need." He turned on a light that was attached to a headband and handed it down to her.

"Thanks, your timing couldn't have been better," she said, slipping it on.

"Well, Della's fixin' to put a big supper on the table. And you know how irritable your mama gets when we don't sit down together." He turned on his own light and pointed it to his face, illuminating a crazy expression, before placing it over his head. He swayed, possibly from the effects of gin or whiskey. "I figured you'd be out here."

"Are you okay?" she asked.

"Yep, I'm feeling real good. Let's go!"

Pivoting, he rode ahead of her, creating a tunnel of light that would lead them home, like he'd done so many times before. Suzanne smiled, feeling the love of a drunk who sometimes came through for her, usually when she least expected it.

Chapter 23

JJ opened his eyes to morning light spilling in through the window of the tack room, aware of the sickening stench of his breath and phlegm stuck in his chest and throat. In front of him were gradations of shadows thrown by a lamp he'd left on. His entire body was stiff and aching from lying on the wooden floor, where he'd been probably since the middle of the night.

Coughing, he raised his left arm with effort and glanced at his wristwatch. Six o'clock. *Damn!* He remembered starting out with noble intentions last evening, rescuing Suzanne from the impending darkness, only to once again succumb to his own.

Sluggishly, he got up on his knees, pressing his hands against the floor with tremendous effort before grabbing hold of the creased leather of an oversized sofa. With every inch of movement, the pain in his abdomen grabbed at him. Cautiously, he sat on the sofa's bulky arm while wiping sweat from his face before staring out the window at the small duck pond. He leaned forward and tried to rise, involuntarily gasping for air. Sitting again, he stilled himself to let the searing pain subside, like it usually did. Yet he knew it was becoming worse with every passing hour.

His girls didn't know about the pancreatic cancer. No one did, except the doctors at the Florida rehab, and its adjoining hospital. He'd checked himself in knowing something more was wrong than his addiction to alcohol. Soon after the doctors confirmed his fears, he checked out, not willing to go through the chemotherapy. *No, siree, bub*, he thought. He'd made the knee-jerk decision, but then he went to the ocean to think it through. After a week of staring at the water and fishing, he knew what he was going to do. *Since I'm going to die, I'll go out my way, with the booze in my hand and my butt in the saddle. No chemo hell for me!*

It hurt to ride, but he could will himself back in the saddle because he believed Hitchcock Woods had the power to bring even a wrecked man like himself a sense of peace and balance, and maybe even some desperately needed pain relief.

He looked for his old stash of alcohol he'd hidden in a drawer behind the saddles. Finding none, he stumbled to the tiny kitchen and gulped water that Randy

kept in the small refrigerator. Sore and hungover, JJ
searched for a bottle he'd secreted under the sink not
long ago, but instead came up with a plastic grocery bag
containing an assortment of wigs. *What the hell is this?*

"Hey, Mr. Clayborn, what you got there?" said
Randy, coming downstairs from his apartment.

"I've no idea," JJ said. "Looks like a rat's nest. Are
these yours?"

"Maybe. What are they?"

"It's a bunch of women's wigs. Did you put them
things in here?"

"Not me," Randy said, taking the bag. "But I'm
happy to get rid of them. Don't worry."

"I'm not going to worry about it, son. Hell, I've
already forgotten it," JJ said, holding his upper left side.
"I couldn't sleep last night, so I came down here. But I
wouldn't have passed out in your digs, so to speak, if I'd
known you were back home." He chuckled. "It's kind of
early; I probably woke you up. And I drank your cold
water. Sorry, but I thought you were still on vacation."

"Oh, that. It turned out that Jimmy didn't want to
be gone the whole month. We came back early, so I
ended up not needing as much time off as I thought." He
wadded up the bag of wigs and tossed them in the
trashcan. "And you didn't wake me; I'm usually up by
six."

"Sounds good. Thanks for taking care of things 'round here." He paused a moment before saying, "Hey, since you're up and all, you wanna tack up Cole for me while I go and change into some fresh clothes?" He stood, wincing visibly as he started to walk.

"If you don't mind me saying, sir, it looks like you're in pain. Maybe you shouldn't ride."

"Thanks for your concern, Randy, but it's not like I'm going out to swing a polo mallet." JJ chuckled. "Besides, Cole has a canter smoother than silk. Sometimes, a ride in the Woods is all I need to feel better. Know what I mean?"

"Sure do. I understand." He was at Cole's stall. "I'll have him ready in fifteen."

At six thirty, JJ used a mounting block to climb into the saddle but still winced as he settled in, pressing his elbow to his side for support. "Thanks, Randy. I won't be that long." Cole turned and trotted into the Woods, finding Clayborn Cut as if he were on autopilot.

Chapter 24

As Randy watched JJ ride away, he got nervous. Jimmy would no doubt raise hell about his books and wigs not being where he put them. Randy would just have to make Jimmy understand that he had to move them because of JJ. He hurried to retrieve the wigs from the trashcan. He wasn't sure why he hadn't come clean to JJ about them belonging to Jimmy. Maybe to protect him. Maybe to protect all three of them.

Randy never wanted to do anything that might jeopardize his working relationship and living arrangements with the Clayborns. Even though Suzanne would sometimes complain about her family's idiosyncrasies to him, the Clayborns had it all: a loving mother, father, daughter and horses. He couldn't think of anything that was better than being a part of the Clayborn clan, surrounded by all things equestrian. The only time

he felt destabilized was when his brother came around
and got in his head, causing so much undo stress and
worry.

Now, though, Randy was worried about JJ. He
knew his employer was sick and still drinking. It was
Randy who'd discovered JJ's liquor under the sink. So, for
JJ's own good, Randy had removed every bottle. It was
unthinkable not to. But then, he'd been cleaning up after
others his whole life.

He trudged to the sofa and sat down, picking up
Jimmy's books on the way. He brightened as he
remembered Suze pointing out how funny it was to have
an Alfred Hitchcock book sitting near Hitchcock Woods.
But just as quickly, he frowned as he wondered if Jimmy
was a psycho, like one of Hitchcock's most famous
characters. They had the mother from hell, for sure, and
no father, since he'd died when they were young. Randy
had turned out okay, but it scared him that Jimmy could
be so moody, dark and unpredictable.

Randy's mind raced back in time to the night his
mother died. She was already drugged out, so he'd ridden
his bike to town to get food. When he returned, she was
slumped in a corner, a needle in her arm. His mother's
dealer was in bed—on top of nine-year-old Jimmy. Randy
nearly killed the man, pulling him off his brother and
beating him with his fists.

Oh, Jimmy.

Randy couldn't stop the nausea from welling up into his throat, then and now.

He ran for the sink and threw up. If only Jimmy hadn't been raped, he'd have been fine. Things would've turned out so much better. If only...

After he cleaned up the sink, Randy sat back down, clutching the vintage books, lost in memories of riding with Suzanne in Hitchcock Woods, when he heard a door open.

"What the hell are you doing with my books? I've been looking all over for them!" Jimmy shouted.

"If you cared so much about them, you shouldn't have left them outside," Randy said. "It wouldn't hurt you to pick up after yourself when you're here. Or better yet, keep your stuff at the place I bought you."

"Why does it matter?"

"Mr. Clayborn was just here and found your bag of wigs. What are they for, anyway?" He scowled, not really wanting an answer.

"Just a project...a class project. What's the big deal? Don't worry. Your precious Clayborn won't fire you for having wigs. You need to get a life, Brother. Stop worrying so much. And stop pining away for Suzy Q."

"Don't call her that. And I'm not pining," Randy said, looking away.

"She finally came home; isn't that what you wanted?"

"Yeah, but I didn't want it to be like this." He could hear the whine in his voice. "I don't want you to mess with her ever again!"

"My advice is you'd better make your move now, Bro, before she picks up another man," Jimmy said. "You don't even realize it, but I heard things are starting to get cozy with her and Nick again. But I have a plan to help you with that. In fact, I've already put it into motion."

"Just stop it. I don't need your kind of help," Randy shouted. "I mean it, Jimmy. Stay out of it!"

"Okay, calm down. So how about I teach you how to ask Suze out instead; you've never even bothered to do that."

"It's not like that with me and Suze. We're best friends."

"I've no problem with the ladies, you know," Jimmy said with a shrug and smirk.

He's just saying that to compensate because he knows what I saw, Randy thought, shaking his head.

Jimmy had been such a sweet kid until the johns started abusing him. Their mother, oblivious or high, didn't even try to stop them. And Randy wasn't always there to intervene. Randy knew when bad things happened to Jimmy. The telltale signs were always there: Jimmy would go disturbingly quiet, his eyes blank, for hours, sometimes days. Or he'd run off and hide in the Woods, where Randy would later find him. Eventually, their horrible situation turned Jimmy mean and into something he was never meant to be.

He couldn't help it. None of us could help it, Randy thought.

"Speaking of your classes, don't you have some studying to do?" he asked. He loved Jimmy more than anyone, even Suze. But at this moment, he didn't want his brother around. JJ would be back soon.

"No, but I've got some planning to do. Now you just go earn our keep like a good big brother should. I'll be upstairs thinking," Jimmy said, heading toward Randy's room.

As Jimmy's footsteps faded and the silence returned, Randy got up for the morning grooming chores. Only the horses could relieve his mind and take away his worries. When the thunder clapped, he was too lost in the joys of brushing Misty's gray-white coat to notice. He paid no attention to the rain as it pelted the stable's tin roof.

Chapter 25

JJ arrived at the inner Horse Show Ring just as the downpour began. He looked toward the forest's edge for refuge, but at the last second, he dashed under one of the open-sided white tents erected for the day's horse show. It was scheduled to start in less than two hours. Spectators were expected to begin flowing in at any second, despite the rain. Or maybe not. *It's coming down pretty hard now,* JJ thought, as sheets of rain fell with a deafening force on the tops of white canvas.

The tent he chose was big enough to accommodate both himself and Cole. Dismounting, he dropped the reins; there was no need to tie up Cole, who stood at ease. JJ leaned on a table and lit a cigarette.

Although quiet for much of the year, the ring and its immediate surroundings bustled at this hour with show workers and volunteers trying their best to dodge the cloudburst while lugging necessities into the main tent, known as Big Hitchcock. Technically, JJ wasn't supposed to be in the Woods yet, much less parking his giant stallion under a spectator show tent. *But then, when did I ever follow the rules?*

No one paid him any mind as he and others continued to wait for the rain to stop. A woman, unidentifiable because she was covered head to foot in a rain poncho, carried in a large clear plastic box of colorful award ribbons; they reminded him of his Suzanne. That girl had won more champion ribbons in this and other Hunter Derby shows than anyone else he knew. She had hundreds of them as well as a glass cabinet full of champion trophies still on display in her childhood bedroom. He had no intention of ever removing them.

He was always bursting with pride over Suzanne. Even as a little tyke, she could handle horse jumps with beauty and grace. She'd made it look so easy. He wondered why he'd never bothered to tell her that and how proud he was of her, and felt a stab of guilt.

A stranger riding a paint-mustang horse dashed in, distracting him from his thoughts. The rider wore a soaked plaid shirt over blue jeans rolled at the bottom. Like JJ, after dismounting, he let go of his reins without concern. His horse stood as quietly as Cole, who accommodated the new horse without concern.

"I haven't seen you or a horse cross like that in the Woods before, and that's pretty unusual. I'm JJ," he said, holding out his hand to the young man with a slight nod of his head.

"Hey, my name is initials too. It's JB," he said. "Funny coincidence." He flashed a friendly smile as they shook hands.

"My mama always said there's no such thing," JJ said, chuckling. JJ noted that the young man's light-brown hands were dry, despite his wet clothes, and that he wore his black hair tied back in a single, long braid. "As a coincidence, I mean."

"Now that I think of it, my mama used to say the same thing," JB said, nodding.

"I'm wondering why you're here and riding like that." JJ's voice was clear and friendly, despite his words. He gestured with his chin to the paint-mustang with no saddle.

"I was just out for a quick ride and, like you, got caught in the downpour. Made a run for the nearest cover."

JJ stared at him.

"And since you were already in here with your magnificent horse, I didn't think anyone would mind if I joined you."

"Well, I hope you don't mind me saying something."

"Not at all," JB said.

"You don't look like you're from around here." JJ looked him up and down through narrowed eyelids.

"You're right. I'm not from here. I enjoy visiting, especially when I can ride in Hitchcock Woods and be of service," JB said, looking at the ring.

"You don't say," JJ said, raising an eyebrow. He extinguished his cigarette in the sand. After it cooled, he put the butt in his shirt pocket and lit another one.

After a few quiet moments, the younger man said, "You don't look like you're ready to leave this place." He could've been talking about the tent, the Woods or life.

"Not yet, but I've been thinking it's about time," JJ said, leaning out of the open side of the tent to look up at the sky. It was starting to clear. He turned toward JB and stared again, thinking that there was something oddly familiar about the young man's face, like someone he'd once known, perhaps from his younger days. But that was impossible. This kid might be twenty years old at the most.

"I hope you don't mind if I hang out with you until then," JB said, smiling easily.

"Nope, assuming you don't mind me asking something else," JJ said, repeating the phrasing in a playful way that also hinted at skepticism. "How in the hell did you find Hitchcock Woods?"

Chapter 26

After having vivid dreams about JB throughout the night, Suzanne woke up at six and immediately dressed to ride. She couldn't remember any of the specifics but believed them to be symbolic with deep meaning. If JB were in the Woods this morning, he'd probably leave before the show began. She'd better hurry.

When she reached the Horse Show Ring, just before seven as she'd intended, the rain had stopped, but the arena was abuzz with activity. Not seeing JB, she continued on, traveling over Bluebird Hill to Peek-a-Boo Lane, Surrey Trace, Whitney Drive and Barton's Pond Path to the end of Cathedral Aisle.

Aggravated that her early-morning hunch had led merely to an aimless, damp chase, Suzanne took an alternate route back, stopping at Bluebird Hill to let her eyes roam over its alabaster crest and toward the open areas of the ring. All she could see were show spectators flowing in, despite the threat of more rain. Low male voices behind her grabbed her attention, and she turned in her saddle. There, settled under the largest live oak in the middle of Bluebird Hill was a pine log bench, where, incredibly, JB sat with her father, of all people, chatting as though they were long-lost buddies.

Suzanne, wide-eyed, turned Misty and walked toward them. They looked up and stared back at her without words. Her father was paler than usual. He held his ribs as if there was a stitch of pain there. Both men's clothes were soaking wet.

"Hey, y'all," she said at last. "Strange finding you here...together."

"Hey, Suze," her father returned. "What a nice surprise. Let me introduce you to this young fella here."

"We've already met," Suzanne said. "Hello, JB."

He gave her an expansive smile. "Good morning, Suzanne."

"So, what are y'all talking about?" she asked.

"Well, it's a funny story," her father said with his usual chuckle. "We both wanted to go on a nice peaceful ride this morning. But we were interrupted with the rain and the horse show fury, so our day turned out to be all wet. Right, JB?" He elbowed him, and they laughed like kids sharing some sort of inside joke.

Suzanne frowned and shook her head, wondering how she could ask her father to leave so she could speak privately to JB. She dismounted and joined them. "Dad, you don't look well. Why're you holding your side like that?"

"Oh, it's nothing. I didn't sleep well."

Suzanne, though, knew better. She felt the misery that showed on his face in her gut. "We'll talk about it…later." Her side twinged, and she pinched it to stem the rise of pain. "JB, I've been looking all over for you," she said. "Do you have a minute for a few questions?"

"I must get back," JB said, rising. He whistled for Raziel, who immediately trotted over.

"Please, before you go. Could I have your cell number? I really need to talk with you." She pulled her cell out of her back pocket.

"Sorry, but I don't own a cell phone." He grinned. "Never found a good use for one. Well, I'll be seeing you." He climbed on Raziel's back.

"Wait," she shouted. "Will you be here later? Can we meet for lunch? Where do you live?"

"Suzy, that's a little forward of you, honey," JJ said. "Let the poor boy go back to his work."

"Your work? Where do you work?" She was speaking faster.

Ignoring her questions, JB said, "I'll be back on Monday afternoon for a ride, after the show, when it's a little quieter. Maybe I'll see you then."

"Can we set a time? How about three o'clock?"

"Sounds good. See you at three." He rode off in the direction of Peek-a-Boo Lane.

Before disappearing on the trail covered with a forested canopy, JB stopped and looked back at Suzanne briefly. The play of light and shadow on his face from the surrounding thicket gave him an otherworldly appearance. She blinked. And he was gone.

"Dad, excuse me, I've got to check something out." She bolted for Misty, jumped on and rode down the trail where she'd seen JB disappear. Not finding him in the wooded areas flanking the trail, she looked down at four hoof marks in the sand that went nowhere.

Chapter 27

"What the hell was that all about?" JJ said, still sitting on the log when Suzanne returned. He took out a pack of cigarettes and lit one.

She dismounted without answering.

"Well?"

Exhaling, she sat down next to him. "It's complicated."

"Try me."

When she finished her story about JB, his dire messages and the riddle, her father asked, "How'd he know so much about you and these here murders?" JJ shook his head. "He said he was just visiting, to ride and be of service. I believed him, too."

"He's quite the mystery man," she said with a loud sigh. "I need to find out if he can tell me more about what might happen."

"I wish I'd known about this earlier. He seemed like such a great guy. Funny, too," JJ said, shaking his head.

"Yeah, he's a real riot." She pursed her lips.

"Well, I'm nervous about him now," JJ snapped. "Maybe he knows what's going to happen because he's the one killing people, and we should tell the police about him."

"Even if JB was the local murderer, I don't think he would've tried to blow me up in Chicago. I never met him before this week."

"Who says those two things are related?"

"You're right. How could they be?" And yet, she felt in her gut that they somehow were. "Do you think the morbid timing of these two events in my life is just a bizarre coincidence?"

"Nah. But the timing isn't great, I'll give you that." JJ looked away and took a drag of his cigarette. "Actually, after spending some time with JB this morning, I don't think he has anything whatsoever to do with these murders. But then, I've never been a very good judge of character." He blew out smoke ringlets.

"I'm not at all sure he's not a ghost."

"Sorry, champ, I'm not exactly a credible witness to prove that theory one way or the other either." He chuckled.

"No, you aren't." She sighed, shaking her head. "Dad, did you ever read Gran's manuscript, the one about the secrets from Bears Repeating?" she asked, changing the subject.

"Yeah, but it's all a lot of mumbo jumbo, just like the other stuff my mother's into."

"She gave me a copy, but I haven't read it all the way through yet. All I know is that if it's anything like Gran, I'm sure it's full of truth and wisdom." Suzanne looked her father in the eyes.

JJ bent over before looking back at her. "Do you have any idea how weird it is to grow up in the South with a mother who talks about soul retrievals and vision quests, who'll quote Jesus but refuses to go to church, who keeps a shaman's altar in her living room with feathers, crystals, and beaded rattles, who burns sage to clean the house of dark spirits and who meditates like Buddha, sometimes even in public?" He shook his head and slapped a hand on his thigh.

"Yeah, I do! But don't forget, the South also loves its eccentric characters," she said, putting her arm around his shoulders. "I think Gran's the wisest person I've ever known. I love that she's a trailblazer." She cocked her head and smiled. "Gran believes nature is better than a church, and I agree." Suzanne kissed her father's cheek. "I think you should give her manuscript another look. It might resonate now more than before."

"Maybe you're right, Suzy Q. You've always been one smart cookie. And truth be told, I've recently felt the need to be at peace with my mother on a number of levels."

That explains why he dug out the manuscript and all those old letters, she thought. "I'm really glad to hear that, Dad. Gran loves you, and I do, too." She kissed him again, feeling tears on his cheeks.

"Well, we'd better get going. The show's starting soon," he said. With considerable effort, JJ got up and climbed into Cole's saddle.

"I'd rather like to stay for a bit, maybe ride on the Cathedral Aisle side," she said, meaning the western end of Hitchcock Woods, where there wasn't as much show traffic.

"Suit yourself. It's going to get jammed up in here real quick. I'll see you back at the ranch." He rode off chuckling, with an elbow pressed to his side.

Suzanne leaned back on the trunk of the live oak, knowing her father didn't feel well. He'd lost weight and muscle. He was pale and, because she'd felt it herself, she knew he was in pain. She sighed, making a mental note to make sure he went to a doctor. And soon. *At least he seems to have finally mellowed to Gran's metaphysical ways and wants to make things better between them.*

Hearing the crackle of leaves and needles under hoof steps, she turned around only to see JB and Raziel emerging from the shadowed trail they'd just vanished from.

When they stood before her, her mouth open, JB announced, "I thought you could use some added insight." A smile touched his lips.

"Well, thank God, something's finally going right today," she said, remembering her dream.

"I can see you have many questions," he added, dismounting. "And you deserve some answers."

"I appreciate that." She gestured for him to sit next to her.

"I shall preface what I'm about to say with this," he said, after assuming a mediation pose on the log bench. "When you had your brief stay in Spirit, your pineal gland was activated and opened by the higher vibrations. That and your inner belief are what enables you to see beyond the veil at times now, although you're seeing only a fraction of the greater reality."

"How do you know that I had a brief stay in Spirit? Are you a part of Aiken's gossip vine? Are you a ghost?"

JB laughed so loud it startled her. "Ghosts don't usually come to offer guidance about essential truths."

She crossed her arms. "They sometimes come with warnings."

"True that," he said, nodding. "But for different reasons."

"Just who are you and how do you know what's happened or might happen to me?"

"I am that I am. That is all. I am here now to remind you of your true heritage, your inner gifts and following your heart to your mission in life. Like you, I have the ability to tap into the universal Source of All That Is and have done so in all of my incarnations."

"You say the strangest things." She threw her hands in the air. "I don't know how to tap into a universal...source of all that is. That's not even a sentence. It doesn't make sense."

"Some people call God the Source of All That Is because God is the source of all that exists. But you already know this. You understand what I'm saying on a deeper level, don't you? You know a lot more than you're willing to admit." He smiled widely.

"If you go around saying stuff like that in the South, you'll be likened to Satan and shown the inside of walls with some extra-thick padding."

"You hear the inner voice and receive strong intuitive and empathic information all the time, don't you? But your core patterns of response are to deflect, joke, ignore, run away. That's okay. It is to be expected in this realm. You'll learn that it's better to face and surrender your shadows and everything that presents as negative. It's the only way to diffuse the focused power that you've given to the undesirable."

Maybe. But I don't want a lecture, she thought. *I want answers.* "Be that as it may, you said that others close to me are going to die by Wednesday, and one may even be me. You've told me to prepare for these deaths by meditating and expanding my psychic abilities. But given the morbidity of the predictions, how can I possibly focus on doing that and not try to do something tangible to stop them? Meanwhile, I ask myself often: Why should I pay any attention to the nonsense of an imaginative young man? But my gut won't let me forget or dismiss it all so easily." She paused to consider how he had once again correctly assessed her abilities before continuing: "How could you possibly know others close to me will die unless you're the one planning to do it? I think you owe me some kind of explanation."

"You're mixing up some of my statements. But I'll attempt to clarify."

"Yay," she said, raising her shoulders with a roll of her eyes.

"I have the ability to align with and tap into God Source, which is all that there is in the universe. This ability helps me to see into future timelines, a looking glass into the future, if you will. He spoke calmly, repeating and rephrasing key points, like a patient teacher. "However, the future is ruled only in probability. Destinies may be altered; nothing is set in stone; changes can be made. That's because no one knows for sure until those involved in an experience make his or her choices. They are always choosing, and we are always choosing, whether we do so consciously or subconsciously. Even when we run away, we're making a choice."

"Does that mean that I could somehow change the probability of someone else dying by the choices I make?"

"Yes and no."

She shook her head. "Still not making sense."

"If someone has chosen to leave this plane of existence and the timing of it, or if certain karma requires it, there's little you could do to prevent it. Everyone has their own exit plans, chosen before human birth."

She exhaled and looked down. "Then what can I or anyone do about it?"

"If it can be helped, it's good to do so. Also, you're assuming that what we know as death is a bad thing. It's but a transition into another dimension, a different level of energetic frequency. You've already learned this is truth through your own near-death experience."

Suzanne swallowed, aware of how young JB looked but how ancient his words sounded. The contrast made him seem ethereal and unreal, like a higher being possessing the power to defy the boundaries of a forest forbidden to ghosts. "How can I really help at all, then?"

"Align with your inner Source in meditation, quiet the mind in golden neutrality, set the intention and get off fluoride and onto a clean organic diet," he said, smiling, almost as if joking.

"I swear you've been talking to my grandmother. She says exactly the same thing. But how can an organic diet help anything? That seems like a trivial thing."

"Not at all. It'll make you feel better, and your stomach won't be upset as much. Your hair and hands will heal," he said. "Eventually, these choices help you see the big picture much better."

"Okay, sure, thanks, I think. But all that sounds more like a long-term plan. I need help—right now."

"Allow your inner guidance to help you make the right choices and act on them at exactly the right time." He rose and stepped next to Raziel. "I must go now."

"But I have so many more questions," Suzanne said, placing her hand at her throat.

"We can continue to meet after the show, as previously discussed. Monday at three still okay?" He jumped on Raziel's bare back.

She nodded. "But what am I supposed to do until then? And what am I supposed to do until Wednesday?" Suzanne held up her palms.

"Don't hesitate to meditate. And don't be careless. The bee offers both the honey and the sting. Sometimes you can get the honey without the sting, or the sting without the honey. At other times, you get both. It depends on how you go about it," he said with an irritatingly sweet smile. "And how much you're listening to your inner guidance."

"But what am I supposed to do until Wednesday?" she repeated, hearing her voice crack.

JB stepped his horse onto Lover's Lane and, without another backward glance, disappeared. After a few seconds, an answer called out from the trails: "Stop looking to others to tell you what to do. You're the only one who can go for the honey where it's hidden. It is within you."

But how do I do that? She closed her eyes, tears of frustration stinging her cheeks. His answers only left her with a fistful of new questions. Trudging over to Misty, Suzanne remembered wanting to read her grandmother's manuscript. *Scratch that,* she corrected herself. *I need to read it. Now.*

Chapter 28

Henrietta carried sandwiches and sweet iced tea on a tray into her living room. Her granddaughter was reclining on one of two facing cream-colored sofas.

She knew Suzanne would be finishing the summary paragraph on the last page of *The Secrets of Bears Repeating* just as she placed the tray on the coffee table, for she'd timed her entry strategically. "I have some lunch for you," Henrietta said, still in her morning workout clothes.

Suzanne sat up and laid the pages next to the tray. "Forgive me for not reading it until now." She nodded toward the manuscript. "Things are just so crazy in Aiken."

"I'm not offended, and don't give it a second thought." Henrietta glanced at Suzanne's troubled frown. "Please help yourself, and we can talk about it."

"Oh, this is delicious," Suzanne said, taking a bite of a sandwich. She lifted the bread, revealing some of Henrietta's favorites: roasted red peppers, zucchini and mushrooms were topped with melted Brie cheese. "Thank you! And also for the Brie on top." She patted her midsection.

Henrietta smiled, pleased to offer her garden's bounty, along with something soothing for her empathic grandchild's often-troubled stomach. "I'm surprised you're not at the Aiken Horse Show today."

"I was there earlier before it started but wasn't in the mood to stay and mingle," Suzanne said. "I've more pressing matters on my mind, like wanting to read and understand *The Secrets of Bears Repeating*."

"Oh?" Henrietta took a bite of her sandwich, silently elated. She knew this day would come. Suzanne was moving toward her inevitable higher calling. She'd seen this transition foretold in a vision quest, not long after Suzanne had been shot so many years ago. Henrietta could hardly contain her excitement at witnessing the vision's unfolding now.

"Let's start with the beginning and how you came upon, um, these ancient secrets worth rediscovering, as you describe them," Suzanne said, pointing to page one.

Henrietta wiped her mouth with a napkin. "I've already told you about my relationship with my spiritual mentors, Joe Loco, known as Bears Repeating, and his wife, Altie."

"Yes. But were you always so open to esoteric teachings like the ones you've described?"

"Not as much as you might think," Henrietta said, sipping the iced tea.

"Do tell," Suzanne said.

"At the start of your grandfather's medical missions in New Mexico, I was still stubbornly holding on to a limited view of myself and spiritual matters," Henrietta said. "And like many people, I wanted to run away from the negative events of my past."

"So, does that mean you didn't understand the secrets you were writing down?"

"I didn't start writing this manuscript until the end of my time on the Medichero reservation, so that is where I'll begin, if that's okay," Henrietta said.

"Please," Suzanne said and took another bite of her sandwich.

"After Jeff passed away and both his parents were gone, too, I moved back to the Clayborn estate, having inherited it all. This is where I thought it best to continue raising our children; your father was only two. It was at that time, I started calling your father JJ, instead of Jeffie Junior." She smiled at the memory. "It was Joe's idea and I liked it."

"I never knew that. So Bears Repeating was the one who coined my father's nickname? Wow."

Henrietta nodded. "It wasn't long after that," she said, pausing briefly before continuing. "I learned that I was pregnant."

"I'm confused. I didn't think you had another child after my father."

"That's correct. I lost the baby." Henrietta's eyes filled with tears.

"Oh! Gran, I'm so sorry. But why haven't I heard about this before now?"

"It was a painful time. And I didn't want to dwell on it, for the sake of my other children, who'd just lost their father." She wiped her eyes.

"I understand." Suzanne hesitated, as though searching for a delicate way to ask her next questions, then finally just asked, "What happened with the baby? And how, then, were you able to write this profound wisdom?"

"I'm getting there. Before losing the baby, as I said, I was having a bad time. I was so overwhelmed with the loss of my beloved husband and then by the affairs of the Clayborn Trust and trying to run a massive peach business." She continued: "I accepted an offer of help from one of Jeff's colleagues who'd worked for the U.S. Department of Interior in New Mexico. His name was Craig Mackenzie."

"Oh yes, Randy's father. I knew that he worked for you and managed the orchards for a brief time; I guess that's in part how Randy eventually ended up working as our barn manager."

"That's right, but there's much more to the story of Craig Mackenzie." Henrietta paused, considering how much to divulge to her granddaughter. "Now that you're an adult, I think you'll be able to handle it."

"Uh-oh, that sounds ominous, and much more serious than I expected."

"Some things are better left unsaid, especially to children," Henrietta said, exhaling.

"I agree. But I think I'm mature enough to hear it now, whatever it might be." Suzanne leaned forward.

"When I offered Craig the job to help with orchard floor management, I also knew he had a crush on me," Henrietta admitted. "He might've thought he was in love with me. But at the same time, I was too preoccupied with my problems to worry about his feelings or mine. I admit to not using good judgment with Craig," she said, sighing.

"I get it. But even so, it seems odd that he would've wanted to change careers like that and move here."

"Well, I wouldn't have thought to offer him the job had he not expressed an interest. And he was very eager about it. He said he'd do anything and everything for me. I reasoned that he had good experience in management, he was smart, and I thought he'd be able to learn orchard floor management quickly. I wasn't wrong about his abilities. But I had completely misjudged his character. I just didn't see it in the beginning, when we were all living on the reservation."

"Unfortunately, I can relate."

"My vulnerability blinded me. In addition to being pregnant and without Jeff, I was also confronted with many of the field workers quitting on me," Henrietta said. "It wasn't as progressive as it is today; a lot of men refused to work for a woman back then. But that was just one of many challenges." She returned her tea glass, dripping with condensation, to the tray.

"I can see how you'd need his help. What happened next?"

"I did something I should not have done with Craig. Regrettably, I actually paid to move him here from New Mexico, knowing I was using his affection for me to help me through a tough situation. I set him up to live in one of the field houses. At first, it went well. He was helpful and easy to have around. But then, as I got to know him better, I sensed there was something off in him. He started to act in strange ways, like he was in competition with me," she said, frowning.

"He'd make demeaning remarks to me in front of the workers, and then try to charm me in private. He wanted to control everything, and it wasn't about being helpful. It was about getting his hands on the money. The family's money." Henrietta shook her head. "He started telling people the baby was his—a huge lie—and he kept pushing me to commit to him before the baby's due date. He wanted to lock me down," Henrietta said, remembering the last day she saw him.

"Why won't you marry me, Henrietta?" Craig had said, pleading. "I want to move in with you, and help you. You need me. I need you."

"Craig, you've been a good friend, but I have to tell you something. I know it'll hurt your feelings, but I need to be honest: I'm not in love with you. I'm not sure if I can ever be in love again. Not after Jeff. I can't marry you. I'm sorry."

"But what about the baby?"

"Craig, you know the baby is Jeff's. And I resent that you've been telling people it's yours."

"Henrietta, I came all this way to South Carolina, for God's sake. You wanted me to."

"It's true. I wanted you here to help me and to be my friend. But I can see that it was wrong of me to do that—to you and to me. I'm so sorry. I can help you move back to New Mexico, if you don't want to keep working here."

As soon as those words came out of her mouth, Henrietta knew he'd turn mean. But she didn't expect to see his eyes turn dark, as if he was possessed by a demon. She was suddenly frightened of him.

"It was wrong to do that to you and *me?*" he sneered. His face took on the vicious, dangerous look of a cornered raccoon. "You used me," he yelled, rushing up to her and grabbing her hard on the arm. He pulled his right hand back as though he'd strike her.

"Don't you dare," Henrietta said, standing her ground.

He let his hand fall away, but he became more enraged, stomping around, accusing her of being responsible for everything wrong in his life. His last words were, "You should know something about your precious Jefferson." He spoke with a hiss. "He wasn't the perfect person you and everyone thought. He wasn't a saint." He pointed his finger at her. "Jeff was a lousy doctor. He cared more about his research than anything. Including you. I bet you didn't know that."

"Just go," Henrietta had said. "And never come back."

Craig's final words were even nastier: "I hope you fall flat on your face. You deserve to fail and suffer, like I have."

"Oh my God, Gran!" Suzanne said. "I'm so sorry you went through that. I had no idea."

"I didn't want to talk about it," Henrietta said. "I was ashamed of the mistakes I made with him. Looking back and knowing more about mental illnesses now than I did then, I believe he definitely had a narcissistic personality disorder. I'm no psychiatrist, but as I said, I studied it."

Henrietta took in a deep breath. "For many years, I couldn't understand how I didn't see or feel the trouble with Craig beforehand. I thought I liked him and wanted his company. But now I know he was intentionally love-bombing me, and I admit, it was hard to resist. It's easy to be fooled by the narcissist's initial love bomb. They're quite accomplished in it."

"Gran, you don't have to tell me any of this," Suzanne said. "I can see how overwhelming your situation must've been."

"Yes, but I wanted to tell you now, and for a number of important reasons. First, I'm at the point in my long life, where I don't want to keep any more secrets—be they good, bad, or divine. No more secrets!" Henrietta breathed deeply, feeling the cathartic release of getting the truth out in the open. "Also, I wanted you to know that I'm able to empathize with you as a way of helping you with your current and past relationships. I know exactly what it's like to get involved with a narcissist. And this one was a real doozy."

"It's good you didn't marry him."

"Although I didn't understand it back then, I was receiving strong intuitive feelings to end it. I'm glad I decided to follow them. It was a bullet dodged and a hard, painful lesson learned. But you're right, it could've been worse. All I knew is that I didn't want his kind of negativity in my home, not then, not ever."

"I totally understand," Suzanne said. "I find it impossible to be around really heavy energy."

"At the same time, I also came to know, beyond a shadow of a doubt, that if I couldn't have Jeff in this life, I didn't want any man. I still feel that way."

"You've had one tremendous love of your life. I've had many shallow ones."

"They simply haven't been right for you. I believe you'll know your true love when you meet him."

"I hope you're right," Suzanne said, surprised her mind went to Nick. "What happened after you sent Craig packing?"

"As you know, he didn't go back to New Mexico. He stayed in Aiken and married a much younger woman. And rather too quickly, I might add."

"Randy's mother."

"No, he actually married and divorced someone else before marrying Randy's mother. I can't remember the first one's name, but they were together for a number of years. After they divorced, Craig got together with Randy's mother, Joyce, who was obviously also much younger than he.

"Anyway, Joyce was a beauty, and I was truly hoping Craig would finally find happiness with her. Later, I found out Joyce had a terrible problem with drugs and other things…or so it was rumored."

"Their story is so tragic. Her addictions apparently got worse, after he died. And it made for a very unstable childhood for poor Randy and his brother."

"Yes," Henrietta said, her voice breaking with sadness. "I always wondered if Craig was the one who brought her down, or vice versa. He may have unwittingly gotten involved with her drug dealers and died tragically from that association."

"How did he die?"

"From a heart attack, possibly brought on by a drug of some sort. Or at least that's what I heard." She shook her head. "I still feel some guilt about my part in handling the situation with him."

"You certainly weren't responsible for his poor choices."

"No, but the dispirited look in his eyes the day he left haunted me, and the weight of everything else made me sick with stress, quite literally. Initially, I attributed the nausea I had to the pregnancy, even though it was much worse and lasted longer than it had before. About a week after Craig left, I started to have severe cramps and I lost the baby later that night. Afterward, I lapsed into a deep depression. All I could think about was how much I'd lost."

"You were clearly suffering. Maybe the stress was the cause of the miscarriage?"

Henrietta nodded. "A few days later, in the depths of my grief, my old friend Bears Repeating called me on the telephone, something he rarely did. But he had a knack for intervening in my life at critical times, precisely when I needed it."

"What a wonderful friend, Gran."

"Yes, and he had a lighthearted way of giving me exactly the healing words I needed. His spirit medicine loosened up the pain and hurt I was holding on to. I started to reach for the speck of light I could still see through the depths of my dark heartache and I remembered what he'd taught me: that healing from trauma is possible."

"Yes!"

"Consequently, I was inspired to return to my daily meditations. Eventually, I began to channel wisdom through the sacred rituals he taught. I recorded his ancient wisdom teachings in a journal, as well as my own epiphanies, and the specifics of what worked for me personally. Through the process, I returned to a life of love and purpose and started to feel whole again. I was smelling the peach blossoms again, so to speak," she said, taking a deep breath. "My parents helped me with the orchards and to find the right help. It all worked out. I didn't fall flat on my face. I didn't fail." She smiled.

"No, you didn't," Suzanne said.

"With my spiritual, mental and physical health renewed, I was able to complete and publish the novels and writings you know well. I also began to travel the country. I took the children back to the Medichero Reservation in New Mexico to visit my friends there and to oversee a healing center that I helped plan and finance through the Clayborn Trust."

"That's so cool!"

"Yes," Henrietta said, nodding. "While there, I welcomed the continued ministrations of Bears Repeating, for he was a gifted shaman healer. Frannie and Annie were especially enthralled with his spirit medicine and they enjoyed learning more about their father's research of it. I'm sure it influenced them to pursue their own medical careers. In any event, it was also during this period of my life that I completed the first draft of *The Secrets of Bears Repeating.*"

"Why didn't you ever publish it?"

"Let's just say that I didn't feel the world was quite ready for it. So, instead, I decided to incorporate many of the secrets symbolically in my novel, *The Soul Retrieval,* which you've already read."

"Yes, it's full of these insights," Suzanne said. "But they never registered as clearly before."

"Truth is sometimes stranger than fiction, but it may be more easily grasped through the lens of storytelling."

"I can see that."

"I feel the time is fast approaching to make it plain in a nonfiction version, like the one you hold in your hands." Henrietta paused. "Oh, that reminds me. After you were here the other day, I added a couple more points to the manuscript. I'll print you a copy of the revised draft," she said, already at her desk. "The edits don't change the secrets you've already read, but rather form an addendum describing the new higher energies coming into the world right now."

Suzanne's eyes widened. "JB said something about new energies coming in."

Henrietta smiled, knowing she didn't have to call attention to yet another synchronicity that was no doubt packed with significance for Suzanne.

"I'm going to study all of this information more at Mom and Dad's," Suzanne said, accepting the new pages. "Thank you, Gran. I'll leave now and get to it."

Arm in arm, they headed toward the circular driveway, where Lita's car was parked. Before she got in, Suzanne stopped to look off in the distance, shielding her eyes from the sun with her hand.

"There are some ghosts out there, but surprisingly, they're staying a respectful distance away,"

Suzanne said, pointing to the end of the property, near the highway.

"What do they look like?" Henrietta asked.

"A big white guy is dressed in overalls, and he's standing in front of what looks like a group of field laborers."

"Could be a foreman we called Jenks and the workers he oversaw, back in Jeff's parents' day," Henrietta said. "Jenks wasn't a very pleasant fellow."

"There are others, but I can't quite make out what they look like. They're all watching us, but it's like they're unable to step any closer."

"I've worked hard to make this estate a sacred sanctuary of light, love, and peace."

Suzanne turned back to her grandmother. "How have you done that?"

"By following the advice of Buddha and Jesus."

"Oh? I was expecting you to say Bears Repeating," Suzanne said with a laugh.

"Where do you think he got it from?" Henrietta giggled.

"Ha!"

"Buddha taught us how to claim our power, space, and our God-given right to be self-sovereign," Henrietta said. "And Jesus taught us how to go within to connect with God and forgive others seventy times seven.

In doing so, we're able to establish healthy boundaries for our personal sanctuaries."

"You've succeeded. These ghosts acknowledge and respect the boundaries you've set. This makes me happier than you can imagine." Suzanne turned back to them. "I'm sensing that they're waiting to pass over but don't know how to do it."

"I've forgiven them, as well as everyone in my past, present and future," Henrietta said. "And I wish them love and peace and freedom. Please tell the ghosts that it's safe for them to pass into God's light."

"You just did. And so they have." Suzanne witnessed them disappearing gracefully. "It isn't always that easy."

"How lovely!" Henrietta said, her hands on her heart. "I feel the truth of it. Thank you!" With a goodbye, she moved slowly toward the front door, giggling as she walked.

Chapter 29

Instead of worrying herself sick about JB's looming deadline and not knowing what else to do, Suzanne planned to spend the remainder of the weekend in her bedroom with Gran's books and *The Secrets of Bears Repeating*. As she stared at the manuscript's title, she felt an inexplicable excitement and anticipation, knowing it had profound meaning for her. She couldn't wait to dig back into it.

One of the primary tenets described in the manuscript was the direct correlation that exists between one's inner and outer worlds. It all started within a person's consciousness, and to change outer experiences, a person had to change his or her inner self-awareness. Though she'd heard Gran say confusing things like this her whole life, she was finally starting to get it. *Yes, I can change the outcomes by changing how I'm thinking about all of this!*

The doorbell rang and her epiphany popped, fading into the ether. She heard Della's muted exchange with male voices, followed by the sound of heavy slippers padding toward her room.

"There's a couple of police officers here for ya," Della said.

Suzanne rubbed the back of her stiff neck before getting up with a deep sigh. She was preparing to receive bad news or defend herself, yet again, so she was surprised when one of the officers said, "We're only here to check in and make sure you and everyone else in the household are safe."

Stunned, Suzanne looked at the officers and said, "Wow, thank you so much. I hadn't expected this." They told her that since the deaths of Mr. Lindley and Mr. Sanchez had been declared homicides and as she had a past association with both of them, it was "just a precaution." Before leaving, they asked her not to hesitate to report anything or anyone appearing suspicious or dangerous in any way.

How refreshing, she thought as she returned to her bedroom. *For once, the police didn't accuse me of being connected to the crimes.*

She sat on her bed and delved back into *The Secrets of Bears Repeating.* Just as she was about to achieve her earlier understanding, the doorbell rang a second time. And once again, Della answered it.

Now what? Suzanne thought with some exasperation as Della approached her bedroom.

"Mr. Nick Vaughn's here for ya," Della said, holding a dishtowel.

She bolted up. "Really?" She felt her heart quicken.

"You want me to send him away?" she said, waving the towel.

"No, that's okay. I'll see him. Thanks, Della," she said, adding, "Tell him I'll be out in a minute." She ran into the bathroom to brush her teeth and hair.

"Nick," Suzanne said, entering the foyer where he stood waiting. "How's the arm?" she asked, noting the sling he was wearing.

"It's better than it looks," he said, gesturing to it. "But that's not why I came over."

"Oh?" She hadn't followed up with him at the hospital like she'd promised, but he seemed unconcerned about it.

"I've just learned something new about the investigation into Tomás' death and Duchess, and I thought you'd like to know," he said.

His smile is beautiful, she thought and nodded for him to proceed.

"You were absolutely right about the horseshoes. The coroner confirmed that Tomás had a partial imprint of a Blue Gem logo on his forehead. Normally it wouldn't be a surprise because it's the brand we've been using on her for years, but after our chat, I checked with Ted Bledsoe, our farrier."

"My parents use him as well."

"Well, guess what Ted said? He admitted to fitting the Circle Forge shoes on Duchess without telling me! And not only that, but he put them on her the day before Tomás died. That means there's no way Duchess kicked Tomás to death. If she had, there'd be a Circle Forge imprint!"

She smiled, feeling her heart's confirmation. "Yeah, it's probably why the police ruled Tomás' death a homicide."

"So, you already know," he said with obvious disappointment.

"The police were here earlier," she said. "I'm glad we were right."

"Me too," he said. "Even though I should be mad as hell at Ted, it's a blessing he changed the shoes. Duchess is off the hook because of him. You and I know she's a good girl." His eyes softened and he touched her waist with his good hand.

"Thank goodness," she said, not moving away.

"But it's frightening to think the killer used a loose Blue Gem horseshoe to kill Tomás because Duchess has worn them for years," he said.

"No offense, but that may implicate you," she said.

"What do you mean?"

"You just admitted that you didn't know the farrier had changed the shoe brand, so you used the horseshoe you thought was on Duchess to hit Tomás on the head."

"Hey, come on! You know me better than that."

Suzanne paused to check her emotions. "Listen, I know you didn't. I'm just trying to say that something out of the ordinary is clearly going on here. Maybe consult with your family attorney about what you know. And just be careful."

"Be careful?"

"I'm completely innocent regarding the Chicago bomb as well as these murders, but the police and some investigators have implied on numerous occasions that I'm somehow connected to it all. Talking to your attorney might be a good idea. That's all I'm saying."

"Thanks," he said, brushing his lips against her cheek. "Actually, you and I are on the same wavelength once again. I'm headed over to see my attorney now about this and other matters."

After he left, Suzanne felt her cheek burning where he'd kissed it, and something unfamiliar but wonderful stirred in her heart. *I'm the one who'd better be careful.*

Chapter 30

On Monday, Suzanne was still too afraid to leave the house, though she hoped to steel herself long enough to ride out to meet with JB at three o'clock in the afternoon, as agreed. After reading and sitting too long in a cross-legged position on her bed, she rose to stretch. A cool breeze floated gently over her forearms, as if the air-conditioning had started a new cycle or a door had opened. It was neither. Framed in the window was the face of the boy ghost who'd been trailing her since Chicago. He shimmered with the colors of moonbeams.

"Congratulations, kid. You got my attention without being scary, although the Peeping Tom routine's getting tiresome. Come on in."

His image flowed inside the window in a varying scale of incandescence and stood next to her. In close proximity for the first time, she felt sure that he was the same boy spirit who'd appeared previously. He had light-brown hair with straight bangs that touched the top of his eyebrows. He wore a blue-and-white plaid shirt over worn blue jeans with knee patches.

"What've you been trying to tell me since Chicago? Spill it, little dude. I'm listening."

He motioned to her using a crude sign language, but that wasn't unusual. Not all ghosts could muster the tremendous amounts of energy required to speak aloud. He moved his hands in a way that conveyed an explosion.

"Are you trying to tell me something about the Chicago bomber?" she asked.

He nodded.

"Do you know who he is?"

He nodded.

"Okay. So you know the identity of the bomber. Was there one or more?

He held up three fingers.

"Three! Oh, my God!" It was exactly as she felt.

He nodded.

"Are they, by chance, involved in these local murders?" she asked because it was something she kept feeling was possible.

He shook his head and mouthed the word *no*. But in the next second, he held up flat hands, palms up, and then did a seesaw movement. He mouthed the words, *maybe*.

"I don't understand. How does that make sense?"

He repeated the sequence.

"Are you saying you don't know?"

No, he motioned.

"Are you saying maybe the bomber guys are the murderers here?"

No, he signaled again.

"I'm sorry, but they're either involved or they're not," she said, exhaling.

He then drew his fingers apart as though he were pulling invisible taffy.

"I don't understand." She paused to purposefully and consciously focus inward, drawing on her ability to empathically feel and see in her mind's eye what he was trying to communicate. Closing her eyes, she breathed in and out deeply, attending to the incoming sensations. In her imagination, she saw a string running between two empty cans, like a telephone experiment she and Clair used to test and play around with when they were children.

"Oh!" Her eyes popped open. "You're saying the bombers and murderers are somehow connected?"

He smiled and nodded, but his image immediately faded as her mother's head popped into the room.

"Suzy Q? Are you on the phone?"

"No, Mama," she said, with her mind still on this new information from the boy ghost. *I knew it!* But how could she explain to the police or anyone that a ghost told her the bombers were connected to the local murders without sounding crazy or looking directly involved?

"Are you talking to yourself?"

"Kind of," Suzanne said, turning back to where the boy had stood. But she already knew he was gone. Under her mother's long, feathery lashes were the eyes of a seasoned ghost buster. *Damn. I need more answers!* His confirmation was deeply disturbing. The bombers had tried to kill her and they were connected with the local murders. She was more scared now than even before.

"Well, I'm going to run some errands. Do you need anything from the drugstore, hon? Or do you wanna come with me?"

"No. I mean, no thanks. I have a meeting with someone at three o'clock at the ring."

"You'd better get going, then. It's two thirty now," Lita said.

"Oh!" Suzanne looked down at the time on her cell phone. "You're right," she said, throwing her riding breeches onto the bed to change.

"Well, okay, toodle-loo," Lita said before closing the door.

When she arrived at the barn, Suzanne was relieved to see that Brad was the only one inside. Gran's story about Randy's father, Craig Mackenzie, had been unsettling, and in that moment, she wasn't in the mood to be reminded about it. Nevertheless, she asked, "Where's Randy?"

"I don't know," Brad said as he groomed Cole.

"Doesn't Randy usually work on Mondays?"

"Yeah, but..." He continued brushing the underside of the great black stallion. "Your dad called me to come in today because he couldn't get in touch with Randy. He's apparently not answering his cell. And your dad wanted Cole exercised. I did, and now I'm cleaning him up."

"Why do you suppose Randy's not answering his phone?" she asked, frowning.

"I'm not sure. Your dad and I both assumed Randy's having Jimmy problems, if you know what I mean."

"You're probably right. Poor Randy. Thank you for helping out," she said.

"Well, Randy's got my back; sometimes I have to be away for family reasons," Brad said.

"Have you been out of town for family, Brad? I mean lately?" she asked, thinking about his Chicago connections, although she wasn't feeling anything off about Brad at the moment.

"No, I was talking about when I had to take a couple of weeks off when my mama fell down some steps and broke her hip." He looked down.

"Oh, I'm sorry to hear that," she said, thinking of how Bobby had died.

"She's okay now."

"Good to hear. So, you haven't seen Randy?"

He shook his head. "Not since yesterday. And he hasn't called in to check on the horses. It's really not like him."

"You're right," she said with a grimace. A fear was starting to take root that Randy might've fallen victim to one of JB's probabilities. "Will you let me know as soon as you hear from him?"

"Sure." Brad smiled. "Happy to. I still have your cell number."

"Thanks. Also, do you mind tacking up Misty for me now? I'm running late for a meeting in the Woods, but I just remembered I need to go back to the house for something."

She returned wearing a holstered .38 snub revolver concealed under a vest just as Brad had Misty ready to go. Even though firearms were prohibited in Hitchcock Woods, given the circumstances, she was more interested in being prepared for whatever might present itself to her between now and Wednesday.

It was a little after three o'clock when she dismounted at the inner Horse Show Ring. Looking over toward Bluebird Hill, she watched JB ride up bareback on Raziel. Incredibly, he was wearing a traditional Native

American costume including leather pants and shirt as well as a full headdress of feathers. He looked magnificent.

"That's some outfit you have on today," she said, grinning.

"Since the fancy horse show is over, I felt like wearing something culturally significant," he said with his baritone drawl, adding to the surreal moment. He looked up, striking an impressive pose.

She laughed. "I bet you got some curious looks on the way out."

"Not really. The Woods are deserted today. And I know how to cloak myself when needed." He smiled with one side of his mouth and chuckled ever so slightly.

"Is that so?"

"You already know I have special abilities." He winked and smiled more broadly.

"But you assured me you're *not* a ghost."

"That is still true; I am not an earth-bound spirit. And I'm not dead. This isn't an episode of *The Ghost Whisperer*." He laughed again, clearly amused at himself.

"Uh-huh." She rolled her eyes.

"In all seriousness, today I want to address the need for you to think better and start paying attention. Like many on Mother Earth right now, your natural psychic abilities are expanding to enable you to peer into other dimensions and see beyond the confines of ordinary reality. Only you're not thinking about what's new or significant about that because you're not being quiet and paying attention."

"That's rather presumptuous of you," she said, crossing her arms. "I believe I am paying attention. Just who do you think you are?"

"I am that I am. And I've let go of what I'm not."

"That's not an answer."

"It's the only true answer I can offer."

"Okay. Should I just guess what you are, then? Let's see, are you an extraterrestrial? A figment of my imagination that can talk?"

"No on both accounts."

"All righty. Let me ask you some very specific questions." She held up her forefinger. "One: Do you know if the bombing incident that happened to me is connected to the murders of my old boyfriends?" she asked, the boy ghost's message fresh in her mind. "Two: Who are the people close to me who might die within the next two days? And three: Has one already happened?" she asked, thinking of Randy's unusual absence.

"I am unable to share any of those specifics with you."

"Ha! Why does that not surprise me? You were just pulling my leg about everything after all!"

"You're drawing the wrong conclusions. It's not what you think."

"Didn't you just advise me to think?"

"Ha! Very good, grasshopper!" He laughed, and it was contagious.

Suzanne laughed, too, noting with amusement his reference to an old TV show. Calming down, she turned somber. "Seriously, what am I thinking that you consider wrong?"

"You're thinking that you're a victim of some kind, caught in an evil scenario not of your own making, and you don't know how to extricate yourself from it or redesign your thoughts in order to change it. You feel bad that others may die, but at the same time, you're mad about being forced out of your life in Chicago."

"It sounds like you've sized me up fairly well." She twisted her lips. "And it doesn't sound pretty."

He continued. "You were thinking you should forfeit your spiritual gifts for the sake of a perceived injustice in your childhood."

"No, I was trying to ignore them into nonexistence."

"But your soul doesn't want that."

"How do you know?"

"Because the universe has organized itself to show you that you must expand and use your abilities for good, to lead by example. Stop being afraid of losing everything you think you've worked for, and accept what you're thinking should not have happened."

"Easy for you to say. Okay, let's say I accept it all. Now what?"

"Acceptance doesn't mean nonaction or to go into some form of false passivity. It means empowering yourself so you can go to the next step and heal the wounds you still carry. A negative mindset and negative emotions about it all keep old wounds in place. You cannot run away from your shadows, but you can make them disappear."

"But how am I supposed to do that?"

"Become neutral and non resistant."

She shook her head. "How is that going to help me take steps to prevent someone close to me from being murdered?"

"Who said they'd be murdered?"

She gasped. "You said that two others close to me would die and one might be me."

"What I said is that a high probability exists for those scenarios. But that's all I know about it, in the present, in the now."

"That's just not helpful. Why can't you tell me the specifics? Why can't you tell me what to do?"

"Suzanne, I am not..." He paused as though searching for the right description. "A fortune-teller, nor am I a taskmaster. It's not my job to tell you exactly what you or others should or will do. It's your job to choose to wake up from the darkness by using your inner light, the divine powers to illuminate your own trails."

"Are you saying I can choose to use my psychic abilities to somehow change the negative outcomes?"

"I'm suggesting that you first have to choose to know truth so that when truth comes, you'll recognize it. Don't rely on me or anyone else for answers. Get quiet and seek your truth from within. When you're finally able to understand this universal truth, you'll know that I am…um, being helpful." He smiled and looked into the wooded areas.

She crossed her arms and pursed her lips. "I don't understand."

He turned back to face her. "Much of life and our true selves are hidden. And I realize it can be confusing." He pointed Raziel west. "So remember this great paradox: To hear divine guidance, you must listen in the golden silence. Yes, it is the silence that speaks! Pay attention to it. And then, it's very important to act as you're guided," he said, repeating the messages he'd given her before. "Adios, amiga." The young man covered in feathers saluted her before walking his horse away.

"Hey, wait a minute, JB."

He halted and turned back.

"Since you don't own a cell phone, and I'm still unclear on whether or not I might be able to *hear* the right steps to take to alter the outcome of your predicted, yet unspecified, death events, would you be willing to meet me here every afternoon this week ... to continue being helpful?" She smiled before frowning and holding her hands out. "At least until we're past these deadlines...no pun intended?"

"I'm happy to do that. Three o'clock works for me this whole week," he said, asking Raziel to move forward. "See you tomorrow."

Perhaps if Suzanne were with JB, because he was clearly not from this dimension, she could change the probabilities.

"Hey, wait, sorry, one last question."

He stopped again, looking back at her through the feathers.

"I'm curious. What does JB stand for, anyway?"

His answer left her with her mouth hanging open and eyes wide.

Chapter 31

Suzanne could hardly wait to tell her grandmother what JB had just said. As soon as she changed out of her riding clothes, she was going to drive over.

She was about to step out of the door when her cell dinged. She didn't recognize the number but answered anyway.

"Miss Suzanne Clayborn?" said a male voice with a thick southern accent.

"Yes?" She cleared her throat. "Who's this?"

"Detective Richard Smith. Aiken Police."

"Oh no, has someone else died?" she asked, terrified he was about to say Randy Mackenzie.

"No. Now hold on. I don't have a new homicide to report," Smith said. "I'm calling with a simple request regarding the Tomás Sanchez case. I'm hoping you'll be able to help me understand a few things better."

"I'm not sure how I can help." She went back into the kitchen and sat at the table. "But I'll try."

"Would you mind coming down to the station, then?"

"I guess not," she said, disappointed she wouldn't get to Gran's as quickly as she wanted, but first things first. Given what the boy ghost had said, she wanted to help, for her own safety as well as others. "I'll be there shortly."

Detective Smith was waiting in the lobby when she arrived at the police station. A medium-height African American, he had a soft, round face, salt-and-pepper hair and a friendly smile. He wore khakis, a white shirt and a black tie. He led her to a sparsely furnished office with a desk and two chairs for guests, although the desk was piled with three-foot-high stacks of file folders awaiting cabinets or banker boxes. He motioned for her to sit down.

He took his chair behind the desk, positioned in a way to enable him to see around the file stacks. "Please, call me Smitty."

"That's a little informal for a detective." She felt his integrity and good humor, and she started to relax after the tense drive over.

"Everyone calls me that, and I rather like it better than answering to the name Dick."

She smiled. "Okay, Smitty."

"May I offer you some coffee? It's kind of like drinking mud, but it's all I have."

He had dark-brown puppy-dog eyes and a disarming manner that made Suzanne think of the famous TV homicide detective from the seventies, Columbo. "As delightful as that sounds, no, thank you."

"Well, then, if you'd be so kind, I'd like to record your input on a couple of things." He placed his cell phone on the desk. "Is that all right?"

"Yes, sir," she said, as he pressed the record button.

"We found a number of fingerprints on the rear shoes of the Vaughns' horse as well as on loose shoes in the stall. Of all the fingerprints found, we've only been able to identify those of the deceased, Mr. Ted Bledsoe, the Vaughns' farrier, who we've already ruled out, and Mr. Jefferson Clayborn Junior."

"*Dad's fingerprints?* No, that can't be right." She immediately felt he was trying to shock her into giving him insights into the case.

"We have your father's prints on file."

"Yeah, yeah, everyone knows he's had DUIs and—" She stopped, not wanting to mention the shooting accident out loud. "There's got to be some reasonable explanation."

"Well, that's part of what I thought you could help me with."

"Why don't you just ask *him*?"

"We're in the process of doing that. In the meantime, we're also collecting the fingerprints of everyone who may have or had ties with those involved. Which is why we'd like yours, too, Miss Clayborn."

"Mine? I had nothing to do with Tomás's murder."

"You recently reported to our officers that you had past relationships with Mr. Sanchez, Mr. Robert Lindley, who may or may not be connected with this case, as well as Mr. Nick Vaughn, the owner of the horse in question. You're familiar with the Vaughns' horse Duchess, and you were actually with Mr. Vaughn in the stables seconds after he was recently shot in the arm by someone unknown at this time—all after just arriving back in town from Chicago." He looked at her with shrewd eyes, suggesting he may have already formed a theory about there being a connection with the two murdered men on the heels of the bombing incident.

"Yes, but—"

"You can speak to your attorney and I could get a warrant, if you'd like."

She exhaled loudly. "No, that's not necessary," she said, now sensing Smitty was a good cop and not trying to harass her, but rather covering all the bases required of him by law. "As I've said, I've nothing to hide. I want these cases solved as much as you do."

"Excellent. Before we go to fingerprinting, then, I'd like to ask you just one more question." He didn't wait for her to answer. "Can you offer any plausible explanation as to why your father's fingerprints were found on horseshoes belonging to the Vaughns' horse?"

"At the moment, no," she said, puzzlement mixing with new worries about what the boy ghost had suggested. "But I'm sure there's got to be one."

"Uh-huh. Now if you'll just follow me down the hall." He stood up.

She was about to get up when a new thought came to her. "Smitty, did you by chance run the prints on the horseshoes for a Jimmy or James Mackenzie?"

"No, although I'm well aware of who James Mackenzie is," Smitty said. "Why do you ask?"

"I've recently found out about his past," she said, remembering how she was also picking up disturbing, yet incomprehensible, vibes about him. "Jimmy was apparently involved in some crimes a few years ago, which means you probably have his prints on file."

"Uh-huh," he said, scribbling a note.

"The thing that's bothering me is this: His brother, Randy, has been missing from work—he's our barn manager—since yesterday, without even a phone call. This is highly unusual. And, frankly, I'm really concerned about them both."

Chapter 32

Early Tuesday morning, Smitty, two officers and a forensics team arrived at the Clayborn stables armed with a search warrant, looking for Randall and James Mackenzie and any evidence of a crime they may or may not have been involved in. The officers combed through Randy's upstairs apartment, the tack room and even the stalls. Loose horseshoes found in the barn were collected and carefully bagged. The fingerprinting dust coated a variety of surfaces.

"Would it be possible for you to point out and confirm something specific that you know the Mackenzie brothers touched?" Smitty asked Suzanne, leading her into Randy's bedroom. "We'd like to confirm their prints, especially since we've been able to rule out you and your father."

"You have?" She smiled broadly.

"Yes, your prints weren't found on any of the shoes collected at the Vaughns immediately after Mr. Sanchez was killed," Smitty said, his shoulders relaxing.

"Of course not."

"And regarding your father's fingerprints..." Smitty glanced at his notes. "Your farrier admitted that he'd been paid by Circle Forge Polo to get his clients to try out their shoes. For this reason, he showed the horseshoe samples to your father. He told us that your father touched the shoes but didn't want to use them on his horses. Later, the farrier nailed the same pair of shoes on Duchess without Mr. Vaughn's direct knowledge."

"I knew there was a logical explanation."

"Furthermore, Mr. Bledsoe admitted that he switched the shoes hoping he might prove to Mr. Vaughn that they were a better fit for Duchess and that her performance on the polo field would improve. It's not ethical, but it's not a crime."

"I see. Good to know," she said. "Thanks for telling me. Now, let's see." She looked around the room. "There." Suzanne pointed to an unwashed cup that had dried coffee in it. "I saw Randy drinking from it."

"Thank you," Smitty said, nodding to a gloved CSI, who took it for processing.

"The only things I personally know that Jimmy touched are those books." She pointed to the stack before continuing. "Randy said they belonged to Jimmy."

"Can't use hearsay," Smitty said.

"Well, I saw Randy touch them. But I'm assuming you found Jimmy's prints on file?"

"About that," Smitty said. "We don't have any prints for any Jimmy or James Mackenzie in our database."

"But Randy said that he'd been in and out of the juvenile penal system throughout his teens." She could feel the rise of a headache forming between her brows.

"What if, and I'm only supposing now," Smitty said in his southern Columbo style. "What if Randy lied about his brother getting into trouble as a juvenile to cover up for something else?"

"No, that doesn't sound right." She shook her head, even as she felt like rocks were in her stomach. "Smitty, actually, I'm beginning to fear something awful has happened to Randy, that maybe he has already met the same fate as Bobby and Tomás. He's been missing without a word for too long." She lowered her head and pressed on her temples to relieve the mounting pressure. "We've all been assuming he's dealing with some emergency with his brother Jimmy. But no one has seen or heard from Randy since Friday. It's not like him at all."

"Okay. We'll issue an APB on Randy...and Jimmy," Smitty said.

"APB?"

"An all-points bulletin. It's a broadcast to law enforcement personnel, typically containing information about a wanted suspect or a person of interest. And right now, I'd say both Randy and his brother are persons of interest. Wouldn't you?"

Chapter 33

Randy was just about to lose it as he cooked eggs and grits in his mobile home on Ascauga Lake. He was beside himself with worry because he'd done the unthinkable: left the Clayborns' barn without a word or ensuring the horses would be taken care of by someone responsible. But then, he remembered that before he had to leave with an out-of-control Jimmy, he'd scheduled Brad to work that week. The thought gave him some relief. Even though Brad liked to act mad and complain about the overtime, he loved the horses. He'd take care of them, no matter what Randy had to do or what happened. After this latest episode with Jimmy was over, Randy intended to make it up to Brad with extra vacation time.

Oh, Jimmy. Randy knew it was getting worse. But he couldn't let anyone know just how bad it was. He also didn't want anyone to know where they were—a small lot at Ascauga Lake he'd bought in secret for Jimmy years ago. Aside from the hospital, it was the best place to keep Jimmy out of trouble—and to keep trouble from finding Jimmy.

Randy liked that the used mobile home he'd put on the small tract of land was mostly secluded with its own little woods. It was a good twenty minutes away from the Clayborns, and there was seldom any traffic on the dirt roads around the lake. Randy would just stay here with Jimmy, until he could pack up his younger brother and return him to the hospital where he belonged. Randy truly loved it when he and Jimmy could do calming and stress-free things together, like fish, away from the rest of the world, and especially the Clayborns. He didn't want Jimmy ruining the good he'd built there.

Just before they had to leave this time, Randy could feel Jimmy's disturbed mental state intensifying. The first sign was when he trash-talked Suzanne. Then he bragged about having a plan to hurt Nick if Suzanne didn't start acting right toward Randy—sign two. The third was more of a haunting sense that Jimmy might have had a hand in some real crimes, although Randy would never say something like that out loud.

He was so tired of pretending about Jimmy. He hated having to lie, like when he'd told Suzanne about Jimmy being a juvenile delinquent. Jimmy wasn't any of the things he'd said. He was sick in the head. The only classes he took were the ones he could sign up for at the state psychiatric hospital in Columbia.

Hearing Jimmy stir from the tiny bedroom, Randy turned from the stove to see the unexpected. "Jimmy, what do you have in your hand?" he shouted, dropping the spatula onto the fry pan. He held out his hand. "Give me that gun."

"You've made me a prisoner here. The scooter doesn't work half the time. And neither does the cell service!" He waved the Colt .45 in the air.

"Hey, be careful with that," Randy said, turning off the stove. It was the pistol he'd stolen from JJ, although Randy had always thought his petty crime to be more of an act of charity toward his boss. JJ didn't want to see the gun he had used to shoot Suzanne years ago.

"I've tried to help you," Jimmy cried, "but nothing's turned out right. Everything's messed up."

"What're you talking about? Of course, everything's messed up with you," Randy said. "We'll just go back to the hospital, and you'll be better. Things will straighten out."

"No! That's not what I'm talking about. We've got to fix it all right now!"

"Fix what?" Randy said, his voice cracking with rising dread.

"We gotta just leave this sick world behind—you, me, Suze."

"The only person who's going somewhere is you, Jimmy. Back to the hospital."

"No. I can't stand it anymore. It has to end," Jimmy said, gesturing with the pistol.

"Stop talking like that," Randy shouted. "Give me that gun now!" He rushed his brother as the Colt fired its second unintentional bullet.

Randy crashed onto the floor, grabbing his foot. "What've you done?" The tip of his white tennis shoe was now bloodred.

Jimmy bolted, disappearing out the door.

As Randy lay on the floor holding his foot, losing consciousness, he heard the Malibu start, instead of Jimmy's scooter. *He's abandoning me? Where's the gun?* Randy looked left, right. *Oh dear Jesus—is he going to shoot Suzanne? Gotta stop. Gotta get up. Have to protect...*

After a time unconscious, Randy wasn't really sure how long, he forced himself up. *The scooter—maybe I can get it to work.* Tentatively, he tried to take a step. *Argh!* He looked down. Throbbing pain. Blood everywhere. He lifted a whiskey bottle to his lips, the one he'd taken from JJ's hiding place under the barn's sink, and gulped it down. He gasped as he pulled off his blood-soaked sock and poured whiskey onto his wound. Given the amount of blood and pain, he was surprised to find only the top of his pinky toe missing. At least it wouldn't need stitches. *No time for that anyway!* He crawled to his first aid kit, bandaged the toe tightly and drank until the pain started to subside. Finally, he felt a kind of numbness that enabled him to regain his footing, but he swore at himself for having to use the liquor, knowing how his mother's addictions to drugs and alcohol had ruined their lives. He'd no doubt inherited that bad trait from her. He'd just have to be more careful than she ever was, that's all.

Their awful mother. She was the reason they had so many problems! She was the reason their dad had died. She deserved to go out with a needle in her arm, for not protecting them from the druggies, the sickos, the pedophiles. He slid back onto the floor, not wanting to go back to the past, but now not being able to stop himself. He chugged the brown liquid.

When he woke up again, he remembered Jimmy taking his car. *How long ago was that? Oh my God!* A hysterical thought now gripped his mind: Jimmy might have gone to Chicago a few weeks ago.

Oh, Jimmy. Randy threw the bottle into the trashcan and pulled himself up. No choice now. *Gotta get the scooter started, get Jimmy back.* Then, he'd make Jimmy go to the hospital for good, with no breaks. Just forever. It made Randy depressed to think about having to do it. But he knew it was the safest thing he could do for everyone, including Jimmy. No one would search for him at the hospital. No one would find him there. And that thought made him feel better.

Randy limped outside. *Wait a minute. What the hell?* His Malibu was still parked in the gravel driveway. He felt his pocket. The keys were still there as well. He looked around for the scooter, but there was no scooter. He scratched his head, his toe pain temporarily forgotten; Randy could've sworn Jimmy had taken the car. Maybe the intense pain had caused him to hear things that weren't really there. Or it might've been that when he passed out, he'd dreamed it all. Fear and paranoia rising, Randy knew he had to get to the Clayborns' before it was too late, before Jimmy did something unforgivable.

Chapter 34

After the police and their forensics team left the stables, Suzanne reasoned that there was nothing else she could do for Randy at the moment, trusting that the search for him and Jimmy was in good hands. She decided to go ahead and update her grandmother about the astonishing admission JB had made yesterday afternoon. And try to get back in time for her three o'clock meeting in the Woods.

Standing on her grandmother's veranda, Suzanne knocked on the massive front door, but there was no answer. With another stab of concern, especially since it was the day before the dreaded Wednesday deadline day, Suzanne let herself in. And with a huge sigh of relief, found her grandmother sitting at her writing desk. Henrietta was wearing earbuds plugged into the computer on which she was typing. Suzanne circled to her grandmother's side and waved.

"Oh, what a lovely surprise," Henrietta said, pulling out the earbuds. "I was just listening to some Chopin, while I work."

"You should keep your doors locked, especially when you're listening to music," Suzanne said.

"Nonsense. It's perfectly safe here."

"Well, it's not safe in Aiken right now. So I wanted to make sure you were okay and also—"

"Suzanne, please forgive me for interrupting you, but I simply must tell you about what I'm working on before I forget," Henrietta said, talking quickly, putting a hand on Suzanne's wrist. "I had the most amazing idea, involving you and your copywriting abilities."

"But, Gran," she said, trying again, "you'll want to hear what I came to tell—"

"Please let me get my proposal out before I forget," Henrietta repeated.

"Well, okay, give it to me."

Henrietta smiled. "You see, I've been feeling the most intense energy during my meditations, especially in the last month. The intelligent power within me has informed me of this: the world's going to need more shamans and soul-healing information than ever before, as victims of heinous childhood abuse come out of the shadows. I've noticed that both arrests and victims speaking out about abuses from clergy, human traffickers, satanic cults and the like are occurring in greater numbers."

"I've noticed that topic being addressed recently on social media as well."

"That's, in part, why I've resurrected *The Secrets of Bears Repeating* and am working to finish it finally, trying to edit it down to make it easier to grasp and internalize."

"So you're thinking more people will need it and be able to relate to it better now?"

"Yes, although it's still true, *The Secrets of Bears Repeating* will have meaning only for those who're ready for its messages. For those who aren't, it'll come across like mumbo jumbo. However, when you're ready, the words will resonate and strike a chord of inner knowing exactly when you need to hear them."

"Hmm," Suzanne uttered, remembering her father's use of *mumbo jumbo*.

"Anyway, I've been trying to make the words simpler and easier to understand. But while editing, it occurred to me that I was attempting to approach the subject matter like an advertising copywriter would. I remembered what you told me, about how a copywriter's job is to distill reams of information down into compelling, easy-to-grasp headlines. Well, that's exactly what's needed!"

"Interesting."

"And then I realized: I've got the best copywriter in the world right here—you!"

Suzanne smiled. "Thanks, Gran."

"Would you be willing to take a stab at it?"

"Sure, Gran. I'll try to do whatever you ask. But it's already concise and reads well." As she spoke, she got goosebumps on her arms, indicating a startling truth was just spoken.

"Thank you, Peaches. I'm pleased to hear that. Even so, I'd still like you to read it with your copywriter's hat on."

"No problem."

"Now what did you want to tell me, dear?"

"I had another meeting with JB yesterday, and you won't believe what he had to say. Also, I'm about to lose my mind over who's in the gravest danger. The first deadline is tomorrow! And I still don't know what I can do about it, if anything."

"Let's have some hot tea, and we can talk about it. But don't forget. You will be my copywriter and editor!" Henrietta rose and lit a burner for a teakettle.

"I won't forget, I promise." Suzanne sat down at the kitchen table.

"So, what did your JB say?" Henrietta asked, pouring hot water over green tea bags. Sitting down, she blew on the steaming brew.

"I asked him what JB stood for. I'm not sure why I hadn't bothered to find out before. But oh! This is incredible!"

Henrietta put down her teacup and leaned forward. Her eyebrows shot up.

"Joseph Beaufort."

"Oh my goodness," Gran said, sitting back, her hand on her heart. "You could just knock me over with a feather."

Suzanne had always loved the full names of her grandfather and father: *Jefferson Beaufort Clayborn.* They had a beautiful, poetic cadence.

"Beaufort was an old family name that went way back in the Clayborn line," Henrietta said. A broad smile spread across her face. She added with a whisper: "It was also Joe Loco's middle name: Joseph Beaufort Loco."

Suzanne gasped. "You've got to be kidding!" Her mouth hung open.

"No, but what a beautiful synchronicity," Gran said, astonishment still in her voice. "And I must say one of the more entertaining!" She was now giggling. "Oh, Suzanne, I have to go to Hitchcock Woods with you and meet your JB. I want to see for myself who he really is. Let's take a ride today."

"A horse ride?"

"Of course!"

"I don't know about that, Gran. It might be too strenuous for you, and I'm still concerned about JB's dire prophecies. I'd feel much better about taking you to meet JB after the deadline, maybe Friday, since he and I agreed to meet at three every afternoon this week. In any event, we could easily drive the small utility vehicle that Dad has out to where I meet JB, at the ring."

"Nonsense. I may be eighty-one years old, but my bones are still strong. And, as you know, I exercise my own horse almost daily, for heaven's sake. I'd like to ride in the Woods. It's been too long since I did. And your Barnie will be quiet and gentle enough for me. It'll be fine."

"Actually," Suzanne said, "to be honest, I'd love for you to meet JB in person, just to confirm that he's not a ghost."

"Oh, I'm so excited," Henrietta said, her eyes glittering. "How about Thursday?"

"Well, it'll only be one day past the deadline, I don't know if that's a good idea."

"I feel it'll be perfect timing." She patted her heart and took a deep breath.

"Well, okay," Suzanne said, although she did not feel the same assurance. "How about you come to the house a little after two on Thursday? I'll have the horses ready to go. But, like I said, we can always take the utility vehicle."

"Yay," Henrietta said, clapping her hands like a schoolgirl.

Chapter 35

Suzanne rode out to meet JB that afternoon and again on the next day, Wednesday, to no avail. On both afternoons, the Woods bustled with riders and walkers, but JB was nowhere to be found. With mounting frustration, she searched the trails for hours, even after people left, but when the rains came late Wednesday, and they came hard, she simply had to give up and return to her room. Randy was still missing and there was no news from Smitty, so she passed the time reading, meditating and praying for the highest good of all involved in her life-or-death riddle. By the time of their meeting on Thursday, she hoped JB would know what had happened, if anything, and be able to give her a more tangible report about what else to expect, even with her grandmother in tow.

It was eerily quiet in the barn on Thursday
morning, and the Woods were cloud shadowed. Thunder
sounded in the distance, but the rain held back. At two
o'clock, it was still gloomy and overcast. Nevertheless,
Henrietta insisted on their riding horses out into
Hitchcock Woods to meet the elusive JB.

"Well, we'd better take some rain slicks, then,"
Suzanne suggested, foraging through the tack room
closet.

"Good idea," Henrietta said, looking out.

"I hope the weather doesn't scare off JB like the
crowds seemed to do the last two afternoons," Suzanne
said. "Ah, here they are." She pulled out two navy-
colored plastic ponchos.

"I feel confidant JB will not be put off. He will be
there today," Henrietta said.

"It may be a bit warm to wear the ponchos, but
we might as well put them on now," Suzanne said, poking
her hand out the window. "It's raining a little. If I didn't
have this standing appointment with JB, I'd say we should
wait it out."

"A little drizzle won't hurt us," Henrietta said
defiantly.

"Hey, Brad," Suzanne said, helping her
grandmother on the mounting block. "Thanks for having
Misty and Barnie all set for us."

"No problem" came Brad's voice from the back stall, where he was mucking up Cole's colossal droppings. "Hopefully, Randy will be back soon."

"Just to be safe, we'll go around Sand River," Suzanne said to Henrietta, planning to take the long way to the inner Horse Show Ring to avoid any potential danger of recent floodwaters. "And I've got my revolver if we run into trouble," she said, patting her holstered gun under her vest. "No one's going to mess with us."

"I've no worries," Henrietta said.

The light rain stopped just as they approached the ring. But the humidity was hot, thick and clingy. Suzanne helped her grandmother off her horse. Since it was clear now, they removed their ponchos, turned them inside out, placed them on the wet picnic table bench, and sat on them.

Suzanne looked at the time on her cell phone. "It's three. We'll see if he shows up today."

"Oh, I hope JB is Bears Repeating. Wouldn't that be something?" Henrietta beamed like a child at Christmas, her hands over her heart.

"Let's not get too excited, Gran. That reminds me, while we wait, I wanted to ask you about *The Secrets of Bears Repeating*. Let's say I give your manuscript a copywriter's edit to your liking. Will you be ready to publish it then?"

"I was thinking you'd publish it for me, since you'll be the coauthor and editor."

"What? No, I don't feel worthy enough to do that. The author has to be someone with your biography, who's internalized and lived the truth it contains, just as you have and do. Don't get me wrong. I'd love to be an authority on life's ancient secrets. But let's be honest. I'm not. I've got serious problems. Ghosts make my life a living hell."

Henrietta frowned and placed her hand over her heart.

"But that's not all. I've probably lost my advertising career. I seem to be unable to attract a nice guy. No offense, but Dad's drunk most of the time. Mama's ...well, she's over-the-top, right? The Chicago bombing and I might be connected to a serial murderer, but I don't know how. Two more people close to me may die soon; one may have already died," she said, exhaling and thinking of poor Randy. "The other may even be me. It's enough to make any sane person want to run away—again."

"Suzanne, you did not come into the world to run away from your fears and the people in your life, as dysfunctional as you describe yourself and them to be. You came here to control the content of your thoughts with pure intent and face your fears. You must embrace your shadows so that you can release and transmute them into light. And to lead with eagle vision. You can do this."

"Gran, you're the only person who's always believed in me and been there for me. You've been my rock—truly the most trustworthy and wise person in my life. I'm not sure I could've made it without you." Tears welled in Suzanne's eyes.

"Of course you would have, and you'll do so in the future. I won't be around forever. I've just been able to see your potential and your gifts as strengths. It's time for you to see them."

"I'm not sure I have enough courage to face my ghosts and the darkness of the past. They still scare me. I wish I couldn't see what no one else sees."

"You've been given tremendous psychic and creative abilities, resources and unlimited personal freedom. What're you going to do with them? The Great Spirit gives us the opportunity to choose experiences that are often seen as being at odds with what we want," she said, referring to God as her Apache friends taught her. "Because our souls know that before you can get what you want in life, you must know precisely what it is you want. We usually need to experience the opposite of what we want in order to ask and thank the Great Spirit in clear terms about it. We can only wake up to the light out of darkness, my dear Suzanne." She patted Suzanne's hand. "You are the light."

"Gran, I've been looking for a hero my entire life, and here you are. You've been here the whole time."

"I think it's high time you stop fighting your spiritual abilities and accept them, and see yourself as your own hero. While you're overly focused on ghosts, the pain of being an empath and the crimes surrounding you, you're missing the Spirit Guides who are talking to you. Listen to them. Feel their resonance and message. Trust it."

"I've been afraid to see and listen to the truth. I don't even know why."

"Back in my days in Medichero, when I first went out West, I wasn't ready to hear about the divine within us either. I had to go through a lot of suffering to get ready. Generally speaking, the public as a whole wasn't ready to hear anything of a metaphysical nature back then; they weren't ready to let go of ancient superstitions, false beliefs and the man-made illusions of extreme religiosity. They weren't ready to listen to the divine speaking to them from within their hearts. I believe the times, they are a changing. We're in the midst of a great human awakening." She coughed, covering her mouth before continuing with a hoarse voice. "Which is how I also know that my son, your father, will ultimately choose wisely for himself and this life. I believe in him and trust that the universe will organize things perfectly for him."

"I hope you're right about Dad."

Henrietta was starting to breathe hard, and her light blue shirt was covered in sweat. She coughed again.

"Gran, you don't look well. Let me get you some water." Suzanne hurried to Misty for a water bottle. A crackling noise came from her left, as if a horse was stepping on wooded underbrush. Her immediate thought was that JB was finally making his grand entrance. She whipped around, but she saw no one. Yet, she felt a presence and lots of commotion going on behind spirit's veil.

"Sorry for the wait, Gran. JB was supposed to be here ten minutes ago," she said, handing her grandmother the bottle.

"Thank you, dear," Henrietta said, attempting to sip the water. But she suddenly bent over, dropping it. "Oh...the pressure." Her hands flew to her chest.

"Gran, I think you should lay down," Suzanne said, growing more alarmed as she felt a tightening in her own heart area. She spread out her poncho on the sand next to the bench. "Let me help you."

"Yes, perhaps that'd be better," Henrietta said. "I'm feeling a little light-headed."

Suzanne eased her grandmother down onto the ground and poncho. Henrietta moaned as she moved.

"I'm calling 911," Suzanne said, fearing her grandmother was having a heart attack right in front of her. She pushed the numbers. "Please send an ambulance for my grandmother. She's in distress…I don't know. She's holding her left arm and her breathing is difficult. We're on the north side of the inner Horse Show Ring…Yes, Hitchcock Woods. Hurry!"

Clutching her shirt, Henrietta said, "Look, he's here! Can you see him?" There was excitement in her strained whisper.

Suzanne turned in the direction of her grandmother's line of focus, but there was no one there. No presence detected, psychically or otherwise. "What?" Suzanne said to the 911 operator, who said she would remain on the line until the EMS arrived. "Yes, she's talking. That's a good sign, right?"

"He's here!" her grandmother cried out again.

Suzanne took in their immediate area. *Nope. No JB. No Bears Repeating.* "I think the pain is making her hallucinate."

"Oh, my friend!" Henrietta said, but her voice was weak, barely a whisper.

"Gran, are you seeing Bears Repeating?" Suzanne looked around, perplexed that she saw no one.

Henrietta's eyes were turning glassy as sirens rang out and through the Woods.

"Gran, the ambulance is on the way—please hold on," Suzanne pleaded.

An EMS vehicle arrived from the direction of South Boundary Avenue. Paramedics jumped out and immediately began lifesaving measures on Henrietta where she lay on the ground. As they placed her on the gurney, Suzanne heard her grandmother say to someone no one else could see: "Will Jeff be there?"

In the next second, Suzanne gasped—right next to her grandmother was a sepia-colored image of a man wearing a full Indigenous American headdress, the kind JB had worn on Monday. The feathers obscured his face, perhaps intentionally so, although Suzanne sensed he was Bears Repeating. He was bending over her grandmother, holding her hand. Another man, whom Suzanne recognized as her Grandfather Jefferson, stepped into the vision, as the feathered man seemed to evaporate before her eyes. When her grandfather picked up Henrietta's wrinkled hand, it immediately turned youthful as a younger, translucent, version of Henrietta rose from the gurney and fell gracefully into his open arms. Together, they disappeared into a cloud of brightness.

There was a smile on her grandmother's lips as the paramedic pronounced Henrietta Smyth Clayborn dead.

"Oh, Gran! I wouldn't have brought you out here if I'd known it was going to be you! I'm so sorry." She hugged Henrietta and kissed her face, sobbing uncontrollably.

"Our condolences, ma'am," said a paramedic.

Suzanne looked up, but her response had nothing to do with what the paramedic had said. What captured her attention was beyond the ordinary and audible. It was the unmistakable, beautiful voice of her grandmother echoing back. With tears pouring and her clairvoyance rekindled, Suzanne heard her grandmother exclaim with a strong voice and the enthusiasm of youth, "Oh, Jeff, my love, I knew you'd come back for me!"

Chapter 36

It rained heavily on Sunday, the day Henrietta was buried under a massive live oak tree on the edge of a peach grove on the Clayborn estate. Her body would reside next to that of her beloved Jefferson Beaufort Clayborn Senior, who'd been laid to rest in this family graveyard near relatives some fifty years ago.

Raindrops on canvas might be soothing and healing to some, like slow requiems and love songs, but they did little to lift Suzanne's somber mood as she stood next to her grieving father and her two aunts under the funeral canopy. JJ's shoulders heaved as he sobbed quietly for their beautiful mother. His sisters, Frannie and Annie, looked more bewildered than sad, though they also cried as they stood on either side of their brother, all three holding hands. The surrounding fields, soaked and haggard from torrential showers and winds, looked equally distressed at the loss of their beloved mistress and having to bear witness to the last of an old dynasty. Inevitably, the orchards would bounce back from their unseasonal sadness and fallen fruit, as Henrietta would wish them to do, teaching by example about how to overcome the heavy hand of a soul's sorrow. For no one understood loss and renaissance better than the peach trees, whose matrons birthed and let go of their offspring annually.

Hundreds of townspeople squeezed under five large canvas tents as the rain poured out of blackened, lightning-struck clouds. It was a pleasant shock to Suzanne that so many in the community had come to pay this kind of homage to Henrietta, especially under these weather conditions. She'd mistakenly believed her grandmother's metaphysical unconventionalism was considered an aberration and a blasphemous embarrassment to many of her southern brethren. How happy she was to stand corrected. It was as if the towns of both Greenfield and Aiken knew they had lost something as rare and irreplaceable as a one-of-a-kind diamond ring heirloom.

Henrietta had specified that her funeral take place not in a church, but rather out in the nature she loved and nourished. An ancient-looking Apache named Big Eagle Feathers, who'd had a mysterious bond with both Jefferson and Henrietta and still lived on the Medichero

Apache Reservation in New Mexico, flew in for the
funeral and delivered a moving eulogy. As he spoke, he
sporadically hit a handheld drum in rhythm to the sounds
of the storm. With an Apache accent and a delivery style
most likely never before heard in Aiken County, Big
Eagle explained how the Clayborns had contributed to his
tribal nation in many ways, including the building of a
medical research and healing center that had helped many
thousands of people.

As the service concluded, ushers with large black
umbrellas ran up to help attendees clad in funeral attire
migrate to the mansion for the wake. Eschewing their
assistance, Suzanne covered her head with the hood of
her raincoat and trudged alongside her parents, who had
their own umbrellas. As they stepped onto the circular
driveway, Randy drove up abruptly in his Malibu. She
bent down at the passenger window, as he rolled it down.

"Suzanne, please forgive me for not being here
sooner," Randy said. "I just found out."

"Where in the hell have you been? I've been
worried sick about you and the police are looking for
you," she shouted, pulling her hood down tighter. "Why
haven't you called?" She was both mad and relieved that
he wasn't dead.

"I'm sorry I worried you, and I know I should
have called. But I've had to deal with Jimmy again. It was
an emergency that I couldn't help."

"Randy, I'm really glad you're okay. I'm grateful for that. But, and I don't mean to offend you, I've got to ask you: Could it be possible that Jimmy's responsible for some of the awful things that've happened?"

"I'll admit that even I thought of that," he said, leaning toward the open window. "But he was in the hospital the whole time. I checked," he said. "I was relieved, I tell you. Also, he doesn't know the first thing about explosives, electronics or even Chicago."

"What?" She shook her head, confused by his answer. "I wasn't thinking of him being involved like that," she said, but her mind flashed to what the boy ghost had said about the incidents being connected. She turned to her parents, who were still standing behind her, looking dazed under their umbrellas. "Mom, Dad, please go ahead. I'll be along in a few minutes." She turned back to the Malibu. "Okay, now I have to ask you something else on this very trying day." She took a breath. "Randy, have you been lying to me about Jimmy?"

He looked down, then up. "Yes."

"You'd better explain fast," she said through gritted teeth.

"But it's not what you think," he said with his voice lowered. "Jimmy's not a college student, and he wasn't a criminal in and out of juvie hall."

"Why did you tell me he was?"

"Because he's in the state psychiatric hospital most of the time. When they let him out occasionally, I have to deal with him, usually at the place I have up on Ascauga Lake. That's where I've been with him. He's back at the hospital now." Randy looked away when he said it.

"Oh my God," Suzanne said. "I'm so sorry." She put her fingers to her forehead. Something still felt off about what he was saying.

"Yeah, it's pretty bad when you'd rather admit that your brother is a criminal than…insane. But I wanted—I have to protect him…" He looked away.

"From what?" She frowned, not as much from what he said, but rather because her emotions were bouncing between sympathy and a growing, inexplicable fear.

Randy shook his head in silence as Nick approached, interrupting her confusing mix of emotions. "Suzanne, let me get you out of this rain," Nick said, holding an umbrella with his good hand.

"Yes, I should go in anyway," she said before turning one more time to the Malibu. "Listen, Randy, we will talk about this later. Okay?"

"Yes, of course," he said with a scowl at Nick, who was nudging her away.

"You've got to stop hanging out with the likes of Randy Mackenzie," Nick said after they entered her grandmother's house.

"Why do you keep saying that?"

"I see him hanging in places where he shouldn't be," Nick said. "And doing things he shouldn't be doing."

"Oh, like what?"

"Like staring at you."

"What's wrong with that?"

"Normally, I'd say nothing. He has good taste," Nick said, smiling in a way that made Suzanne's heart flutter. "But there's a creep factor in the way he does it. He's been that way since before high school. I'm not sure why you've never seen it...or felt it."

"Oh, you're just jealous," she said, dismissing him with a wave of her hand. "Randy's a trusted friend, and one of the nicest men I've ever known." Then she grimaced, remembering that he'd just confessed to lying about Jimmy. And he'd been a very good liar, at that.

Chapter 37

Gran is gone, Suzanne thought as she cried in her bedroom. She hoped her grandmother might at some point be able to visit her from Spirit, but the loss of her physical presence was great and irreplaceable.

As she finished getting dressed for the day, Suzanne wondered if JB would be gone from her world, too.

Wait a minute—it suddenly hit her that JB's prophecy was not yet completed. When Randy had gone missing, she'd assumed incorrectly that he might have been the first one close to her to die and Gran was then the second person. But now Randy was back. Which would make Gran the first. And JB had said the second would die *soon thereafter!*

"Suzy," her mother said, knocking and opening the bedroom door. "We're fixing to head off to the attorney." The family was going to hear the official reading of Henrietta's trust and will. "You'll ride over with us, won't you?"

Under black umbrellas once again, the Clayborn family made long strides toward a historic redbrick building in the heart of Aiken that held the offices of Leonard E. Drake, Esquire. Wet sidewalks and bruise-colored skies created an absence of pedestrians. The winds had died down, though a miasma of gloom lingered. Smells of lunchtime hamburgers and barbeque wafted on the damp breeze from the ovens of Laurens Street's diners and bistros. Store windows were gauzed in glassy humidity, glistening with the golden backlights of hopeful shopkeepers, their awnings dripping as though crying.

Inside the attorney's office, the family settled solemnly into the leather chairs of a wood-paneled conference room. Brown- and maroon-colored leather spines faced them from wall-length bookshelves as Suzanne wondered if her grandmother's trust and will documents would hold any last secrets of Bears Repeating. After reviewing what seemed like volumes of legalese, Mr. Drake at last pulled out and read a typewritten letter, and Suzanne's wonder turned into astonishment.

"And now for some final words from Henrietta that she wished, and I quote, for only the eyes and ears of my beloved family members, end quote," Mr. Drake said. Because the letter was composed on a typewriter—not a computer keyboard—Suzanne assumed Gran had written it many years before. She imagined her grandmother sitting at her writing desk behind her old typewriter instead of her new computer. As Mr. Drake continued reading the words, it became apparent that they were indeed written many years before—the letter was dated exactly thirteen years ago, a couple of months after Suzanne's shooting accident. Everyone sat in stunned silence, as, incredibly, the content that Mr. Drake read had a direct impact on Suzanne and the decisions she was currently in the process of making, once again confirming the tremendous spirit and amazing prescience of Henrietta S. Clayborn.

Chapter 38

A month and half ago, Suzanne had been a dreamer in love with words, who wanted nothing more than to write compelling, award-winning advertising copy in a big city. Now, she imagined creating healing words and sanctuary for dreamers on the lands of her ancestors. And this filled her with a surprising emotion: joy.

Sitting in the Clayborn estate's grand living room, Suzanne considered how her grandmother had stressed in her typewritten note that there was no pressure for her granddaughter to agree to her plan to transform the estate into something she'd dubbed "the Aiken Artists' Colony" and running it with Annie, Frannie, and JJ, if they chose to participate. But, unlike the others in her family, Suzanne felt her grandmother's intentions instinctively, like a call from the wild she couldn't possibly resist. As Suzanne expected, her aunts were unable to relocate back

to South Carolina because of their medical work. And as
they had little in common with artists, her aunts were
happy just to continue receiving their trust funds and
asked their brother to manage everything else.

Gran had a glorious rationale for creating a place
for artists. Her note had read: "As humans continue to
awaken from and transmute the darkness and false
programming of the past, I foresee there will be a
growing consumer demand for artistic products of a
higher vibration, which are both entertaining and
enlightening, even while artists are guided to create them.
Realistically, however, I know firsthand how challenging
it is for artists of all kinds—writers, painters, singers,
musicians, actors and the like—to support themselves
financially during the creative process. Thus, it is my hope
and wish for the artists' colony to be fiscally self-
sustaining, through peach farming and the other
businesses of the Clayborn Trust. Furthermore, I hope
that the Aiken Artists' Colony will inspire and encourage
other patrons of the arts to follow suit in their own
unique ways, so that creative people with noble intentions
might produce inspirational works in safe, nurturing
environments—without fears, financial burdens,
malevolent controls or negative influences."

Although it was not mentioned in Henrietta's
prophetic note, Suzanne also planned to give *The Secrets of
Bears Repeating* a copywriter's spin, as her grandmother

had requested just before she'd passed away. But having read and studied the manuscript, Suzanne didn't see how she could possibly improve upon it. In that second, she grasped that Gran was asking her to work on the manuscript because she knew the editing process would cause Suzanne to better internalize its metaphysical teachings. She'd even suggested that Suzanne would be the one who published it. Suzanne smiled. Even from the grave, her grandmother was the ceaseless teacher, someone who was always aware of the importance of helping others. What a tremendous creative legacy she was leaving for Suzanne and other creative people.

The first week after Gran died, Suzanne stopped looking for the JB of Hitchcock Woods at three o'clock in the afternoon. By the second week, she was no longer scratching her scaly, chapped hands. They'd healed, thanks to JB's essential oil remedy and a more relaxed state of mind. She wasn't constantly searching online for news or checking the clock. There was something indescribably freeing about living in the present without feeling obligated to make social media broadcasts about her life and times. That there had not been a second death, as JB warned was possible, was still a nagging concern. But perhaps, she reasoned, they were past the "soon thereafter" time period, and the choices made by those involved had been effective in changing the outcomes. *Soon thereafter*, she repeated in her mind. It was such a nebulous phrase. What did it really mean, anyway?

She reached for her dinging cell phone on the side table. "Hello? Oh, hi, Shane. How's the campaign going without me?" She was quiet as he filled her in. Eventually, he asked if there was any chance she would return to Chicago.

"Only to sell the condo and take care of some personal matters." She didn't feel the need to get into the specifics, like that she'd already broken up with Dan. She did feel obliged to give him the gist of her grandmother's trust and her wish for Suzanne to start and run a community for budding artists on the family's peach orchard estate.

"I've decided to do it, to continue my grandmother's legacy, and I'm excited about it— surprisingly so." She paused to feel the resonance of its truth, and smiled. "I think we'll be able to do a lot of good, and I'll have the time for a writing project I'm eager to finish," Suzanne said, thinking of *The Secrets of Bears Repeating*. "But I'll admit to feeling a little sad about leaving the agency and my work there."

"I see," Shane said. "That's very interesting," he added, growing quiet, his habit when he was in the process of formulating a new idea.

"I'm sorry I won't be able to produce the Americos Oil campaign with you. It would've been fun," she continued. "But that's how it goes sometimes. This is what I'm meant to do."

"Now hold on. Don't give up on your own advertising life so soon!" Shane said with enthusiasm. "I was calling to make you an offer. But I just had an idea that might work well with grandmama's wishes."

"I'm listening."

"What if we started an ad agency together? I was initially thinking in Atlanta, but with our Internet-connected world, it could easily be in Aiken. Sure it can—why not? I have some clients that will move virtually with me anywhere. And you may not realize this right now, but you do too!"

"I do?" And she remembered one of her former clients expressing an interest in hiring Suzanne to work on his new business venture.

"Yes! And now that I hear about your plans for an artists' community, this might work out better than I thought," he said. "Your family estate might make the perfect location for a boutique ad agency. It's certainly creative and unexpected. I like it! You could kill two birds with one stone: maintain your creative life, but also run the Aiken Artists' Colony for your grandmother."

"I must say I'm intrigued with your idea," she said.

"As you know, I'm full of 'em."

"Yeah, you're full of something, all right," she said, feeling her own wide grin as they fell easily back into their usual repartee. "Hashtag BS."

He busted out laughing, and she realized how much she had missed him and their camaraderie.

"But seriously, you know how much I've always wanted to live in the South. I've had about all I can take of the cold and gray weather, not to mention the ongoing city violence. This would suit me just fine," Shane said, affecting a southern drawl.

"I must say it always surprised me just how much you were attracted to the South. I'll definitely consider it. I'll talk to the attorney, too. In the meantime, why don't you come down for a visit, see the place and we can brainstorm more about it?"

"Deal, partner. How about next weekend?"

"That'll work."

"Do you mind if I bring my girlfriend, Theresa? You've met her, right? She's a terrific graphic designer."

"How perfect, yes, please bring her! We've plenty of room."

After Suzanne clicked off, she could feel her heartbeat accelerating. *What an incredible solution!* It was a beautiful blending of her old creative life and what felt like her new life's mission unfolding. Or as Gran would've said: *What a beautiful synchronicity!* Suddenly, she saw the big picture of it. And it felt glorious.

Chapter 39

Suzanne was humming as she walked toward the barn, but stopped abruptly when she caught sight of the tail end of a black spoiler, no doubt belonging to the modified Honda she'd seen once before. It was tucked discreetly under a magnolia on the barn's eastern side.

Tiptoeing to the barn's window, she peeked in, thinking she might at last see the elusive Jimmy. But Randy was standing with two older men who looked neither familiar nor friendly. Scary guy number one was a lean, fortysomething, white, bald guy with a snake tattoo slithering up the back of his head. Scary guy number two, also white, was tall and muscular, with large forearms covered in tattoos of guns and skulls. He wore a black cap over long, black, curly hair and a black T-shirt over blue jeans. He was holding something, but she couldn't tell what it was from her angle.

Every hair on her neck and arms stood up. Before she could decide whether or not to intervene for Randy's sake or run back to the house for her revolver, the strangers turned abruptly in her direction. She ducked behind the barn door. Misty, probably sensing her presence and possible danger, started stomping and snorting loudly before making a high-pitched neigh.

Don't give me away, girl! Suzanne thought, wishing to convey it telepathically.

"You'd better quiet that horse and remember to keep your fucking mouth shut, or…you don't want to know," the bald guy said before departing. Through cracks in the wood door, she saw Randy limp over to attend Misty just before the Honda took off, kicking up gravel onto the barn siding like the pellet spray from a shotgun.

Letting out the breath she'd been holding, Suzanne slipped out of her hiding place and walked briskly into the barn. "Who were those men?" she demanded, pointing toward the door.

Randy jumped and whipped around. "Oh, Suzanne, you scared me to death."

"I should think those men are the ones you should be scared of. And maybe my father for letting them onto our property."

"You got that right." He exhaled and put his hand over his heart.

"What did they want?" Suzanne patted Misty's nose to help calm her down. "It's okay, girl. I'm here. I'm okay."

"They wanted to know...um," he started, limping over. His voice was small and cracking, as though he were confessing to an awful crime. "Um...about Jimmy."

"Did they hurt you? Why are you limping?"

"No, um, I hurt my toe by accident the other day."

"Why do those men care about Jimmy?"

"They're concerned that I...I mean Jimmy...I mean *we* will...um...testify." He looked around with paranoid eyes.

"Testify? About what?"

"Do you know a police detective named Richard Smith?" he asked.

"You mean Smitty?"

Randy nodded. "He's apparently reopened my mother's case. He thinks her death was a murder, not an accident, and that it was part of some bigger crimes."

"Why would those men care about that?" she asked, holding her palms up, but already knew the answer would be bad. "Randy, we need to call Smitty about their visit as soon as possible."

"That's not a good idea." He shook his head.

"I heard them threaten you," she said.

He lifted a dark, worried and tired gaze to her. "They do it all the time, Suzanne. And now that you know about them, I'm scared to death they'll find out you know." He put his face in his hands. Even though the noisy car was gone, the horses were still snorting in alarm from the men's visit.

She went to each one, patting and calming them with her voice and hands, before turning back to Randy. "Could those two men be responsible for the deaths of Bobby and Tomás?"

"I don't know. Maybe. Probably." Randy was trembling.

She was reminded of the second part of JB's apocalyptic reading, the death that could happen "soon thereafter" the first and that it might be her. Suzanne was suddenly terrified for Randy and herself like never before. "That does it. I'm going to call Smitty about those scary guys, and then I'm getting a security service as soon as possible to protect us twenty-four/seven." She turned to leave.

"Wait, Suzanne. I've got to tell you...I'm so, so sorry to involve you in this," he said. His face was red, and his eyes watered. "I hate that my horrible past is now touching you and your family. But since you know, I've got to tell you something else. But I don't want to." Tears poured down his cheeks.

She stopped. "It's okay, Randy. You can tell me. I can help you." *Would the bullying of this poor man ever stop?*

"It's so terrible and shocking. But, but...you must know for your own protection, and I can't keep this in anymore." He shook his head. "There're a lot of bad people like those two. They're sick and twisted...evil. They do horrible things to women and children. They raped and tortured Jimmy. They create sickness in everyone they touch. I escaped it, but I was hurt because of what I saw them do to Jimmy...and others. They've kept me quiet about it by threatening me...and Jimmy."

"Oh my God!" She gasped when she recalled Gran bringing up the very same topic about abused children and people right before she died.

"I'm so afraid," Randy said. "It's an evil you cannot even imagine. Or ever get away from. They also came up to Spartanburg when we lived with Aunt Jane and threatened us there."

"Oh, you poor things," she said. "Will Jimmy testify about what they did to him?"

"He should. But I won't let him. He can't!"

"Don't y'all want to help put them away?"

"Of course! But they aren't the only ones, and we wouldn't stand a chance against the whole lot of them. We'd be dead before getting to the witness stand. That's why I've got Jimmy hidden someplace where they won't be able to find him ever again."

"And where is that?"

"Well…um…it's the state psychiatric hospital in Columbia." He tapped his forehead as if this was an ingenious idea.

"You said that before."

"I did?" He looked truly perplexed. "I don't think so."

"Yes, at Gran's funeral."

"Oh yeah," he said, but didn't really seem to remember. "This whole thing with Silas has got me messed up again."

"Silas?"

"The one with the snake tattoo."

"I still think we should inform Smitty," Suzanne said. "He can take care of this Silas and that other guy."

"No! I'm telling you, it won't end well if we do that. There're a lot of good people who've died trying to stop them. I can't lose Jimmy!"

"This is just so awful for you, Randy—and us. It's not at all fair what you and Jimmy went through as children."

"Suze, sometimes, I just want to give up…and die. It's just not possible to escape them. Or be saved somehow." He was crying harder now.

"Don't give up," she said. "I believe it's up to us to save ourselves from evil like this." She took in a gulp of air. "It comes from within here," she said, thumping her fist over her heart before doing the same to his chest.

"How do you know?" He looked at her with wet, swollen eyes.

"Let's just say I know in my 'knower' that I know." She smiled with her hands crossed on her chest, remembering JB's coining the lilting phrase.

"You've always been the brave one, Suzanne. You've got more courage than any person I've ever known, but you're also the kindest. The best I could ever do was to be your shadow. You're the reason I came back to Aiken from Spartanburg. I feel your protection, even when you're not here, just by living where you lived and taking care of your Misty. This barn and Hitchcock Woods are the only places I've ever felt safe in the entire world."

"You're braver than you think, Randy. Or you wouldn't have survived this far. We just have to face the situation and take the right actions," she said, as JB's advice about following her inner guidance also came to mind. "And then afterward, we have to be there to help our brothers and sisters who've been so hurt by these horrible predators." She patted his arm and gave it a tender squeeze.

"Thank you, Suzanne." He took a breath and seemed to gain some equilibrium.

"Randy, I hate to leave you right now, but as I said, it's time to step up. I'm getting a security guard service immediately, and I've got to take care of some other things that can't wait," she said. "Will you be all right for a while?"

"I have a gun." He wiped his wet face with the sleeve of his T-shirt. But something in his voice had changed. It was more confident, yet his eyes were vacant, empty.

"Okay, good. I'll check on you in a bit," she said, not comprehending a new feeling of discomfort in her gut. "Let the horses calm you, and you them."

He nodded with a strange, forced smile. "I will."

She turned and marched to the main house. She planned to make three calls: one to a security guard company, one to Smitty and the third to Shane—she'd have to tell him not to come right now, for his and Theresa's safety.

Smitty confirmed the Aiken Police Department had indeed reopened the Joyce Mackenzie case based on new witness testimony. He also informed Suzanne that he'd dug deeper in the files for any records pertaining to James Mackenzie.

But what he'd discovered was as shocking as what she'd just learned from Randy.

Chapter 40

According to Spartanburg County's Public Safety records, a missing person's report had been filed for James Mackenzie seven years ago. "But here's the thing," Smitty said. "He's still considered a missing person."

"Clearly the records are wrong," Suzanne said, stunned. "Randy talks about his brother being very much around."

"It could be there was an error in the record-keeping," Smitty said with some awkwardness.

"I don't understand," she said.

"Even when they lived in Aiken, Jimmy Mackenzie was known to run away from time to time. He might've continued with that pattern in Spartanburg. It's possible a report was filed and he was later found, but the records were never reconciled. When I get a chance, I'll look more into it."

Suzanne was getting a different feeling about it. "Or maybe Randy used the missing person's report as a way to hide Jimmy from Silas."

"Uh-huh, could be," Smitty said, as if he were considering her theory. "Had Randy ever mentioned Jimmy prior to your arrival back in town?"

"A little, he mainly just acknowledged he had a sweet kid brother." She paused to consider their past together. "To be honest, I've never actually met Jimmy."

"Is that right?" he said, before quieting as though taking notes.

"You said you were able to reopen the Joyce Mackenzie case because of new witness testimony," Suzanne said. "I'm curious, why now?"

"This case has always bothered me; things just never added up," Smitty said. "I've kept it on my radar, even though I wasn't able to do more about it. That is, until we arrested Robert Lindley for trying to solicit minors."

"Bobby was involved with that Silas guy?" She could hardly believe it.

"All I can say is that Mr. Lindley had some knowledge of the case from his own tragic childhood experiences. He was going to turn state's evidence."

Suzanne gasped. "Oh, dear Lord!" She understood immediately. Bobby had been a victim. Jimmy and Randy were victims. This was about human trafficking and child exploitation, just as Gran had talked about. Now she wondered about the other murder.

"Smitty, was Tomás Sanchez, by chance, also involved in this?" In truth, she didn't want to know if Tomás had been involved with a human trafficking ring, but she had to ask.

"I can say that Mr. Sanchez did offer information relative to this case."

"Smitty, I find it inconceivable Tomás was raping minors or involved with Silas."

"He wasn't. Let's just say, he witnessed some things that haunted him and he came to see us. He agreed to testify in court. I regret it may have cost him his life."

"But isn't that enough to make some arrests?"

"Not yet, but we're very close. So, I want to thank you for calling me about Silas's visit to Randy. This helps more than you know."

"I understand. Um, there's one more thing I should tell you." She didn't want to betray Randy's confidence, but she felt she simply had to report Randy's claim about hiding Jimmy in the state mental hospital.

"Okay," Smitty said. "I'll check into it."

As their call ended, she remembered how the boy ghost suggested the murders were connected to the Chicago bomb event. *But the murders weren't about me at all.* So how could they be connected? *They wouldn't be*, she thought as she darted back to the barn.

Alarmed that Randy wasn't in the barn, she called him on her cell. He answered promptly, assuring her he was okay, that he had a plan and he'd be back soon.

Satisfied Randy was safe for the time being, she tacked up Misty, since Brad was also absent. She wondered what Randy had meant by having a plan. She felt a cramp in her abdomen that didn't subside during her ride, so she cut it short.

With the barn still vacant, Suzanne started the methodical process of removing Misty's saddle and bridle. As she brushed out Misty's perspiration and saddle marks with a curry comb, she decided that since Bobby's and Tomás's deaths weren't about her, it might be safe enough for Shane and Theresa to visit this weekend as planned. She intended to put them at Gran's place, anyway. She wondered if they'd feel comfortable staying at such a large estate home all by themselves. Maybe she should hire a security guard for them as well. *What else?* She'd ask one of Della's friends to help out in the kitchen. And she'd make sure to fill their rooms with some good books. "Of course, they won't mind," she said aloud when Misty's head jerked back.

"Who won't mind?" Randy said, running into the barn.

"Oh hey, I was just thinking out loud."

"Okay," he said, panting. He was wearing jogging shorts, a T-shirt and running shoes. He wheezed between breaths, as though he had an allergy. "I didn't know you were going out for a ride. Here, let me take care of tacking up Misty," Randy said, putting down a backpack.

"Actually, I'm just getting back," she said, shocked that he didn't notice she was brushing out Misty's sweat marks, making it obvious, especially to someone like Randy, that she had already ridden her horse.

"Oh, yeah," he said, helping her finish.

Given his previous agitated state of mind and all she'd learned, she decided to dismiss it.

"I didn't know you were a jogger, and besides, I thought you said you'd injured your toe."

"It doesn't hurt anymore," he said with an uncharacteristically flippant tone. "Jogging helps me cope with stress." Despite having just come back from a run, his face had taken on the color of eggshell.

"I hope you're feeling better, then," she said.

"I'm fine," he said, but clearly he wasn't. His body slumped, his sadness palpable.

"Hey, I want to let you know that we'll have a security guard service twenty-four/seven, starting tonight," she said to change the subject. "And until things calm down."

He nodded, seemingly relieved. "Thank you."

"Oh, and I've a colleague coming to visit from Chicago next weekend. I certainly don't want him to feel uncomfortable, given the scary things going on, so that's another reason for hiring security. But he'll be staying out at Gran's."

"That's nice," Randy said. His mind now seemed to be elsewhere.

"Also, I plan to take Misty out to Gran's place while he's there." She patted Misty's head.

"Who?"

"My colleague who's coming next weekend. His name is Shane Morgan. And I'm thinking of having him stay at Gran's 'cause I don't want to put his life in jeopardy, if you know what I mean. He's coming because we might start an ad agency together. Isn't that exciting?"

"I suppose," Randy said. "Is that why you're taking Misty away? And moving out there with him?" His voice quivered with obvious confusion.

"I'm not moving out there with Shane, silly, but we'll have business meetings while he's here," she said, trying to remain upbeat for Randy's sake. "He likes horses, so I thought we could ride when he visits. Also, I'm responsible for Gran's property and her horses now. I have a caretaker for them, of course, but I need to figure out what's going on with them and the orchards, anyway. Consequently, I may have to spend more time out there. But that'll be later, after Shane goes back to Chicago."

"That's nice," Randy repeated, his voice dipping lower. He pulled out a peppermint from his pocket and held it up to Misty. His movements were mechanical. Unexpectedly, the mare yanked her head up, refusing it.

Suzanne had never seen Misty reject an offered mint, especially one from Randy. She opened Misty's mouth and searched her teeth for a dental issue. "Let's have the vet take a look at Misty's mouth."

"Okay," Randy said, his voice monotone. Unexpectedly, he reached up and touched Suzanne's cheek. His hands smelled of peppermint and burnt paper. Misty snorted, her head bobbing, causing them both to take a step back.

"Randy," she snapped, jerking away sideways.

"Aww, don't worry. I'm not trying to be another one of your boyfriends, like Nick Vaughn is," he sneered.

"Randy, Nick is not my boyfriend," she said, confused that he would even care if she had a boyfriend or not. Randy was not acting like himself.

"I was just trying to let you know how much I appreciate everything you and your parents have done for us. I hate to hear that you might not live here anymore." His tone was uncharacteristically whiny—bratty even. He looked down, avoiding eye contact.

"I'm not getting involved with anyone right now, and I'm not moving," she said, hating that he was taking everything she said wrong.

"Why're you bringing Shane in, then?" His mouth pinched. He stared at her with blank eyes.

"As I said, Shane's a colleague from Chicago, and he's bringing his girlfriend here with him. Her name is Theresa," she added with emphasis, growing more worried by the minute about Randy's mental state. "I'm getting a water," she said to break the tension. Stepping into the tack room, she opened the refrigerator. "You want one?" Turning, she caught sight of the boy ghost lurking in the shadows.

"I guess," Randy said. "Thanks." He walked Misty into her stall.

When he came out, Suzanne handed Randy the water bottle. "Well, I've got to get going," she said. "Will you be okay?"

She watched him nod.

"I'll check in with you in a bit." As she headed toward the barn door, they both heard a car coming down the gravel driveway—Nick in his British racing green Jaguar XK-E.

Randy blew out a breath of annoyance. "I wonder what he wants."

"Suzanne," Nick said, after powering down the window. "Is everything alright here?"

"Yeah, why do you ask?" She leaned down to be eye level with him.

"I just had another incident at my house. I came over here to warn you about it."

"Not another shooting?" She backed up as he opened the door and got out. He'd replaced his sling with a shoulder holster.

"No, but I saw a suspicious-looking character running on our property." Nick reached out and put both hands on Suzanne's waist. "He was very much out of place."

She swung around, paranoid that Randy had seen Nick's intimate move. She saw the boy ghost instead. His attention was locked onto her like a tractor beam.

"When I yelled at him, he ran off," Nick said.

"Could you tell who he was?" She was breathing faster, anxiety creeping in with the ghost's energies feeling heavy on her back.

"No. It was from a distance. But I could tell he was white and had long, black hair."

She covered her mouth, reminded of the Chicago bomber and the scary guy she'd seen with Silas.

"I was already carrying my Beretta, and I went after him, but lost him. From his tracks, it appeared he might've headed this way. I warned Emma before coming over here straightaway."

"He had long, dark hair?"

"Yes. And he was wearing a baseball cap," Nick said. "Oh, and he had a backpack. He was jogging, but his gait was odd."

Suzanne sucked in a breath and went quiet.

"I feel better now that I see you're safe," Nick said, looking around. He removed his holster and laid it on the car seat. He turned, touching her waist again, and pulled her closer. "Sorry, but I can't keep my hands off you." He leaned in to kiss her.

She stepped back, brushing his hands away. "What about Pam?"

"I told you before, I broke up with her. What about your Chicago boyfriend?"

"Same," she whispered.

"So, what's the problem?" He stepped closer.

"Nick, this isn't a good time—" She whipped around.

Randy was there, staring at them; the ghost was right next to him. "I thought you weren't getting close to anyone, Suzanne," Randy blurted out, starting to shake. "But it's just what I suspected." He ran back into the barn. She followed.

"Randy, no, it's not!" The boy ghost was no longer trying to get her attention. His focus was on Randy, who had thrown on his backpack and was pulling Barnie out of his stall. Randy jumped on Barnie's bare back and rode out into Hitchcock Woods. Unexpectedly, the ghost disappeared.

Suzanne stood there trying to decide if she and Nick should follow them. But for the first time in her life, she was afraid of Randy.

Chapter 41

"Sorry, Suze, but I'd say let him go," Nick said, waving his hand. "Everyone knows he's in love with you and has been since middle school, poor bastard." He threaded his fingers through hers and guided her into the sitting area of the tack room. "He'll get over what he just saw."

"It's not like that with us," she said, but didn't feel like telling Nick that Randy was gay, although she didn't at all understand why he was acting so jealous. "Listen, I have to tell you something, but I didn't want to do it in front of Randy," she said, pulling her hands away. "The guy who attacked me in Chicago had long, black hair."

"Was it curly?"

"Yes, and he also wore a baseball cap, a Cubs hat to be exact, and yellow rubber gloves."

Nick stood up. "Like these?" He held up a pair lying next to the sink.

"Don't touch them. They may be evidence."

"What're you saying?"

"I think we should go after him…right now," she said, feeling as if she were seeing part of the big picture with Randy. She led Misty back out of the stall. "No time to explain, but Randy's very upset. He might even be sick…in the head. Come on. Let's get the horses ready. You can ride Juice."

Just as they were mounting their horses, Nick said, "Do you smell smoke?"

Suzanne nodded, fearing the worst.

"I didn't receive any notices about a prescribed burning in the Woods. Have you?" he asked, referring to the regularly controlled burns designed to ensure ecosystem health and help reduce wildfire risk.

"No."

The boy ghost appeared, motioning for them to follow. He pointed to Clayborn Cut.

"Let's go," she shouted.

"I'm calling 911," he said, already on his cell.

"Make sure they notify Smitty," she shouted.

"What? Why?"

"Please, just do it," she cried, knowing in her knower that Smitty and his team would be desperately needed.

They galloped toward the source of the smoke billowing in the trees. In the thickest part of the forest surrounding the inner Horse Show Ring, Randy was using a handheld fire starter. Unbelievably, he was wearing a curly black wig and Cubs baseball cap as he set areas aflame.

Dismounting, she raced toward him, shouting: "Randy! Of all people, how could you do this to the place you love the most…and to me?"

"I'm not Randy."

"What? What're you talking about?" she yelled, pulling on his arm. "Just stop what you're doing. Give me that fire starter. Now!"

"You sick piece of shit," Nick yelled, tackling and pummeling him. They were rolling on the ground as the fires grew higher.

The horses backed up, ready to bolt. Suzanne didn't want them to get hurt. "Go home," she commanded them, pointing and hitting them on the rears. Immediately, the horses obeyed, running back toward the Clayborn barn. *They know what's best, thank God,* Suzanne thought.

Sirens screamed in the distance as her heart beat wildly, feeling like it was about to explode. Then she spotted her father riding in on Cole bareback. For a moment, it looked like JB was on Raziel riding in tandem with her father, but when she blinked and shook her head, the vision was gone. She waved her arms, calling him over, as Nick pinned Randy down. JJ slid off Cole and attempted to tackle both of the younger men. But he fumbled, writhing in pain, enabling Randy to wiggle out of Nick's grasping hands. Randy ran to the place he'd thrown down his backpack.

Suzanne chased him, fast on his heels. "Randy, don't you dare run away from me!"

"Stop right there," he said, pulling out the Colt .45 from his backpack and pointing it at her. "I'm not Randy."

"What? No! Listen to me. Put down the gun. Don't ruin everything you love. And that includes me."

"With Silas threatening us again, you've no idea how much we needed you to see us...protect us. But it's too late for that. We'll all be together soon...finally safe—in heaven." He raised the gun, pointing it at her heart as Nick and JJ ran toward them.

"Stop right there," Randy shouted at JJ and Nick, while pointing his gun at Nick. They halted.

"Put that goddamn gun down, Randy!" JJ shouted back, clutching his side.

"No! And y'all better stand still."

"Listen, Randy," Suzanne said, holding up her palms. "You and I are friends, forever friends. You know I love you. Please, put down the gun. We've got to get help, to put these fires out."

"I told you I'm not Randy!" he repeated, tears running down his cheeks as the sirens grew closer.

"You're not making any sense. If you're not Randy, who are you?" she shouted.

"I'm Jimmy." He lowered the gun slightly and released the cock.

"No, you're not, sweetie." She shook her head.

"Wait a minute," Randy said. His voice shifted lower and he looked up as if remembering something temporarily forgotten. "That's right. I'm Johnny! Johnny Johns!" He lifted the gun, pointed it at Nick, then Suzanne and re-cocked it. "I'm about to buy us all a one-way ticket straight out of this hell."

"No, no, Johnny, I know there's good in you, too," Suzanne said, immediately intuiting how the bombing, the three watchers she'd felt that day and the murders were all connected—Randy's mind had fractured into multiple personas because of his horrifying childhood. "You couldn't really hurt Jill or me in Chicago when you put us in the closet in the Americos Building. Could you?"

"That wasn't me; it was Randy. I didn't care at all about what happened to that redheaded Yankee. She just got in the way. And I was thrilled when the others got themselves dead," he said.

"Does that mean you killed Tomás?" Nick shouted.

"No. He and Lindley—they were just happy coincidences," he said. "But I might've killed them—I should've! They were perverts," he said, his voice rising and becoming higher pitched. "Just like the ones our mother was involved with, the ones who tortured us. God knows how she got involved in that sick cult. She just couldn't see it before it was too late, before they trapped her in it, along with us. Most people can't see how evil the pedos are until it's too late. You can't, either, Suze! But now, even with everything we did, you go off and get back with him," he said, pointing the gun at Nick. "And on top of that, you're even bringing in another guy, Shane." He sneered and spit.

"Listen to me! Nick and Shane are not pedophiles," she said.

"Maybe not, but they're still bad!"

She could feel his hysteria escalating. "Randy, please, just calm down," calling out the name of her friend, trying to get him to return.

"But I've got a plan to get out of this, even though we keep having to make changes," he said, spitting out the words.

"What do you mean by changes?"

"We wanted to exit out of this dark world...with you, Suze...in Chicago. We were all set. We were going to shoot ourselves right when the bomb exploded. But Randy wouldn't let us and ruined it. He made us let you and that redhead out of that closet! Then we were going to off Nick to make it look like the others. But Randy wouldn't let us go through with that either. So now, it's back to the original plan. We'll exit out now."

"Randy!" she shouted, trying again to pull her friend out of his delusion.

"Sorry, Suze, but you and me, I mean us, we're going to leave this sick world together, once and for all. I'm going to have to shoot you, then us. It's the only way."

"Now, you just simmer down, Randy Mackenzie," JJ said. "You aren't going to shoot nobody."

"Stand back, Mr. Clayborn. Or you're going to get it, too. We don't want to do it. But we will." His body shook and twisted, as though he were fighting the different voices in his head.

"Randy, I want to talk to Randy!" Suzanne said, pointing her finger at him. "There's a way out of this nightmare. It's possible to heal from the crimes committed against you and Jimmy. I'll help you," she said. "You're no longer my shadow, Randy. Stand in the light with me." She stepped in front of her father, intentionally choosing to put her body between him and the gun, holding out her hand. "I'm here, Randy."

His chest heaved as the boy ghost appeared behind him, frantically waving and jumping up and down.

"No, no, ghosts can't be in here. Ghosts aren't allowed!" she yelled to the boy no one else could see. But in a flash, she knew with utter certainty who the boy was and how he'd been desperately trying to save his brother—and her from his brother. Because the truth of it was felt in her heart: the boy ghost was Jimmy.

Randy turned in the direction Suzanne was speaking. But not seeing anything, he jerked back, hesitating just before firing the Colt, giving JJ the split second he needed to wrap his arms around Suzanne and turn, so his back was toward the gunfire.

Suzanne heard her father's "ow" and the whoosh of air from his lung deflating as they hit the ground, his arms still around her. Sirens wailed as police cars, a small brushfire truck with a water tank and an ambulance bounced on the sandy paths toward them.

Randy, in his delirium, threw the gun down beside Suzanne and ran toward Bluebird Hill, as if begging to be shot.

Although groaning loudly in pain, JJ rolled over to reach for Randy's gun.

"Daddy!" Suzanne cried.

JJ's hands were covered in blood, and useless. In the next second, Nick grabbed the Colt and sprinted after Randy.

When the two men reached the top of Bluebird Hill, Suzanne heard gunfire. Randy fell. But Nick's body also hit the ground. Suzanne screamed.

Chapter 42

Suzanne held her father in her arms, her hands over his wound, as she sobbed uncontrollably. From the sheriff's EMS vehicle, two uniformed paramedics ran toward them holding medical bags. Men from the brush truck were rushing to put out the fires.

A paramedic kneeled beside them, wearing a badge identifying him as Tom. "What's happened? What's going on, bud?" Tom asked in an unhurried, calm voice. Her father tried to respond, but he sputtered blood instead.

"He was shot in the back," Suzanne said.

"His name?" Tom asked.

"JJ."

"Okay, Mr. JJ, stay with me. We're going to fix you right up, right here," Tom said, continuing calmly.

"Active shooter! Stop," yelled an officer, holding another paramedic back from attending to Randy and Nick. Waiting for the go-ahead from Smitty, the paramedic stared at him with the intensity of a pit bull on high alert.

Ignoring the chaos surrounding them, Tom opened a bag and pulled out some medical shears. "Now you just hang on, Mr. JJ. I've got to take a look," Tom said, cutting JJ's shirt off.

Pulling away from his phone, Smitty shouted: "Got him, got him! Shooter apprehended!"

Another officer repeated: "Shooter apprehended!"

"Go! Go!" Smitty shouted, motioning to the waiting paramedic and two officers, pointing toward Randy and Nick, who were still on the ground.

In the confusion, Suzanne didn't understand why Smitty would be talking about another shooter. Hadn't Nick just shot Randy?

"Please stand back, miss," said Tom, unfolding an emergency blanket on the ground.

"I'm Suzanne. This is my father."

JJ winced as Tom rolled him over on the blanket to his left side. Carefully, Tom removed the blood-soaked shirt to find the source of blood flow. Suzanne could now see that it was between the right shoulder blade and spine. It didn't look good for his right lung. JJ was losing a tremendous amount of blood, even as the paramedic tried to stop it. "Please stand back, Miss Suzanne," he repeated.

"Of course," she said. She was covered in her father's blood. "Please, you have to save him."

As she waited helplessly, she saw that, at least, the firefighters were able to put out the blazes. The Woods were shrouded in eerie, smoldering smoke as she heard the wails of another ambulance arriving.

Suzanne watched as Randy, wounded on his right thigh, was placed on a gurney. A paramedic had already applied a tourniquet to his leg. Yet he seemed to be covered in more blood than her father. His eyes were closed and his body jerked in spasm. His paramedic was on a cell phone describing Randy's symptoms to someone on the other end.

"Didn't you just shoot Randy?" she asked Nick, who was walking fast and seemed okay apart from being disheveled and covered in sand.

"No, actually, I didn't," Nick said, looking at Smitty.

"What? I don't understand," she said.

"We have the shooter in custody," said Smitty.

"Are you sure?" Nick said.

"We had a tail on him, fortunately. In large part because of your recent report, Suzanne."

"Are you talking about that Silas guy?" she asked.

"When I saw Randy get hit, I dove to the ground," Nick said.

"That was the right decision and it probably saved your life," Smitty said. "Suzanne, rest assured, we've got it all under control. I'll fill you in later. Let's take care of these emergencies here first." His cell rang again.

"Yes," Suzanne said, her hands over her heart, its beat frantic, as she tried to keep her fears from taking hold of it.

When the paramedic finished with Randy's care, an officer read him his rights.

"I told you already. I'm not Randy. I'm Jimmy," Randy said, now restrained with plastic zip-tie handcuffs.

"I thought you said you were Johnny," Nick said. "Clearly, you're neither. What you are, dude, is a fucking psycho."

"You're right. I'm Johnny," Randy said, his face vacant and ashen. "I forgot for a minute. Jimmy's in the hospital. We put him there."

"No, Randy," said Smitty. "He's not." He turned to Suzanne and nodded before addressing Randy. "We'll get you the help you need. And then you can help us end this trafficking ring for good."

"Yes, Randy, you're the one who can finally help end it," Suzanne said.

"No, no, no," Randy said, still delusional. "What are you talking about? Jimmy's in the hospital. I put him in there to protect him from Silas."

"Oh, Randy," she said, shaking her head. She still felt an overwhelming pity and sorrow for him, and it hurt all over. He and his brother had been the victims of such heinous acts. It didn't seem fair that he should be punished further. Child abusers were monsters that created monsters in a vicious cycle of tragic proportions. It had to stop now.

Randy continued babbling incoherently about being Jimmy and Johnny when they loaded him into the ambulance. As it drove away, Suzanne turned back to her father, reaching again for his hand.

"Got it," Smitty said on his cell. "Excellent. Hold on." He turned back to Suzanne. "Our men have Silas, the man who just shot Randy. We suspect him of killing the others. He was a big player, if not the leader of the human trafficking ring. This is the break we needed. Excuse me." He turned back to his phone.

But that isn't going to save my father, Suzanne thought, catching sight of the boy ghost again, standing next to Smitty. Her heart confirmed he was Jimmy, but she was no longer alarmed by his presence in the Woods. Spirit had permitted it temporarily. *I feel it. I know it.* With her strong imagination, she envisioned sending him a note telepathically, one saying that she'd make sure Randy got the mental health care he needed. She watched Jimmy nod to her—he had obviously received her message—before a gloriole of light enfolded him and he disappeared. *I feel it. I know it*, she repeated in her mind.

Turning again to the paramedic working on her father, she asked, "Shouldn't you take my father to the hospital?"

"No time, too critical," said Tom after readying JJ's arm for an IV drip, while the other medic assisted. "When the bleeding stops, we'll start the IV. We can't risk moving him on the uneven surface of the trails until he has fluids," Tom said.

Suzanne reached for her father's booted ankles, being the only parts she could touch without getting in the way. "Daddy, please don't go; stay with me." She cried as she remembered how Gran had held a sacred trust and belief about her son, that he'd ultimately make the right choice for his life. Incredibly, in a strange turn of events that she never would've predicted, her father had chosen to take a bullet to the back near the right shoulder, saving her from being shot twice.

"Hang on, Mr. JJ," Tom said reassuringly. But when he turned and looked Suzanne directly in the eye, she knew that Tom understood he wouldn't.

"Daddy, please stay with me," she repeated, wishing she didn't know what was about to happen again because of what JB had prophesized. She now understood JB's awful riddle, *how two people close to her would die, although one might be her.* "Daddy—" The tears flowed down her cheeks.

"Now, don't you fret, my Suzy Q," JJ gasped out. "Funny thing, I've been meaning to tell you. I was prepared for this…'cause…I got myself pan…pancreatic cancer. It's bad…Wasn't gonna last…long. So this here…saved me…a lot of pain." He chuckled through coughs and faded in and out of consciousness.

"Keep him talking," Tom said, still holding the untapped IV drip.

"Daddy! You saved me. You're my hero! I love you so much. Stay here with me!"

His eyes were closed when he said, "You tell your mama I love her. And…" His voice was now a mere whisper. "I never meant to hurt you ever…I've always been so proud of you…love you, Peaches."

"Please don't—"

"No, baby, I'm glad to go now…for your good, my good, the highest good of—" He coughed.

"All," she whispered, remembering the phrase written in *The Secrets of Bears Repeating*. He'd read and internalized the teachings from his mother's writing after all.

"Hey, looky there," JJ said as if he would say more. He didn't.

She turned, but only saw the sunlight filtering softly through the trees and smoke, like slender peaceful spirits. In the aching silence that followed, her father's eyes opened wide once more before turning still. A stream of blood rolled from the corner of his mouth.

"He has passed," Tom said, even as both of the medics continued to try to bring him back. After their failed attempts, Tom turned to Suzanne and said, "I'm very sorry."

She nodded amid unstoppable tears, feeling the awful truth of it.

"Do you want to ride over to the hospital with us?" Tom asked, his voice soft. "Or meet us there?"

"Please...can you just give me a moment with him now...before we go?"

"Of course." They stood back before Tom pulled off his gloves and lumbered away with his cell phone to his ear.

Suzanne touched her father's hair and said a silent prayer for his soul. She also prayed for her mother, who'd be beyond devastated and lost without her soul mate.

With a gentle hand, Nick touched her shoulder. "I'm so sorry, Suzanne," he said. They embraced tenderly through a waterfall of tears. He looked up and pulled away as if something unexpected caught his eye. "Wow, can you see those?" He pointed to the area above JJ's body. "The round balls of light above your dad? That's amazing!"

Suzanne turned. "Yes," she said, but she saw more than just orbs; she saw the extraordinary. There, surrounding them in ethereal light, were the full-bodied spirits of her grandmother, grandfather and the man she recognized as Bears Repeating. They were shimmering as they encircled her father's body. Then she saw her father's young adult self, pink-cheeked, blond and strong, getting up from the gurney and stepping into a group hug with them. Just before he vanished in the mist with them, he turned and stepped back to her, smiling broadly, his deep dimples showing. He reached out to her cheek, and she felt his loving touch as a cool breeze. He came back like a gift, relieving her of the horror of having just watched him die in such a painful, violent way. With a wink, he rejoined the others and disappeared with them in sunbeams.

In the immediate wake of her father's physical death, her heart filled with a surprising emotion— gratitude, for being able to see this miracle with her accidental psychic gifts. Even more astounding was that Nick had also seen what was outside of his ordinary reality, even though to his eyes, the spirits appeared as glowing balls of light. To Suzanne, it was a good sign for their rekindled relationship.

They stood spellbound in the dead silence until, from behind the curtain of smoke still clinging to the humid air, Suzanne heard a voice. It was rich, baritone and southern. She smiled knowing that it was JB's singular voice, speaking for many, perhaps even for Bears Repeating and for the heart and soul of Hitchcock Woods. The voice said: "We're not ghosts and never have been. We, who love you more than you know, are your spirit team now."

Chapter 43

A year after Jefferson Beaufort Clayborn Junior was laid to rest in the Clayborn family cemetery, Suzanne entered the state psychiatric hospital in Columbia, South Carolina. Randy had been confined there after having been charged with numerous crimes and diagnosed with dissociative identity disorder, previously known as multiple personality disorder. The court's forensic psychologists stated that the disorder was characterized by the presence and maintenance of at least two distinct personality states within a person. Randy had at least three. Memory gaps beyond ordinary forgetfulness were typical. And in 90 percent of the cases, the disorder was caused by overwhelming trauma, such as extreme childhood abuse.

Randy's charges included one count of involuntary manslaughter that resulted in her father's death, two counts of possession of an illegally acquired firearm during the commission of attempted murder and two counts of conspiracy to use illegally acquired explosive materials for attempted murder and to cause destruction in the Americos Building, Chicago. The jury later found him not guilty by way of insanity on all counts, but he was ordered to remain in the psychiatric facility for up to ten years. The state of Illinois had agreed to the verdict so Randy wasn't required to be extradited for another trial out of state.

"Hello, Randy," Suzanne said when she sat down with him in the facility's conference room. The walls, tables and chairs were all white. The space smelled of disinfectant. A male attendant in hunter-green scrubs stood quietly and observant in the corner. "How're you doing?"

"Better, I guess," he said softly. Randy wore a navy-blue sweatshirt and sweatpants. "Since I've been here, I've finally been able to mourn Jimmy...and your father. I loved them both...very much...despite," he said, tears welling in his eyes.

"I know, Randy," she said, her hand over her throat.

He looked at her blankly before hiding his face with his hands. "Oh, Suzanne, I'm so, so sorry for what I did to you." His breathing was labored through his fingers. "I can't believe you're even here, that you'd ever want anything else to do with me," he cried. "I don't deserve it." He looked up, his lips trembling.

Alarmed, the attendant started toward them, but Suzanne motioned for him to halt. *It's okay*, she mouthed, her palm held out. Surprisingly, the attendant returned to his corner.

Prior to her visit, Smitty and a court psychologist had prepared Suzanne for what to expect from Randy, that clinically insane defendants with dissociative identity disorder might be able to act perfectly normal, rational and remorseful, even while remaining in delusional states of mind. They might not remember the crimes committed by their alter personalities, but even if they do, they might deny they ever happened. Randy seemed to understand the crimes his alter personalities had committed and was taking full responsibility for them. Perhaps his meds and therapies had already been effective.

"Granted, some folks might not understand why I'm here," Suzanne said, looking sideways at the attendant. It was difficult to explain to others the unnamable allegiance and pity she still felt for her childhood friend. But holding Randy responsible for being a victim of heinous child abuse would've been like blaming newborn sparrows for falling from the nest too soon. "I came today because I want you to know that we've forgiven you," she said, exhaling.

"I don't know how. I'm not sure how I can ever face your mama again. I'm so ashamed," he said, shaking his head.

"Well, I'm not gonna lie," she said. "It took Mama a whole lot longer to forgive you for what you did to me…and Dad. But after the shock of it all started to wear off a bit, and the Florida doctors confirmed that Dad had less than a month to live anyway, she was able to see the big picture. In my case, she's come to understand what extreme childhood trauma can do and cause. And with Dad, she's come to appreciate that he went out of this life the way he wanted—as a hero." She felt tears rising and swallowed.

Randy nodded with a half-smile.

"But the main reason we can forgive you is because we know the real you. And the Randy we know would never do anything to hurt me, my coworkers, my father or even Nick."

"No, I never wanted to hurt you or anyone."

She breathed deep and placed her hands flat on the table. "In truth, I don't blame you…at least not completely. I blame mostly Silas and all the evil predators involved in human trafficking and child exploitation." She made fists before relaxing them.

"Thank you, Suzanne. Your forgiveness means the world to me," he said.

She had learned in the trials of Randy, Silas and the others that Randy and his brother had both been raped and tortured in their childhoods by their mother's handlers. Other evidence proved Silas had kidnapped Jimmy in Spartanburg, before ultimately killing him with a horseshoe, in almost identical fashion to the way he'd murdered Tomás. Randy admitted that he'd found Jimmy's body in the stables where they lived with their aunt, removed it and drove to Aiken to bury it in Hitchcock Woods.

"Even before the trial, I knew Jimmy must've been buried somewhere in Hitchcock Woods," Suzanne said. "It was the only way he would've been allowed in."

"Allowed in?"

When Suzanne explained to Randy about her ability to see ghosts and how they were not allowed in Hitchcock Woods, as well as sharing the backstory about Jimmy's ghost, Randy didn't even look surprised. He accepted the idea as if it weren't unusual. He simply said, "Well, that explains why you've always been so brave."

"I'm not following," she said.

"Anyone who can see ghosts like you has got to be more courageous than the average person," he said. "Or God wouldn't have given you that gift."

"I've never thought of it in that way," she said, taken aback by the insightfulness of Randy, even though he was a mental patient. "Thank you for that," she said with genuine appreciation.

He nodded; his eyes downcast.

"I've learned a lot about my gift, as you call it, since leaving Chicago."

He looked up. "Like what?"

"Like all along, I was seeing more than what I called ghosts." She shook her head. "There are, in fact, many types of beings which exist on varying realms all around us. They're invisible to most people. But sometimes, I can see or just feel them all. There are dark beings, and I'm not gonna lie about that either: they're scary as hell. But what excites me about my ability and gives me the most hope is that, incredibly, I've also been seeing and encountering angels and other higher spiritual beings. Only I didn't realize I was doing that," she said, thinking of JB as well as the spirit children dancing around the homeless guy in Chicago. "But then, I've never bothered to learn about my psychic abilities before. Mainly, because I was scared of having them. I didn't see them as gifts. I didn't want to have them," she said, breathing out hard. "It wasn't like they came wrapped in colorful paper and tied up with pretty bows."

"Ha, I got you." He nodded.

"I just wanted to be normal. So I tried to do the impossible."

"The impossible?"

"I tried to run away from myself."

"Is that why you left South Carolina?"

"In part." She nodded. "But here's the thing I learned. You can't heal your wounds or use your abilities by running away from them...without a lot of suffering."

"I get that." He rested his chin in his palm.

"Ironically, because of the nightmares in my life, I was finally able to know who I am, accept my God-given psychic and creative abilities with gratitude, and start using them correctly, which, in effect, has solved my own life's riddle," she said.

He smiled with what looked like astounding empathy, but just as quickly, turned his head and stared out the window with a blank expression.

She wanted to ask him more about Jimmy. There were still a few unanswered questions that hadn't come out in the trials. As she was trying to form the proper words, Randy spoke. "I can tell you want to ask me something," he said as if reading her mind.

"Yes," she said, nodding. "There is something I wanted to better understand...about Jimmy. But I don't want to put you back in a bad space."

"Don't worry. I won't get upset. I promise."

"Well, I was curious: Why did you move Jimmy's body from Spartanburg? Why didn't you go to your aunt and just let the police handle it?"

"Because, Suze, I wasn't in my right mind, remember?" He grinned and looked at her sideways, like he'd done so many times before.

"You must be getting better to make jokes. But I'm serious."

"Jimmy went missing for a few days, and Aunt Jane filed a missing person's report. A week later, I found him in the stables at the farm where my Aunt Jane worked. And I knew Silas had killed him after doing God knows what to him. When I realized it, I think that's when my mind really snapped apart."

"How'd you know it was Silas who did it?"

"There was a dead snake next to Jimmy when I found him, like a calling card."

"Oh, dear Lord," she said, recalling the snake tattoo on the back of Silas' bald head.

"It happened just before we planned to come back to Aiken together. And we'd almost made it back to you, where I thought we'd be safe from them," he said breathing hard. "I didn't want to face life without Jimmy, even in Aiken," he said, tears falling.

"It's okay. You don't have to explain."

"No, I want to," he said. "I didn't want Jimmy to be gone, and I especially didn't want Silas to know where to find Jimmy ever again. So, I bundled up his body and brought him back with me to Aiken. I buried him deep in the Woods, where we hid out the night Mama died.

Obviously, I was messed up in a lot of ways to do that, to think it was a good idea. It made sense at the time. Because it sort of helped me to pretend Jimmy was still alive. After a while, I didn't have to pretend. I believed he was alive. In me."

She held her stomach without comment, feeling his deep wounds and the great love for his brother.

"Hey, I've been making progress on the renovation plans for opening Gran's artists' colony," Suzanne said, breaking the silence with a lighter subject.

"Yeah, I heard about it." He wiped his eyes.

She was also in the process of creating the boutique advertising agency with Shane, but decided not to mention it. "We're aiming for the New Year to open. We've already been interviewing a variety of artist candidates to sponsor."

"That's wonderful, Suze. Your grandmother would be so proud of you. That reminds me," he said. "Did I ever tell you that Jimmy was an artist?" He pulled out a folded, wrinkled paper from his pocket. "Well, sort of," he said, handing it to her. "He liked to draw, and I like keeping this with me." He unfolded the paper and handed it to her.

"Wow, it's good." A black-ink illustration showed a teenaged Randy with his arm around someone who looked identical to the boy ghost she'd last seen in

Hitchcock Woods. "You're standing in front of the Masters sign at the Augusta National Golf Club."

"Yeah, we were able to go to the Practice Rounds that year, thanks to your mama."

"My mama? I didn't know that!"

"It was through a special wish program at the church," he said. "Your mama was always helping out people like us," he said, looking down. "She even bought the clothes we wore that day."

"As flashy as Mama can be, you and I are probably the only ones who know she prefers her giving to be in secret."

He nodded. "I've always loved her. She's such a good mother. Anyway, Jimmy drew that picture from a photograph taken outside the gates."

"I must say this drawing's excellent. Randy, your brother was a true artist," she said with a nod of astonishment. Looking at the illustration again, a granite memorial took shape in Suzanne's imagination.

"Yeah, I thought so too, especially for a little kid. I was proud of him."

"Randy, I don't want to upset or offend you, but I have to ask," she said, wanting to tread lightly. She softened her voice. "Have you decided what to do with Jimmy's body...um...after?"

"I guess you know that it's been approved for me to accompany Detective Smitty out to Hitchcock Woods to get him," he said. "No one can find Jimmy's body but me." He shook his head and his eyes dimmed. "I don't know what to do…after. I'd like to give him a proper burial, but don't know how or where."

"Well, I've just had an idea about it. How about the Clayborn estate graveyard? Or better yet, we can start a new one next to it, especially for our artists. That way, Jimmy would be our first official artist to reside at the Aiken Artists' Colony."

"You're too good to us," he said, tears again marking his face.

"Oh, Randy. I'm not trying to be good…it's more like…I'm at a place where I'm no longer running away from myself or my abilities," she said. "But to get there, I had to get quiet for hours and hours, listening to my heart in silent meditation. That's where all of our answers and masterpieces are waiting for us to find. Right here," she said, patting her heart. "You don't even have to be psychic to do it."

He smiled.

"In any event, right now, I feel very strongly about creating a memorial for Jimmy. And I'm already seeing a special, beautiful monument in my mind's eye. It could be designed, perhaps even by one of our resident artists, as a way to honor Jimmy and all the poor souls who've been so terribly hurt by the evil people who prey on innocent children." She paused to take a breath.

"Well…whether that idea works out or not, whatever we end up doing, I just want to make sure we never forget about the Jimmys of the world," she said, handing the drawing back.

"Please, I'd like you to have it," he said, holding up his palms. "Consider it a thank-you for all you've done for us—from me and Jimmy."

"Your hour's about up, ma'am," the attendant said.

"Just a few more minutes, please," Suzanne said before turning back to Randy. "I've one last thing to share with you before I have to leave. I'm not sure you got the full story about Silas and the others in here," she said, handing him an article she'd clipped from the *Aiken Standard* newspaper. "But I wanted you to know that this justice happened primarily because of you…and your testimony."

Aiken Police Bust Human Trafficking Ring and End Murder Spree

A man convicted on two counts of first-degree murder, one count of attempted murder and of leading a human trafficking, prostitution and child exploitation ring will be spending the rest of his life in federal prison with no chance for parole.

Silas Collins, 49, a resident of Aiken County was found guilty of murdering Robert Lindley, 35, a professor at the University of South Carolina Aiken (campus); and Tomás Sanchez, 28, an Argentinian polo

player on the international circuit and temporary
resident of Aiken, according to a joint statement issued
Wednesday by the U.S. Attorney's Office, Aiken Police
Department and the Aiken County Sheriff's Office.

Collins was found guilty by a jury on all counts,
along with ten other codefendants, including his
primary partner in crime, Darrell Boggs, 45, a former
resident of Atlanta, who received two forty-year
sentences to be served consecutively, according to the
statement.

Collins was apprehended in Hitchcock Woods
while he was in the process of attempting to murder
another unnamed victim, who was a key witness to
many of Collins' crimes and provided the necessary
testimony for these convictions.

In addition to two local murders that sent shock
waves through the community, evidence presented at
the trial established that Collins and his codefendants
were running a South Carolina branch of a human
trafficking ring based in Atlanta. They preyed on mostly
female victims and minors, forcing them on an almost
daily basis to have sex with numerous "johns" each
night for years, until they were either murdered or able
to escape.

The ten other defendants named in the case also
were found guilty of the crimes related to the
conspiracy to commit human trafficking and received
prison sentences ranging from twenty to forty years,
according to the statement.

"These long sentences are just, and they send a
clear message that human trafficking, prostitution and
child exploitation will not be tolerated in South

Carolina," said Detective Richard Smith, Aiken Police
Department. "The defendants in this case preyed on
some of the most vulnerable among us. Their heinous
crimes have a devastating impact, especially on child
victims who are left with severe emotional scars.
Without the coordinated efforts of the investigative
team and the brave testimony of numerous key
witnesses, these atrocities may never have come to light
and been prosecuted. I'm pleased to announce the ring
has been busted, here and in Atlanta, and the victims
rescued are receiving the medical care and services
needed."

Smith concluded the statement by saying:
"Many folks have asked us what they can do to help
prevent human trafficking and child exploitation crimes
in the future. And my answer is always this: if you see
something suspicious in this regard, please say
something. Report it to your local Human Trafficking
Task Force as soon as possible." #

Randy looked up from the article with a sense of
relief and bewilderment, as if he'd awakened from a dark
nightmare into morning sunlight. "Thank you, Suzanne,"
he said with quivering lips, standing up. He held the
article to his heart and wept silently, as the attendant led
him out of the room.

As she exited the facility, Suzanne wiped away her
own tears as she saw two light orbs hovering under a tree
near the entrance. In the next instant, they expanded and
transformed into the full-bodied images of Henrietta and

Bears Repeating, smiling and waving. They looked like real people, only with an otherworldly glow about them.

Bears Repeating wore sunglasses, his bangs combed into a pompadour with braids on the sides, and a dress jacket like in the one photo she'd seen of him. Her grandmother appeared as a happy, beautiful thirtysomething from the 1950s. No one else in the parking lot could see them, of course. She waved back, as their images faded from her sight. But in that luminous moment, Suzanne knew they weren't ghosts. She understood that JB was not only her Joe Loco, as her grandmother had suggested, but also the true Joe Loco, a spirit guide or perhaps even her guardian angel, who'd taken on a different appearance for her benefit.

Their presence felt like a blessing of what she'd just done, of coming to the hospital and offering both forgiveness to Randy and a final resting place for the real Jimmy. It also seemed to be a confirmation of her life's direction. That she was finally on the right path, embracing and sharing her gifts for good, even as her spirit team continued to whisper and show guidance from somewhere in the ethers, and between her heart and the heart of the Woods.

Acknowledgments

In bringing a novel to life, which can take many years, there are myriad obstacles to overcome. But writing the Acknowledgments is not one of them. It's here that I'm finally able to express gratitude publicly to all the wonderful and gracious people who've helped me along the way.

First and foremost, I want to thank my husband and first beta reader Paul Jarvie, and our sons, Dane and Luke. Your love has always moved me in profound ways, and I am forever thankful for your presence in my life and work. I also want to recognize my sister Leigh Weibel Everett, brother Marc Weibel and sister-in-law Sharon Welch Weibel, extended Weibel family as well as my extra-large Jarvie family for being the greatest of cheerleaders.

To my brilliant circle of editors and writer friends who have supported this novel, I must say I'm both lucky and grateful to be the beneficiary of your excellent input. Rita Robinson, your editorial wisdom is greatly appreciated. Madeline Hopkins, your eagle eyes and stamp of approval have always given me the confidence to proceed with the Great American Novel. Gretchen Stelter, I am in awe of you and your editing talents. And to Lesley Ward, thank you for sharing your equestrian knowledge, enthusiasm and editorial expertise with me. I thank you all!

A round of applause goes to all of my beta readers including Susan Jarvie, Margaret McKibben Key and Mary Ruczko Pate. Susan, thank you for always offering to read anything I write and for your analytical approach to every detail. This helps more than you know. Mary, only you and I know the backstory of the "bam-bam" scene, and it still makes me smile. But it was your specific suggestions for the end that helped make the final chapter really sing, and I appreciate it. Heather Locke Cairney and the "Ladies of the Book Club" in Phoenix earn special praise for reading an early rough draft. And to my friend and essential oil specialist, Allison Contris, thank you for providing the oil recipes used in this novel (and by me).

Long trails of appreciation go to my lifetime friend, equestrian go-to, and fellow Hitchcock Woods' lover, Margaret McKibben Key. Margaret, you're always there to lend an ear and provide help and encouragement. I'm also grateful to you for introducing me to a number of people in Aiken who ended up playing starring roles in my story as author of this novel.

Aiken's Greg and Betty Ryberg are two of the most generous, bright and entertaining people I've ever met. When they heard about my "Hitchcock Woods writing project," they immediately offered their lovely carriage house apartment, with close proximity to the Woods, for my research and writing. I am especially appreciative of them and for the opportunity.

Much gratitude goes to Aiken and its equestrian community, including Barbara Morgan (of Morgan Cut trail fame) along with the talented Aiken photographer Shelly Schmidt. Both of these lovely women walked the sandy wooded trails of Hitchcock with me, pointing out key features and introducing me to their entertaining Tao of Dinky Donkey. For sharing their local realty knowledge and equestrian adventures with me years ago when this novel was a mere concept, I also want to acknowledge and thank Charles and Tara Bostwick, Deirdre Stoker Vaillancourt and Tracey Turner.

A special note of appreciation goes to the Hitchcock Woods Foundation for continuing to give the public such a beautiful slice of forested heaven to enjoy. Dear readers, this is a foundation worthy of support, and I'd like to invite you to contribute to it by visiting hitchcockwoods.org/support.

And last but not least, I thank YOU for reading *The Woods of Hitchcock*, which has been a labor of love. As with my first novel, it's my wish and prayer that you have been entertained and found something useful and inspiring within…yourself.

Interview with the Author
Ann W. Jarvie

What is your novel about?

The Woods of Hitchcock is a thriller about a psychically gifted Chicago copywriter and victim of violence who returns to South Carolina's equestrian country to solve a riddle involving murder, the metaphysical and the secrets of her eccentric family.

Thematically, it could be described as a hero's journey of a woman running away from the literal ghosts of her past until she discovers the secret gifts of spirit within herself.

Is *The Woods of Hitchcock* the sequel to your first novel, *The Soul Retrieval*?

Yes, although it's not a direct sequel, and the styles are much different. The heroine of *The Soul Retrieval,* Henrietta Clayborn, was a thirtysomething in the 1950s in an epic novel, but she plays a mentoring role as an eightysomething in this contemporary thriller. *The Woods of Hitchcock* centers on Henrietta's granddaughter, Suzanne Clayborn, but it's also a story that can stand on its own.

What was the inspiration for this novel?

When I was growing up in Aiken County, South Carolina, and first heard the name "Hitchcock Woods," even as a young teen, I honestly thought it sounded more like a suspense novel than the enchanting equestrian forest preserve that it is. Perhaps I was seeing into my own future. While I was living in Chicago and started writing novels, I kept coming back to Hitchcock Woods, walking and riding horses in it with family and friends, eventually realizing it, as well as Chicago, would be the ideal settings for my fictional character, Suzanne Clayborn, and her suspenseful hero's journey. Also, I enjoy paying homage to my southern roots, bringing attention to admirable highlights such as the Hitchcock Woods Foundation, which provides, maintains and protects a wonderful natural resource for public use.

Does Hitchcock Woods have anything to do with the filmmaker, Alfred Hitchcock?
Not at all. But I've intentionally included a few subtle Hitchcockian film themes and plot devices in *The Woods of Hitchcock*—for fun, surprise and added suspense. I've even included something that might be likened to one of Alfred's famous "cameo" appearances, and I challenge readers to find it!

Hitchcock Woods was in fact named after its founder, Thomas Hitchcock, who was one of the leading American polo players in the latter part of the nineteenth century and a hall-of-fame horse trainer known as the father of American steeplechase horse racing. In 1939, the Thomas Hitchcock family donated 1,120 acres of its land for public use, while establishing a foundation (now Hitchcock Woods Foundation) to protect and preserve the land in perpetuity. Later, the Foundation added other lands for a total of 2,100 acres today, making it the largest privately owned urban forest preserves in the country.

Are the horse trails you describe in Hitchcock Woods real or imaginary? Does the Americos Building in Chicago exist?

With the exception of the fictional Clayborn, Davidson and Vaughn homes and the Clayborn Cut, I have tried to present Hitchcock Woods, its trails, features and urban surroundings as true to life as possible. If there is an error, I respectfully ask forgiveness from those who know better.

The Americos Building is pure fiction, although my descriptions of its surroundings in Chicago's Loop are based upon my experience working and living in that area.

Why do you use bird themes and symbols in your novels?

The use of birds is not only a Hitchcockian theme element, it's also something I enjoy. Unlike Alfred's films, however, I've featured birds as positive symbols in my novels mainly because they remind me of my late father. My dad was an Eagle Scout who had earned a Bird Study

Merit Badge. His love of birds stayed with him throughout his life, and he inspired a fondness for them in me. He regularly fed and treated as pets the wild birds in the backyard of our Carolina home, although the thought of caging them was abhorrent to him. If he were ever late in feeding his "pets," numerous sets of cardinals would gather just outside the windows looking for him. And he's the only person I've ever seen who could pick up and hold a wild duck that came to him.

Why did you include ghosts in this novel?
I've always loved a good ghost story and also tales with forbidden secrets and metaphysical elements. But rather than writing about them in the horror genre, I wanted to create a contemporary thriller. So, I started to imagine what it was truly like to see, feel and hear ghosts as well as higher spiritual beings. Consequently, these psychic abilities kept creeping into my main character's profile. I decided to go with them in a big way to satisfy my own interests and to enhance overall suspense.

Is *The Secrets of Bears Repeating* manuscript, mentioned in this novel, something that is written?
In part, yes. Like my character Henrietta, I started compiling my list of ancient universal truths worth repeating as I wrote *The Soul Retrieval*. Also, like Henrietta, my intention is to publish it one day…when it's ready.

How might book clubs and readers connect with you?

I'd love to hear from readers through my website and social media. I also welcome the opportunity to speak with book clubs online or in person. There's a contact form, especially for book clubs, on my website. My book news and links to my current social media pages also can be found on my website. Looking forward to visiting with you there! **ANNWJARVIE.COM**

Afterward

Thank you for reading **The Woods of Hitchcock**, which is the sequel to **The Soul Retrieval: A Novel**, where the story of Henrietta and Joe Loco/Bears Repeating begins.

To stay posted on the third novel in this series, be sure to follow Ann on her website, where you'll also find her social media and retailer links. ANNWJARVIE.COM

In the meantime, please enjoy this overview and first-chapter excerpt from the award-winning novel, **The Soul Retrieval** by Ann W. Jarvie.

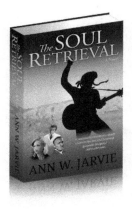

Inspired by a true story, ***The Soul Retrieval*** is a suspenseful tale of love, loss and healing which follows traumatized southern beauty Henrietta Clayborn as she moves between her home in a small South Carolina town and the New Mexico Apache reservation whose spontaneous healings keep drawing her physician husband back. Tortured by her awful secrets, Henrietta struggles to thrive in either locale, but it is her unlikely friendship with Joe Loco—an eccentric Native American mystic with an Elvis fetish and a gift for healing—that shows her the way to be whole again.

Set in the late 1950s, ***The Soul Retrieval*** is richly woven with spiritual insights but also deadly secrets, forbidden healings, a murder mystery, stunning scenery and an unforgettable cast of characters.

A story of transcendent and inspiring power that is both entertaining and enlightening, readers will be cheering for the uptight woman from South Carolina to push through her fears of the forbidden as she searches for truth and healing, faces great obstacles on the frontier of self and ultimately becomes more than she ever thought possible.

Chapter 1

Something in the air shifted when Joe Loco limped into the doctor's cottage. Maybe because the sun shot through the window just as he opened the door, and light was now spilling over the kitchen table like a radiant tablecloth. Or maybe it was because of the way Joe was dressed. Today, he wore a trendy sport coat, colorful striped shirt and baggy black pants—all over blue-suede moccasins. He had coaxed his black bangs into a soaring pompadour, higher than Henrietta had ever seen. Granted it was all the craze for fashionable young men that year. Everything Elvis—people just couldn't get enough of the hot young singer. But Joe wore his puffed-up hair with a shoulder-length braid on each side of his light-brown face.

"Henrietta, you remember Joe, right?" her husband said.

"Yes, Jeff, of course," she replied. *How could I possibly forget someone so … so strange?* she thought. "We met on your first mission here. How've you been, Joe?"

Joe shifted a full brown paper bag into his left arm. "Never been better, thanks for asking, Mrs. Clayborn. And you?" He reached for her hand.

Joe's baritone voice was exactly as Henrietta remembered it: surprisingly accent-free, though he occasionally sprinkled his speech with a few Apache words. His smile was as sweet as melted milk chocolate and, unlike most Apaches she'd met, his face held delicate features. Some might say he was downright pretty. He moved with a childlike enthusiasm despite a limp. His clothes were usually colorful and fashion-forward, but always with a native twist. He was an attractive oddball and a happy curiosity—Henrietta was glad to see him again.

But when their hands touched, his brow furrowed and his eyes narrowed.

"Wait. You're the same, but different, *ha'aa*, yes?" Joe said. His hand lingered on hers. He cocked his head to the left then right, studying Henrietta's eyes and the area around her perfectly coiffed blond hair.

"Well, um, I suppose," she said. She pulled her hand away and looked down. *Dear God, what's that nut looking at?* Henrietta thought.

Out of the corner of her eye, she peeked over at her husband, who'd thankfully returned to his seat at the table and was reading the newspaper.

"You're still off today, I presume?" Jeff asked, eyes on his paper. He either didn't hear Joe's question to Henrietta or had chosen to ignore it.

"*Ha'aa*, yes. I'm needed at the Sunrise Ceremonies most of the week," Joe said. "I hope that's still okay, Doc." He smiled, returning to his previous upbeat manner.

Henrietta let out the breath she was holding.

"Yes, of course," Jeff answered as he looked up. "So, what brings you by this morning?"

"Well, I had a meeting with the elders earlier today and wanted to see Altie before going to—" Joe was interrupted by a knock on the door. "Ah, here she is now."

Altie, Joe's petite wife, glided in like a graceful Apache ballerina. She wore a simple blue and green cotton dress with matching jacket, but also a stunning large turquoise-stone necklace. "*Yati' dahbidá'*, good morning," she said, speaking in the stilted, almost inflectionless way so common among Apaches. "The stars and sun are in agreeable positions for the ceremonies." Although she had learned English words and grammar perfectly—albeit a bit formally—at the Agency school on the reservation, Altie, like most

Apaches, pronounced her "th" sounds with a "da" giving her speech a distinctive accent.

"Henrietta tells me you offered to take the kids to the Sunrise Ceremonies," Jeff said, after they all greeted her. "That's an incredible honor for them, Altie."

"*Ha'aa*, the honor is mine. I should get the little one ready," Altie said, but Henrietta knew it was meant as a question. Altie never seemed to ask anything in a direct way.

"Thanks, Altie," Henrietta said, "but if you don't mind, I'll keep him here until he wakes up from his morning nap." She was referring to Jefferson Junior, her eighteen-month-old son. "We'll join up with you and the girls down at the ceremonies in a little while." Unexpectedly, tears stung Henrietta's eyes, but she discreetly rubbed them with a handkerchief from her pocket.

When Henrietta looked up, Joe was staring at her while whispering something to Altie in Athabascan, their native Apache language. When his eyes turned away from hers and met Altie's, Henrietta sensed some invisible communication passing between them. Her stomach churned.

In the uncomfortable silence that followed, Henrietta walked out of the kitchen toward the staircase. "Girls," she called out, "Miss Altie's here; let's make it snappy."

"We'll be down in a minute, Mama," one of the twins yelled.

"Sorry for the wait, Altie," Henrietta said. She fanned her face, feeling a rush of heat on her neck and perspiration forming between her breasts despite the summer morning's cool breeze.

"On the way over, I picked up my costume for tonight's ceremonies," Joe said, turning to Jeff. "Do you mind if I try it on here?"

"Not at all," Jeff said, taking a sip of coffee. "There's a bathroom around that wall; help yourself."

Joe limped out as Henrietta and Altie chatted about the Sunrise festivities. After a few minutes, Henrietta paused.

"Whew, I don't know why I'm so hot this morning." She pulled her hair up off her shoulders before searching the refrigerator for ice tea. Shutting it as she straightened, she stopped abruptly, stunned by what she saw: Joe Loco was standing in the middle of their kitchen wearing nothing more than old work boots and what appeared to be a giant flannel diaper.

"Looks good, *ha'aa*?" Joe said with an impish grin.

For a moment, everyone was speechless.

Joe's skin was a shade lighter than most Apaches living in Medichero. Henrietta thought of it as being more like the tawny color of sunbaked straw. On the skinny side, with that piled-up hair, and in the ridiculous diaper,

Joe looked like he might have been an escapee from a mental institution for half-naked scarecrows, rather than a Medichero Apaches. He was also sockless and Henrietta saw for the first time why he limped: most of his left calf muscle was missing.

"That's your costume?" Henrietta said with eyes still wide. She had expected Joe to come out of the bathroom wearing the typical fringed buckskin and a headdress made of eagle feathers. She covered her mouth with her hands as she looked over at Jeff, who was snickering like a schoolboy and shaking his head.

"Not quite," Joe Loco said, donning a mask with the face and long ears of a donkey.

Jeff was laughing out loud now.

"Joe is dancing the part of the sacred *Libayé* this year," Altie said, as though that explained everything.

"I thought the Sunrise Ceremonies were a rite of passage for your tribe's teenage girls, not, um, incontinent donkeys," Henrietta said. She laughed, unable to resist being pulled into Joe's indigenous comedy.

"The *Libayé* teaches many lessons," Joe said. He removed his mask.

Jeff smiled and gave Henrietta a wink.

"The *Libayé* is a clown-like character who is supposed to look contrary to four beautiful and powerful Mountain Spirit dancers," Altie said. "They will perform together for the maidens and an audience at sunset tonight around a great bonfire."

"I see. Then why are you dressing so early?" Henrietta asked. She looked down at his heavy work boots. They were oversized and had no shoelaces; their tongues arched out grotesquely like some rotting, leathered form of aloe vera leaves.

"I wanted to make sure my diaper and boots fit well enough for this evening's dance now because I'll be tied up for most of the afternoon as one of the singers." He headed back toward the bathroom to change.

After he left, Frannie ran into the kitchen, breathless. "I'm here, Miss Altie!"

"Me, too," Annie seconded.

The nine-year-old twins with blond braids were dressed identically in blue dungarees, pink plaid blouses tied at the waist, and white sneakers. They sat next to their dad and started eating the egg biscuits Henrietta had laid out earlier.

Joe returned fully dressed, but he had replaced his sport coat with a white, fringed buckskin overshirt. His pompadour had been re-combed and pomaded into a noticeably higher crest.

"Altie, I forgot to ask, do you or Joe want anything to drink, or how about some breakfast?" Henrietta asked. She tried not to stare at Joe's big hair.

"I've got coffee and plenty of eggs and bacon left. Have y'all ever had grits?"

"Sweet hero. If you feed me …" Joe said and struck the pose made famous by Elvis Presley. He began strumming an invisible guitar, bobbing his shoulders and singing a slightly altered version of a hit song: "I'll be your teddy bear, put a chain around my neck, and lead me anywhere … oh just let me eat … and I'll be your teddy bear."

The girls squealed and applauded.

"Thank you, thank you very much," Joe said, taking a dramatic bow.

Altie rolled her eyes. Jeff was laughing again.

"Okay, Joe, I get it. You'd like some breakfast. How about you, Altie?" Henrietta said, smiling.

"No, thank you. We ate earlier, but it is hard for Joe to say no to food. The girls and I can go now," Altie said. They were kissed and out the door just as the telephone rang.

"I'll get it; it's probably Dr. Belzer," Jeff said.

Henrietta watched her husband as he left the kitchen, and kept staring long after he had disappeared from the room. When she turned back to Joe, he was giving her that intense look once again.

"It's just as Bear foretold," the Apache said. He closed his eyes and moved his hands in small circles with palms out. "The fire's burning, but no one's home in your teepee."

"Excuse me?"

"You don't feel like yourself, you're feeling vacant and disconnected, like something's missing." Joe spoke as he opened his eyes.

She gaped at him in stunned silence before whispering: "How ... why would you say something like that?" Henrietta's heart thumped in her chest as she nervously glanced toward the living room. Jeff was still talking on the phone.

"Your soul speaks volumes through your eyes."

"You see something in my eyes?" And she rubbed them again with her handkerchief.

"I see what was there, what should be there, but is not now."

"Don't be silly. I'm fine. My eyes were just watering, that's all." She winced, knowing that it wasn't true, hating that she'd become such a liar.

"It's okay, I'm here to help," he said. He placed his folded hands on the table after sitting down.

His smile and disarming empathy surprised Henrietta, but she wasn't going to be moved by what seemed like a sweet and insightful gesture. Joe Loco was absolutely the last person in the world she'd choose to confide in.

"Thanks, but there's really nothing to help with. I'm fine." She was determined to maintain her fiction, though her stomach tightened and jumped as if trying to digest rocks. Mechanically, she started to reheat some cooked bacon in the fry pan, stirred the grits she'd kept warm and cracked open a few fresh eggs next to the bacon. "Your breakfast will be ready in a few minutes." She diverted her eyes to avoid his continued scrutiny but could not help stealing a look back at him. *What is it with that guy? Doesn't he know it's rude to stare?* she thought.

Joe continued to look fixedly at her as he hummed and tapped an accompanying tune on the table. He quieted for a moment without shifting his gaze. "It's okay, I'm here to help," he repeated.

No! Henrietta didn't want to be charmed or disturbed into divulging any sordid details of her past. She had simply wanted to be friendly to this man, and only in a neighborly sort of way because he worked with Jeff at the hospital and was Altie's husband. *But, dadgummit, he is pushing all kinds of buttons!*

Still hearing Jeff talking on the phone, she exhaled dramatically and turned to face Joe. Before she could stop herself Henrietta blurted out in a strained whisper: "Okay, I don't know how you know it, but you're right. Something awful's happened to me since our first mission here. And now, I feel like I'm not all here. Something is missing. And I don't know what." *Oh dear God! What am I doing? What am I saying?* She blushed, feeling exposed and vulnerable by her sudden candor. She jerked her hands up and covered her mouth.

"Don't worry. It's obvious your soul has fragmented and is in need of repair," Joe said with a calm certainty, as if it was an everyday matter to be dealt with.

"What?" Henrietta put her hands down and stared into space, bewildered by his words. In the quietude, the sizzle of the frying eggs and bacon filled the room like a choir of rattlers. *My soul has what?* When she looked again at Joe, planning to demand exactly what he meant, his eyes were closed, and he was whispering and holding his palms up as though in prayer.

So she placed the cooked food on a plate, poured a glass of milk and put both down in front of him. He opened his eyes and smiled up at her.

"That's one of the strangest things I've ever heard—a soul fragmenting," she said. "How would something like that even be possible?"

"It can happen when we believe or experience something bad we don't want to face." He took a bite of eggs and grits, closing his eyes again to savor the combination. "Oh, this is yum-yum," he said.

When he looked up, it was Henrietta who was staring.

"The good news is that lost soul fragments can be recovered and healed. It's not hard, if you know how, if you know the secret," Joe said.

"Are you saying you know how to do that? That you know the secret?"

"The Great Spirit works hitherto and I work."

She crossed her arms. "So what are you, some kind of soul repairman?"

"Ho, ha!" He laughed out loud. "In truth, I'm a practitioner of the Great Spirit's bear medicine, which in your case, would start with a ritual called the soul retrieval. It's something that could really help you." Joe took a sip of milk while nodding to himself.

"Bear medicine? Soul retrieval? I was raised in a church where just saying that kind of stuff could get you tarred and feathered." Henrietta tried to say it like a devil's advocate and a joke, but she wasn't kidding.

"I wasn't aware your people use feathers in rituals," Joe responded with no overt sarcasm, wiping his mouth with a napkin.

"Ha! That's not exactly it." She gave a false laugh, shaking her head. "I'm from a place where saying or even thinking things like that is considered blasphemous and will get you into a lot of trouble with Baptist ministers. Do you know what I'm saying?"

"Apaches consider asking questions to be so rude, it's like a sacrilege," he said, his voice uncharacteristically stern.

"Oh!" Henrietta blushed again as she realized she was still ignorant of many of the life-ways and traditions governing Medichero Apaches. "I'm sorry, I didn't know."

"Please, there's no need to apologize. I was just trying to make a point: sometimes it makes sense to discard old rules that no longer serve. I actually believe asking questions is a great way to learn and grow. Do some of our elders consider me a heretic for thinking that?" He shrugged his shoulders. "Probably."

"And that doesn't bother you?" She'd never met someone so audacious or unconcerned about what others thought. Especially about what religious leaders thought.

"Religious dogma that's become too rigid is like a hound dog with rigor mortis—not good for much." He squeezed his nose between his fingers. "Smells bad, too."

It didn't exactly answer her question. Still she couldn't help but smile.

"We must not fear questioning anything, even outdated rules of etiquette or what some consider forbidden," the Apache continued. "We must not let dead dogs dictate our paths. We must follow the Great Spirit's Truth wherever it may lead us."

For several seconds, Henrietta stared out of the window at nothing, trying to assimilate all that he'd said, wondering if she should just dismiss it as nonsense. But she had to admit, given the horrible things she'd experienced, there was something undeniably intriguing, comforting and perhaps even tempting about his concept of retrieving and healing lost soul fragments. She realized she wanted to know more. *Could something like the soul retrieval really be possible? And could it help me?* Henrietta shook her head to clear it of this foolishness.

"Please keep eating before it gets cold," she said, turning back to face him. It was all she could think of to say.

After finishing, Joe tidied up where he'd eaten, limped over to the sink with his dishes and rinsed them off. "That was a delightful breakfast—many thanks," he said, bowing. "And those grits, they were terrific."

"I'm glad you liked them. I brought them with us, all the way from South Carolina."

"Please allow me to return the favor," he said.

"Oh, you want to cook something for me?"

He shook his head, grinning. "If you want to experience the soul retrieval and more, please come to our teepee tomorrow; it's right behind our house. At about noon would be good; my singing's not required at the ceremonies then."

Me? Take part in a soul retrieval? Her stomach fluttered, and Henrietta wasn't sure if that meant the idea was appealing or if it just plain scared her.

"Um, thanks ..." she started. But the thought of letting Joe Loco tinker around in her soul gave her more than pause. "I'll have to think about your offer."

"Altie can tell you more about it," Joe said. "And, because we've already agreed, she won't mind if you ask her any rude questions about it." He smiled as he picked up the paper bag that contained his diaper costume, sport coat, work boots and, apparently, some hair supplies.

"What do you mean, you've already agreed?" she asked, once again taken aback.

Joe had no time to respond since Jeff returned and changed the subject. "Sorry, but Dr. Belzer wanted to fill me in on Billy Santana's condition."

"You were on the phone quite a while. Is everything okay?" Henrietta frowned, knowing that this favored child within the tribe had been in the hospital for about a week and his condition was critical, as he was among those affected by the influenza epidemic that had recently swept through the reservation.

"Let's just say the boy's stable for now," Jeff said. He glanced at Joe with a frown, as if to belie his statement.

"I can go with you now and help," Joe offered.

Jeff held up his palms. "You've got the ceremonies today, and I think we can handle it."

"If you change your mind or if the situation changes, you know where I'll be," Joe said before turning back to Henrietta. "Again, thank you for a most delicious breakfast. *Ka-dish-day*, farewell, for now."

"Ka-dish-day," Henrietta and Jeff said at the same time as Joe limped out the door.

Her husband looked down at his watch. "I'm relieving Dr. Belzer in about forty-five minutes. Why don't we go into the living room until I have to go?" He walked over and nibbled on her neck. His voice was both warm and animated as he added, "I've so much to tell you about my research."

"Um," she started. "There's something I need to tell you, too." *Maybe I can get it out this time.* She pushed back the wilting blond curls falling over her stinging eyes; her hands trembled. But how could she do it to him? *How can I do it to us?*

"Well first, how about a little concerto? Just for you, Peaches," he said, calling her his favorite pet name. He pulled her toward the living room piano.

To purchase your copy of the award-winning novel, **The Soul Retrieval** by Ann W. Jarvie, please visit ANNWJARVIE.COM for a list of retailers.

Photo Credit: Dane Jarvie

Ann W. Jarvie has a B.A. in journalism and twenty-five years' experience as a copywriter in advertising and public relations agencies, both in Chicago and South Carolina. Her debut novel, *The Soul Retrieval*, received four literary awards, the highest score by Writer's Digest E-book Awards' judges (5 out of 5 on all points) as well as myriad positive reviews. She currently lives in Paradise Valley, Arizona with her husband, their boxer dog and boxer mix rescue.